SLEUTHS

SLEUTHS

Bill Pronzini

Five Star
Unity, Maine

Five Star Mystery.
Published in conjunction with Tekno-Books.

Cover photograph by Jason Johnson.

February 1999
Standard Print Hardcover Edition.

Five Star Standard Print Mystery Series.

The text of this edition is unabridged.

Set in 11 pt. Plantin.

Printed in the United States on permanent paper.

Library of Congress Cataloging in Publication Data

Pronzini, Bill.
    Sleuths / Bill Pronzini.
        p.   cm.
    ISBN 0-7862-1702-2 (hc : alk. paper)
     1. Detective and mystery stories, American. I. Title.
PS3566.R67S58   1999
813'.54—dc21   98-44598

Acknowledgments

"Fergus O'Hara, Detective." Copyright © 1974, 1990 by the Pronzini-Muller Family Trust. First published in *Alfred Hitchcock's Mystery Magazine*.

"The Desert Limited." Copyright © 1995 by the Pronzini-Muller Family Trust. First published in *Louis L'Amour Western Magazine*.

"Medium Rare." Copyright © 1998 by the Pronzini-Muller Family Trust. First published in *Ellery Queen's Mystery Magazine*.

"Jade." Copyright © 1970 by H.S.D. Publications; revised version copyright © 1999 by the Pronzini-Muller Family Trust. First published in *Alfred Hitchcock's Mystery Magazine* as "The Jade Figurine."

"Vanishing Act." Copyright © 1975 by H.S.D. Publications, Inc. First published in *Alfred Hitchcock's Mystery Magazine*.

"The Desperate Ones." Copyright © 1971, 1992 by the Pronzini-Muller Family Trust. First published in *Alfred Hitchcock's Mystery Magazine*.

"Blood Money." Copyright © 1975, 1992 by the Pronzini-Muller Family Trust. First published in *Alfred Hitchcock's Mystery Magazine*.

"Dead Man's Slough." Copyright © 1980, 1983 by the Pronzini-Muller Family Trust. First published in *Alfred Hitchcock's Mystery Magazine*.

"A Killing in Xanadu." Copyright © 1980 by the Pronzini-Muller Family Trust. First published in a limited edition by Waves Press.

"Stakeout." Copyright © 1990 by the Pronzini-Muller Family Trust. First published in *Justice for Hire*.

"La Bellezza delle Bellezze." Copyright © 1991 by the Pronzini-Muller Family Trust. First published in *Invitation to Murder*.

Contents

Preface

Over the past thirty-some years I've had the pleasure of creating a variety of fictional sleuths for both novels and short stories. One of them has fared quite well; the others have been less successful, though a couple have had careers which exceeded my modest expectations. Each has led an interesting life (at least to me) and each has been different in fundamental ways.

Foremost among them, of course, is the fellow who has been around almost as long as I have — my first story was published in 1966, his first recorded case a year later — and who is better known than I am in spite of the fact that he doesn't have a name. The San Francisco private investigator dubbed the "Nameless Detective" (by a former editor, not by me) has appeared in twenty-five novels and numerous short stories spanning four decades.

My other series detectives run the gamut of fictional types: professional and amateur, historical and contemporary, humorous and deadly serious, honorable and notorious, soft-boiled, medium-boiled, and hard-boiled. There is Fergus O'Hara, a roguish individualist who, with his wife Hattie, plies his trade during the time of the Civil War. There are John Quincannon and Sabina Carpenter, an affectionately mismatched pair who operate a private agency called Carpenter and Quincannon, Professional Detective Services, in 1890s San Francisco. There is Dan Connell, ex-pilot and reformed black marketeer whose bailiwick is Singapore and Malaysia. There is Christopher Steele, magician extraordinary, who specializes in solving seemingly impossible crimes — a joint creation with Michael Kurland. And there is Carmody, a freelance bodyguard and supplier of legal and extralegal services, who is based on the Mediterranean island of Majorca and whose adventures take him to such locales as Vienna, Venice, Amsterdam, North Africa, and Spain's Costa del Sol.

Each of these characters, and his (and her) special brand of detection, is represented here — a sort of detectives' round table. You may not like all of them or their methods, but I hope you'll find their company stimulating. None of them gave *me* a dull moment, anyway . . .

Bill Pronzini
Petaluma, California

Fergus O'Hara, Detective

On a balmy March afternoon in the third full year of the War Between the States, while that conflict continued to rage bloodily some two thousand miles distant, Fergus and Hattie O'Hara jostled their way along San Francisco's Embarcadero toward Long Wharf and the riverboat *Delta Star*. The half-plank, half-dirt roads and plank walks were choked with horses, mules, cargo-laden wagons — and with all manner of humanity: bearded miners and burly roustabouts and sun-darkened farmers; rope-muscled Kanakas and Filipino laborers and coolie-hatted Chinese; shrewd-eyed merchants and ruffle-shirted gamblers and bonneted ladies who might have been the wives of prominent citizens or trollops on their way to the gold fields of the Mother Lode. Both the pace and the din were furious. At exactly four P.M. some twenty steamers would leave the waterfront, bound upriver for Sacramento and Stockton and points in between.

O'Hara clung to their carpetbags and Hattie clung to O'Hara as they pushed through the throng. They could see the *Delta Star* the moment they reached Long Wharf. She was an impressive side-wheeler, one of the "floating palaces" that had adorned the Sacramento and San Joaquin rivers for more than ten years. Powered by a single-cylinder, vertical-beam engine, she was 245 feet long and had slim, graceful lines. The long rows of windows running full length both starboard and larboard along her deckhouse, where the Gentlemen's and Dining Saloons and most of the staterooms were located, refracted jewellike the rays of the

11

afternoon sun. Above, to the stern, was the weather deck, on which stretched the "texas"; this housed luxury state-rooms and cabins for the packet's officers. Some distance forward of the texas was the oblong glassed-in structure of the pilothouse.

Smiling as they approached, O'Hara said, "Now ain't she a fine lady?" He spoke with a careless brogue, the result of a strict ethnic upbringing in the Irish Channel section of New Orleans. At times this caused certain individuals to under-estimate his capabilities and intelligence, which in his pro-fession was a major asset.

"She *is* fine, Fergus," Hattie agreed. "As fine as any on the Mississippi before the war. How far did you say it was to Stockton?"

O'Hara laughed. "A hundred twenty-seven miles. One night in the lap of luxury is all we'll be having this trip, me lady."

"Pity," Hattie said. She was in her late twenties, five years younger than her husband; dark-complected, buxom. Thick black hair, worn in ringlets, was covered by a lace-decorated bonnet. She wore a gray serge traveling dress, the hem of which was now coated with dust.

O'Hara was tall and plump, and sported a luxuriant red beard of which he was inordinately proud and on which he doted every morning with scissors and comb. Like Hattie, he had mild blue eyes; unlike Hattie, and as a result of a fondness for spirits, he possessed a nose that approximated the color of his beard. He was dressed in a black frock coat, striped trousers, and a flowered vest. He carried no visible weapons, but in a holster inside his coat was a double-action revolver.

The *Delta Star*'s stageplank, set aft to the main deck, was jammed with passengers and wagons; it was not twenty till

12

four. A large group of nankeen-dressed men were congregated near the foot of the plank. All of them wore green felt shamrocks pinned to the lapels of their coats, and several were smoking thin, "long-nine" seegars. Fluttering above them on a pole held by one was a green banner with the words *Mulrooney Guards, San Francisco Company A* crudely printed on it in white.

Four of the group were struggling to lift a massive wooden crate that appeared to be quite heavy. They managed to get it aloft, grunting, and began to stagger with it to the plank. As they started up, two members of the *Delta Star*'s deck crew came down and blocked their way. One of them said, "Before you go any farther, gents, show us your manifest on that box."

One of the other Mulrooneys stepped up the plank. "What manifest?" he demanded. "This ain't cargo, it's personal belongings."

"Anything heavy as that pays cargo," the deckhand said. "Rules is rules and they apply to Bluebellies same as to better folks."

"Bluebellies, is it? Ye damned Copperhead, I'll pound ye up into horsemeat!" And the Mulrooney hit the deckhand on the side of the head and knocked him down.

The second crew member stepped forward and hit the Mulrooney on the side of the head and knocked *him* down.

Another of the Guards jumped in and hit the second crewman on the side of the head and knocked *him* down.

The first deckhand got up and the first Mulrooney got up, minus his hat, and began swinging at each other. The second crewman got up and began swinging at the second Mulrooney. The other members of the Guards, shouting encouragement, formed a tight circle around the fighting men — all except for the four carrying the heavy wooden crate.

Those Mulrooneys struggled up the stageplank with their burden and disappeared among the confusion on the main deck.

The fight did not last long. Several roustabouts and one of the steamer's mates hurried onto the landing and broke it up. No one seemed to have been injured, save for the two deckhands who were both unconscious. The mate seemed undecided as to what to do, finally concluded that to do nothing at all was the best recourse; he turned up the plank again. Four roustabouts carried the limp crewmen up after him, followed by the Guards who were all now loudly singing "John Brown's Body."

Hattie asked O'Hara, "Now what was *that* all about?"

"War business," he told her solemnly. "California's a long way from the battlefields, but feelings and loyalties are as strong here as in the East."

"But who are the Mulrooney Guards?"

Before O'Hara could answer, a tall man wearing a Prince Albert, who was standing next to Hattie, swung toward them and smiled and said, "I couldn't help overhearing the lady's question. If you'll pardon the intrusion, I can supply an answer."

O'Hara looked the tall man over and decided he was a gambler. He had no particular liking for gamblers, but for the most part he was tolerant of them. He said the intrusion was pardoned, introduced himself and Hattie, and learned that the tall man was John A. Colfax, of San Francisco.

Colfax had gray eyes that were both congenial and cunning. In his left hand he continually shuffled half a dozen small bronze war-issue cents — coinage that was not often seen in the West. He said, "The Mulrooney Guards is a more or less official militia company, one of several supporting the Union cause. They have two companies, one in

14

San Francisco and one in Stockton. I imagine this one is joining the other for some sort of celebration."

"Tomorrow is St. Patrick's Day," O'Hara told him.

"Ah, yes, of course."

"Ye seem to know quite a bit about these lads, Mr. Colfax."

"I am a regular passenger on the *Delta Star*," Colfax said. "On the Sacramento packets as well. A traveling man picks up a good deal of information."

O'Hara said blandly, "Aye, that he does."

Hattie said, "I wonder what the Mulrooneys have in that crate?"

Colfax allowed as how he had no idea. He seemed about to say something further, but the appearance of three closely grouped men, hurrying through the crowd toward the stageplank, claimed his attention. The one in the middle, O'Hara saw, wore a broadcloth suit and a nervous, harried expression; cradled in both hands against his body was a large and apparently heavy valise. The two men on either side were more roughly dressed, had revolvers holstered at their hips. Their expressions were dispassionate, their eyes watchful.

O'Hara frowned and glanced at Colfax. The gambler watched the trio climb the plank and hurry up the aft stairway; then he said quietly, as if to himself, "It appears we'll be carrying more than passengers and cargo this trip." He regarded the O'Haras again, touched his hat, said it had been a pleasure talking to them, and moved away to board the riverboat.

Hattie looked at her husband inquiringly. He said, "Gold."

"Gold, Fergus?"

"That nervous chap had the look of a banker, the other

15

two of deputies. A bank transfer of specie or dust from here to Stockton — or so I'm thinking."

"Where will they keep it?"

"Purser's office, mayhap. Or the pilothouse."

Hattie and O'Hara climbed the plank. As they were crossing the main deck, the three men appeared again on the stairway; the one in the broadcloth suit looked considerably less nervous now. O'Hara watched them go down onto the landing. Then, shrugging, he followed Hattie up the stairs to the weather deck. They stopped at the starboard rail to await departure.

Hattie said, "What did you think of Mr. Colfax?"

"A slick-tongued lad, even for a gambler. But ye'd not want to be giving him a coin to put in a village poor box for ye."

She laughed. "He seemed rather interested in the delivery of gold, if that's what it was."

"Aye, so he did."

At exactly four o'clock the *Delta Star*'s whistle sounded; her buckets churned the water, steam poured from her twin stacks. She began to move slowly away from the wharf. All up and down the Embarcadero now, whistles sounded and the other packets commenced backing down from their landings. The waters of the bay took on a chaotic appearance as the boats maneuvered for right-of-way. Clouds of steam filled the sky; the sound of pilot whistles was angry and shrill.

Once the *Delta Star* was clear of the wharves and of other riverboats, her speed increased steadily. Hattie and O'Hara remained at the rail until San Francisco's low, sun-washed skyline had receded into the distance; then they went in search of a steward, who took them to their stateroom. Its windows faced larboard, but its entrance was located inside

16

a tunnellike hallway down the center of the texas. Spacious and opulent, the cabin contained carved rosewood paneling and red plush upholstery. Hattie said she thought it was grand. O'Hara, who had never been particularly impressed by Victorian elegance, said he imagined she would be wanting to freshen up a bit — and that, so as not to be disturbing her, he would take a stroll about the decks.

"Stay away from the liquor buffet," Hattie said. "The day is young, if I make my meaning clear."

O'Hara sighed. "I had no intention of visiting the liquor buffet," he lied, and sighed again, and left the stateroom.

He wandered aft, past the officers' quarters. When he emerged from the texas he found himself confronted by the huge A-shaped gallows frame that housed the cylinder, valve gear, beam and crank of the walking-beam engine. Each stroke of the piston produced a mighty roar and hiss of escaping steam. The noise turned O'Hara around and sent him back through the texas to the forward stairway.

Ahead of him as he started down were two men who had come out of the pilothouse. One was tall, with bushy black hair and a thick mustache — apparently a passenger. The second wore a square-billed cap and the sort of stern, authoritative look that would have identified him as the *Delta Star*'s pilot even without the cap. At this untroubled point in the journey, the packet would be in the hands of a cub apprentice.

The door to the Gentlemen's Saloon kept intruding on O'Hara's thoughts as he walked about the deckhouse. Finally he went down to the main deck. Here, in the open areas and in the shedlike expanse beneath the superstructures, deck passengers and cargo were pressed together in noisy confusion: men and women and children, wagons and animals and chickens in coops; sacks, bales, boxes, hogs-heads, cords of bull pine for the roaring fireboxes under the boilers. And, too, the Mulrooney Guards, who were loosely grouped near the taffrail, alternately singing "The Girl I Left Behind Me" and passing around jugs of what was likely poteen — a powerful homemade Irish whiskey.

O'Hara sauntered near the group, stood with his back against a stanchion, and began to shave cuttings from his tobacco plug into his briar. One of the Mulrooneys — small and fair and feisty looking — noticed him, studied his luxuriant red beard, and then approached him carrying one of the jugs. Without preamble he demanded to know if the gentleman were Irish. O'Hara said he was, with great dignity. The Mulrooney slapped him on the back. "I knew it!" he said effusively. "Me name's Billy Culligan. Have a drap of the crayture."

O'Hara decided Hattie had told him only to stay away from the buffet. There was no deceit in accepting hospitality from fellows of the Auld Sod. He took the jug, drank deeply, and allowed as how it was a fine crayture, indeed. Then he introduced himself, saying that he and the missus were traveling to Stockton on a business matter.

"Ye won't be conducting business on the morrow, will ye?"

"On St. Pat's Day?" O'Hara was properly shocked.

"Boyo, I like ye," Culligan said. "How would ye like to join in on the biggest St. Pat's Day celebration in the entire sovereign state of California?"

"I'd like nothing better."

"Then come to Green Park, on the north of Stockton, 'twixt nine and ten and tell the lads ye're a friend of Billy Culligan. There'll be a parade, and all the food and liquor ye can hold. Oh, it'll be a fine celebration, lad!"

O'Hara said he and the missus would be there, meaning it. Culligan offered another drink of poteen, which O'Hara casually accepted. Then the little Mulrooney stepped forward and said in a conspiratorial voice, "Come round here to the taffrail just before we steam into Stockton on the morrow. We've a plan to start off St. Pat's Day with a mighty salute — part of the reason we sent our wives and wee ones ahead on the *San Joaquin*. Ye won't want to be missing that either." Before O'Hara could ask him what he meant by "mighty salute," he and his jug were gone into the midst of the other Guards.

"Me lady," O'Hara said contentedly, "that was a meal fit for royalty and no doubt about it."

Hattie agreed that it had been a sumptuous repast as they walked from the Dining Saloon to the texas stairway. The evening was mild, with little breeze and no sign of the thick tule fog that often made Northern California riverboating a hazardous proposition. The *Delta Star* — aglow with hundreds of lights — had come through the Carquinez Straits, passed Chipp's Island, and was now entering the San Joaquin River. A pale moon silvered the water, turned a ghostly white the long stretches of fields along both banks.

On the weather deck, they stood close together at the larboard rail, not far from the pilothouse. For a couple of minutes they were alone. Then footsteps sounded and O'Hara turned to see the ship's captain and pilot returning from their dinner. Touching his cap, the captain — a lean, graying man of fifty-odd — wished them good evening. The pilot merely grunted.

The O'Haras continued to stand looking out at the willows and cottonwoods along the riverbank. Then, suddenly, an explosive, angry cry came from the pilothouse, startling them both. This was followed by muffled voices, another sharp exclamation, movement not clearly perceived through the window glass and beyond partially drawn rear curtains, and several sharp blasts on the pilot whistle.

Natural curiosity drew O'Hara away from the rail, hurrying; Hattie was close behind him. The door to the pilothouse stood open when they reached it, and O'Hara turned inside by one step. The enclosure was almost as opulent as their stateroom, but he noticed its appointments only peripherally. What captured his full attention was three men now grouped before the wheel, and the four items on the floor close to and against the starboard bulkhead.

The pilot stood clutching two of the wheel spokes, red-faced with anger; the captain was bending over the kneeling figure of the third man — a young blond individual wearing a buttoned-up sack coat and baggy trousers, both of which were streaked with dust and soot and grease. The blond lad was making soft moaning sounds, holding the back of his head cupped in one palm.

One of the items on the floor was a steel pry bar. The others were a small safe bolted to the bulkhead, a black valise — the one O'Hara had seen carried by the nervous man and his two bodyguards — and a medium-sized iron strongbox, just large enough to have fit inside the valise. The safe door, minus its combination dial, stood wide open; the valise and a strongbox were also open. All three were quite obviously empty.

The pilot jerked the bell knobs, signaling an urgent request to the engineer for a lessening of speed, and began barking stand-by orders into a speaking tube. His was the voice which had startled Hattie and O'Hara. The captain was saying to the blond man, "It's a miracle we didn't drift

20

out of the channel and run afoul of a snag — a miracle, Chadwick."

"I can't be held to blame, sir," Chadwick said defensively. "Whoever it was hit me from behind. I was sitting at the wheel when I heard the door open and thought it was you and Mr. Bridgeman returning from supper, so I didn't even bother to turn. The next thing, my head seemed to explode. That is all I know."

He managed to regain his feet and moved stiffly to a red plush sofa, hitching up his trousers with one hand; the other still held the back of his head. Bridgeman, the pilot, banged down the speaking tube, then spun the wheel a half-turn to larboard. As he did the last, he glanced over his shoulder and saw O'Hara and Hattie. "Get out of here!" he shouted at them. "There is nothing here for you."

"Perhaps, now, that isn't true," O'Hara said mildly. "Ye've had a robbery, have ye not?"

"That is none of your affair."

Boldly O'Hara came deeper into the pilothouse, motioning Hattie to close the door. She did so. Bridgeman yelled, "I told you to get out of here! Who do you think you are?"

"Fergus O'Hara — operative of the Pinkerton Police Agency."

Bridgeman stared at him, open-mouthed. The captain and Chadwick had shifted their attention to him as well. At length, in a less harsh tone, the pilot said, "Pinkerton Agency?"

"Of Chicago, Illinois; Allan Pinkerton, Principal."

O'Hara produced his billfold, extracted from it the letter from Allan Pinkerton and the Chicago & Eastern Central Railroad Pass, both of which identified him, as the bearer of these documents, to be a Pinkerton Police agent. He showed them to both Bridgeman and the captain.

"What would a Pinkerton man be doing way out here in California?" the captain asked.

"Me wife Hattie and me are on the trail of a gang that has been terrorizing Adams Express coaches. We've traced them to San Francisco and now have reliable information they're to be found in Stockton."

"Your *wife* is a Pinkerton agent too? A *woman* . . . ?"

O'Hara looked at him as if he might be a dullard. "Ye've never heard of Miss Kate Warne, one of the agency's most trusted Chicago operatives? No, I don't suppose ye have. Well, me wife has no official capacity, but since one of the leaders of this gang is reputed to be a woman, and since Hattie has assisted me in the past, women being able to obtain information in places men cannot, I've brought her along."

Bridgeman said from the wheel, "Well, we can use a trained detective after what has happened here."

O'Hara nodded. "Is it gold ye've had stolen?"

"Gold — yes. How did you know that?"

He told them of witnessing the delivery of the valise at Long Wharf. He asked then, "How large an amount is involved?"

"Forty thousand dollars," the captain said.

O'Hara whistled. "That's a fair considerable sum."

"To put it mildly, sir."

"Was it specie or dust?"

"Dust. An urgent consignment from the California Merchant's Bank to their branch in Stockton."

"How many men had foreknowledge of the shipment?"

"The officials of the bank, Mr. Bridgeman, and myself."

"No other officers of the packet?"

"No."

"Would you be telling me, Captain, who was present

22

when the delivery was made this afternoon?"

"Mr. Bridgeman and I, and a friend of his visiting in San Francisco — a newspaperman from Nevada."

O'Hara remembered the tall man with bushy hair who had been with the pilot earlier. "Can ye vouch for this newspaperman?" he asked Bridgeman.

"I can. His reputation is unimpeachable."

"Has anyone other than he been here since the gold was brought aboard?"

"Not to my knowledge."

Chadwick said that no one had come by while he was on duty; and none of them had noticed anyone shirking about at any time. The captain said sourly, "It appears as though almost any man on this packet could be the culprit. Just how do you propose we find out which one, Mr. O'Hara?"

O'Hara did not reply. He bent to examine the safe. The combination dial appeared to have been snapped off, by a hand with experience at such villainous business. The valise and the strongbox had also been forced. The pry bar was an ordinary tool and had likely also been used as a weapon to knock Chadwick unconscious.

He straightened and moved about the enclosure, studying each fixture. Then he got down on hands and knees and peered under both the sofa and a blackened winter stove. It was under the stove that he found the coin.

His fingers grasped it, closed it into his palm. Standing again, he glanced at the coin and saw that it was made of bronze, a small war-issue cent piece shinily new and free of dust or soot. A smile plucked at the edges of his mouth as he slipped the coin into his vest pocket.

Bridgeman said, "Did you find something?"

"Perhaps. Then again, perhaps not."

O'Hara came forward, paused near where Bridgeman

23

stood at the wheel. Through the windshield he could see the moonlit waters of the San Joaquin. He could also see, as a result of the pilothouse lamps and the darkness without, his own dim reflection in the glass. He thought his stern expression was rather like the one Allan Pinkerton himself possessed.

Bridgeman suggested that crewmen be posted on the lower decks throughout the night, as a precaution in the event the culprit had a confederate with a boat somewhere along the route and intended to leave the packet in the wee hours. The captain thought this was a good idea; so did O'Hara.

He was ready to leave, but the captain had a few more words for him. "I am grateful for your professional assistance, Mr. O'Hara, but as master of the *Delta Star* the primary investigative responsibility is mine. Please inform me immediately if you learn anything of significance."

O'Hara said he would.

"Also, I intend my inquiries to be discreet, so as not to alarm the passengers. I'll expect yours to be the same."

"Discretion is me middle name," O'Hara assured him.

A few moments later, he and Hattie were on their way back along the larboard rail to the texas. Hattie, who had been silent during their time in the pilothouse, started to speak, but O'Hara overrode her. "I know what ye're going to say, me lady, and it'll do no good. Me mind's made up. The opportunity to sniff out forty thousand in missing gold is one I'll not pass up."

He left Hattie at the door to their stateroom and hurried to the deckhouse, where he entered the Gentlemen's Saloon. It was a long room, with a liquor buffet at one end and private tables and card layouts spread throughout. A pall of tobacco smoke as thick as tule fog hung in the crowded enclosure.

O'Hara located the shrewd, handsome features of John A. Colfax at a table aft. Two other men were with him: a portly individual with sideburns like miniature tumbleweeds, and the mustached Nevada reporter. They were playing draw poker. O'Hara was not surprised to see that most of the stakes — gold specie and greenbacks — were in front of Colfax.

Casually, O'Hara approached the table and stopped behind an empty chair next to the portly man, just as Colfax claimed a pot with four treys. He said, "Good evening, gentlemen."

Colfax greeted him unctuously, asked if he were enjoying the voyage thus far. O'Hara said he was, and observed that the gambler seemed to be enjoying it too, judging from the stack of legal tender before him. Colfax just smiled. But the portly man said in grumbling tones, "I should damned well say so. He has been taking my money for three solid hours."

"Aye? That long?"

"Since just after dinner."

"Ye've been playing without pause since then?"

"Nearly so," the newspaperman said. Through the tendrils of smoke from his cigar, he studied O'Hara with mild blue eyes. "Why do you ask, sir?"

"Oh, I was thinking I saw Mr. Colfax up on the weather deck about an hour ago. Near the pilothouse."

"You must have mistaken someone else for me," Colfax said. Now that the draw game had been momentarily suspended, he had produced a handful of war-issue coins and begun to toy with them as he had done at Long Wharf. "I did leave the table for a few minutes about an hour ago, but only to use the lavatory. I haven't been on the weather deck at all this trip."

O'Hara saw no advantage in pressing the matter. He pretended to notice for the first time the one-cent pieces Colfax was shuffling. "Lucky coins, Mr. Colfax?"

"These? Why, yes. I won a sackful of them on a wager once and my luck has been good ever since." Disarming smile. "Gamblers are superstitious about such things, you know."

"Ye don't see many coins like that in California."

"True. They are practically worthless out here."

"So worthless," the reporter said, "that I have seen them used to decorate various leather goods."

The portly man said irritably, "To hell with lucky coins and such nonsense. Are we going to play poker or have a gabfest?"

"Poker, by all means," Colfax said. He slipped the war-issue cents into a pocket of his Prince Albert and reached for the cards. His interest in O'Hara seemed to have vanished.

The reporter, however, was still looking at him with curiosity. "Perhaps you'd care to join us?"

O'Hara declined, saying he had never had any luck with the pasteboards. Then he left the saloon and went in search of the *Delta Star*'s purser. It took him ten minutes to find the man, and thirty seconds to learn that John A. Colfax did not have a stateroom either in the texas or on the deckhouse. The purser, who knew Colfax as a regular passenger, said wryly that the gambler would spend the entire voyage in the Gentlemen's Saloon, having gullible citizens for a ride.

O'Hara returned to the saloon, this time to avail himself of the liquor buffet. He ordered a shot of rye from a bartender who owned a resplendent handlebar moustache, and tossed it down without his customary enjoyment. Immediately he ordered another.

Colfax might well be his man; there was the war-issue coin he'd found under the pilothouse stove, and the fact that Colfax had left the poker game at about the time of the robbery. And yet . . . what could he have done with the gold? The weight of forty thousand in dust was considerable; he could not very well carry it in his pockets. He had been gone from the poker game long enough to commit the robbery, perhaps, but hardly long enough to have also hidden the spoils.

There were other factors weighing against Colfax, too. One: gentlemen gamblers made considerable sums of money at their trade; they seldom found it necessary to resort to baser thievery. Two: how could Colfax, while sitting here in the saloon, have known when only one man would be present in the pilothouse? An accomplice might have been on watch — but if there were such a second party, why hadn't *he* committed the robbery himself?

O'Hara scowled, put away his second rye. If Colfax wasn't the culprit, then who was? And what was the significance of the coin he had found in the pilothouse?

Perhaps the coin had no significance at all; but his instincts told him it did, and he had always trusted his instincts. If not to Colfax, then to whom did it point? Answer: to no one, and to everyone. Even though war-issue cents were uncommon in California, at least half a dozen men presently on board might have one or two in their pockets.

A remark passed by the newspaperman came back to him: such coins were used to decorate various leather goods. Aye, that was a possibility. If the guilty man had been wearing a holster or vest or some other article adorned with the cent pieces, one might have popped loose unnoticed.

27

O'Hara slid the coin from his pocket and examined it carefully. There were small scratches on its surface that might have been made by stud fasteners, but he couldn't be sure. The scratches might also have been caused by any one of a hundred other means — and the coin could still belong to John A. Colfax.

Returning it to his vest pocket, O'Hara considered the idea of conducting a search for a man wearing leather ornamented with bronze war coins. And dismissed it immediately as folly. He could roam the *Delta Star* all night and not encounter even two-thirds of the passengers. Or he might find someone wearing such an article who would turn out to be completely innocent. And what if the robber had discovered the loss of the coin and chucked the article overboard?

Frustration began to assail him now. But it did not dull his determination. If any man aboard the *Delta Star* could fetch up both the thief and the gold before the packet reached Stockton, that man was Fergus O'Hara; and by damn, if such were humanly possible, he meant to do it!

He left the saloon again and went up to the pilothouse. Bridgeman was alone at the wheel. "What news, O'Hara?" he asked.

"None as yet. Would ye know where the captain is?"

Bridgeman shook his head. "Young fool Chadwick was feeling dizzy from that blow on the head; the captain took him to his quarters just after you and your wife left, and then went to make his inquiries. I expect he's still making 'em."

O'Hara sat on the red plush sofa, packed and lighted his pipe, and let his mind drift along various channels. After a time something in his memory flickered like a guttering candle — and then died before he could steady the flame.

28

When he was unable to rekindle the flame he roared forth with a venomous ten-jointed oath that startled even Bridgeman.

Presently the captain returned to the pilothouse. He and O'Hara exchanged identical expectant looks, which immediately told each that the other had uncovered nothing of significance. Verbal confirmation of this was brief, after which the captain said bleakly, "The prospects are grim, Mr. O'Hara. Grim, indeed."

"We've not yet come into Stockton," O'Hara reminded him.

The captain sighed. "We have no idea of who is guilty, thus no idea of where to find the gold . . . if in fact it is still on board. We haven't the manpower for a search of packet and passengers before our arrival. And afterward — I don't see how we can hope to hold everyone on board while the authorities are summoned and a search mounted. Miners are a hotheaded lot; so are those Irish militiamen. We would likely have a riot on our hands."

O'Hara had nothing more to say. By all the saints, *he* was not yet ready to admit defeat. He bid the captain and Bridgeman good night, and spent the next hour prowling the decks and cudgeling his brain. It seemed to him that he had seen and heard enough since the robbery to *know* who it was he was after and where the missing gold could be found. If only he could bring forth one scrap of this knowledge from his memory, he was certain the others would follow . . .

Maddeningly, however, no scrap was forthcoming. Not while he prowled the decks, not after he returned to his stateroom (Hattie, he was relieved to find, was already fast asleep) — and not when the first light of dawn crept into the sky beyond the window.

★ ★ ★ ★ ★

When the *Delta Star* came out of one of the snakelike bends in the river and started down the last long reach to Stockton, O'Hara was standing with Hattie at the starboard deckhouse rail. It was just past seven-thirty — a spring-crisp, cloudless St. Patrick's Day morning — and the steamer would dock in another thirty minutes.

O'Hara was in a foul humor: three-quarters frustration and one-quarter lack of sleep. He had left the stateroom at six o'clock and gone up to the pilothouse and found the captain, Bridgeman, and Chadwick drinking coffee thickened with molasses. They had nothing to tell him. And their humors had been no better than his; it seemed that as a result of O'Hara's failure to perform as advertised, he had fallen out of favor with them.

Staring down at the slow-moving waters frothed by the sidewheel, he told himself for the thousandth time: Ye've got the answer, ye know ye do. Think, lad! Dredge it up before it's too late . . .

A voice beside him said, "Fine morning, isn't it?"

Irritably O'Hara turned his head and found himself looking into the cheerfully smiling visage of the Nevada newspaperman. The bushy-haired lad's eyes were red-veined from a long night in the Gentlemen's Saloon, but this did not seem to have had any effect on his disposition.

O'Hara grunted. "Is it?" he said grumpily. "Ye sound as if ye have cause for rejoicing. Did ye win a hatful of specie from the gambler Colfax last night?"

"Unfortunately, no. I lost a fair sum, as a matter of fact. Gambling is one of my sadder vices, along with a fondness for the social drink. But then, a man may have no bad habits and have worse."

O'Hara grunted again and looked out over the broad,

yellowish land of the San Joaquin Valley.

The reporter's gaze was on the river. "Clear as a mirror, isn't it?" he said nostalgically. "Not at all like the Mississippi. I remember when I was a boy . . ."

O'Hara had jerked upright, into a posture as rigid as an obelisk. He stood that way for several seconds. Then he said explosively, "In the name of Patrick and all the saints!"

Hattie said with alarm in her voice, "Fergus, what is it?"

O'Hara grinned at her, swung around to the newspaperman and clapped him exuberantly on the shoulder. "Lad, it may yet be a fine a morning. It may yet be, indeed."

He told Hattie to wait there for him, left her and the bewildered reporter at the rail, and hurried down to the aft stairway. On the weather deck, he moved aft of the texas and stopped before the gallows frame.

There was no one in the immediate vicinity. O'Hara stepped up close to the frame and eased his head and both arms inside the vent opening, avoiding the machinery of the massive walking-beam. Heat and the heavy odor of cylinder oil assailed him; the throb of the piston was almost deafening.

With his left hand he felt along the interior wall of the frame, his fingertips encountering a greasy build-up of oil and dust. It was only a few seconds before they located a metal hook screwed into the wood. A new hook, free of grease; he was able to determine that by touching it with the clean fingers of his right hand. Nothing was suspended from the hook, but O'Hara was now certain that something had been during most of the night.

He was also certain that he knew where it could be found at this very moment.

When he withdrew his head and arms from the vent opening, grease stained his hands and his coat and shirt

31

sleeves, and he was sweating from the heat. He used his handkerchief, then hastened across to enter the texas. There were identifying plates screwed to the doors of the officers' cabins; he stopped before the one he wanted, drew his coat away from his revolver and laid the fingers of his right hand on its grip. With his left hand he rapped on the door panel.

There was no response.

He knocked again, waited, then took out his pocket knife. The door latch yielded in short order to rapid manipulations with one of the blades. He slipped inside and shut the door behind him.

A brief look around convinced him that the most likely hiding place was a dark corner formed by the single bunkbed and an open-topped wooden tool carrier. And that in fact was where he found what he was looking for: a wide leather belt ornamented with bronze war-issue coins, and a greasy calfskin grip. He drew the bag out, worked at the locked catch with his knife, and got it open.

The missing gold was inside, in two-score small pouches.

O'Hara looked at the sacks for several seconds, smiling. Then he found himself thinking of the captain, and of the bank in Stockton that urgently awaited the consignment. He sobered, shook himself mentally. This was neither the time nor the place for rumination; there was still much to be done. He refastened the grip, hefted it, and started to rise.

Scraping noise on the deck outside. Then the cabin door burst open, and the man whose quarters these were, the man who had stolen the gold, stood framed in the opening.

Chadwick, the cub pilot.

Recognition darkened his face with the blood of rage. He growled, "So you found out, did you? You damned

Pinkerton meddler!" And he launched himself across the cabin.

O'Hara moved to draw his revolver too late. By then Chadwick was on him. The young pilot's shoulder struck the carpetbag that O'Hara thrust up defensively, sandwiched it between them as they went crashing into the larboard bulkhead. The impact broke them apart. O'Hara spilled sideways across the bunk, with the grip between his legs, and cracked his head on the rounded projection of wood that served as headboard. An eruption of pain blurred his vision, kept him from reacting as quickly as he might have. Chadwick was on him again before he could disengage himself from the bag.

A wild blow grazed the side of O'Hara's head. He threw up a forearm, succeeded in warding off a second blow but not a third. That one connected solidly with his jaw, and his vision went cockeyed again.

He was still conscious, but he seemed to have momentarily lost all power of movement. The flailing weight that was Chadwick lifted from him. There were scuffling sounds, then the sharp running slap of boots receding across the cabin and on the deck outside.

O'Hara's jaw and the back of his head began a simultaneous and painful throbbing; at the same time strength seemed to flow back into his arms and legs. Shaking his head to clear his vision, he swung off the bunk and let loose with a many-jointed oath that even his grandfather, who had always sworn he could out-cuss Old Nick himself, would have been proud to call his own. When he could see again he realized that Chadwick had caught up the calfskin grip and taken it with him. He hobbled to the door and turned to larboard out of it, the way the running steps had gone.

33

Chadwick, hampered by the weight and bulk of the grip, was at the bottom of the aft stairway when O'Hara reached the top. He glanced upward, saw O'Hara, and began to race frantically toward the nearby main-deck staircase. He banged into passengers, scattering them; whirled a fat woman around like a ballerina executing a pirouette and sent the reticule she had been carrying over the rail into the river.

Men commenced calling in angry voices and milling about as O'Hara tumbled down the stairs to the deckhouse. A bearded, red-shirted miner stepped into Chadwick's path at the top of the main-deck stairway; without slowing, the cub pilot bowled him over as if he were a giant ninepin and went down the stairs in a headlong dash. O'Hara lurched through the confusion of passengers and descended after him, cursing eloquently all the while.

Chadwick shoved two startled Chinese out of the way at the foot of the stairs and raced toward the taffrail, looking back over his shoulder. The bloody fool was going to jump into the river, O'Hara thought. And when he did, the weight of the gold would take both him and the bag straight to the bottom —

All at once O'Hara became aware that there were not many passengers inhabiting the aft section of the main deck, when there should have been a clotted mass of them. Some of those who were present had heard the commotion on the upper deck and been drawn to the staircase; the rest were split into two groups, one lining the larboard rail and the other lining the starboard, and their attention was held by a different spectacle. Some were murmuring excitedly; others looked amused; still others wore apprehensive expressions. The center section of the deck opposite the taffrail was completely cleared.

The reason for this was that a small, rusted, and very old half-pounder had been set up on wooden chocks at the taffrail, aimed downriver like an impolitely pointing finger.

Beside the cannon was a keg of black powder and a charred-looking ramrod.

And surrounding the cannon were the Mulrooney Guards, one of whom held a firebrand poised above the fuse vent and all of whom were now loudly singing "The Wearing of the Green."

O'Hara knew in that moment what it was the Mulrooneys had had secreted inside their wooden crate, and why they had been so anxious to get it aboard without having the contents examined; and he knew the meaning of Billy Culligan's remark about planning to start off St. Patrick's day with a mighty salute. He stopped running and opened his mouth to shout at Chadwick, who was still fleeing and still looking back over his shoulder. He could not recall afterward if he actually *did* shout or not; if so, it was akin to whispering in a thunderstorm.

The Mulrooney cannoneer touched off the fuse. The other Mulrooney Guards scattered, still singing. The watching passengers huddled farther back, some averting their eyes. Chadwick kept on running toward the taffrail.

And the cannon, as well as the keg of black powder, promptly blew up.

The *Delta Star* lurched and rolled with the sudden concussion. A great sweeping cloud of sulfurous black smoke enveloped the riverboat. O'Hara caught hold of one of the uprights in the starboard rail and clung to it, coughing and choking. Too much black powder and not enough bracing, he thought. Then he thought: I hope Hattie had the good sense to stay where she was on the deckhouse.

The steamer was in a state of bedlam: everyone on each

of the three decks screaming or shouting. Some of the passengers thought a boiler had exploded, a common steamboat hazard. When the smoke finally began to dissipate, O'Hara looked in the direction of the center taffrail and discovered that most of it, like the cannon, was missing. The deck in that area was blackened and scarred, some of the boarding torn into splinters.

But there did not seem to have been any casualties. A few passengers had received minor injuries, most of them Mulrooney Guards, and several were speckled with black soot. No one had fallen overboard. Even Chadwick had miraculously managed to survive the concussion, despite his proximity to the cannon when it and the powder keg had gone up. He was moaning feebly and moving his arms and legs, looking like a bedraggled chimney sweep, when O'Hara reached his side.

The grip containing the gold had fared somewhat better. Chadwick had been shielding it with his body at the moment of the blast, and while it was torn open and the leather pouches scattered about, most of the sacks were intact. One or two had split open, and particles of gold dust glittered in the sooty air. The preponderance of passengers were too concerned with their own welfare to notice; those who did stared with disbelief but kept their distance, for no sooner had O'Hara reached Chadwick than the captain and half a dozen of the deck crew arrived.

"Chadwick?" the captain said in amazement. "*Chadwick's* the thief?"

"Aye, he's the one."

"But . . . what happened? What was he doing here with the gold?"

"I was chasing him, the spalpeen."

"You were? Then . . . you knew of his guilt before the

explosion? How?"

"I'll explain it all to ye later," O'Hara said. "Right now there's me wife to consider."

He left the bewildered captain and his crew to attend to Chadwick and the gold, and went to find Hattie.

Shortly past nine, an hour after the *Delta Star* had docked at the foot of Stockton's Center Street, O'Hara stood with Hattie and a group of men on the landing. He wore his last clean suit, a broadcloth, and a bright green tie in honor of St. Patrick's Day. The others, clustered around him, were Bridgeman, the captain, the Nevada reporter, a hawkish man who was Stockton's sheriff, and two officials of the California Merchants Bank. Chadwick had been removed to the local jail in the company of a pair of deputies and a doctor. The Mulrooney Guards, after medical treatment, a severe reprimand, and a promise to pay all damages to the packet, had been released to continue their merrymaking in Green Park.

The captain was saying, "We are all deeply indebted to you, Mr. O'Hara. It would have been a black day if Chadwick had succeeded in escaping with the gold — a black day for us all."

"I only did me duty," O'Hara said solemnly.

"It is unfortunate that the California Merchants Bank cannot offer you a reward," one of the bank officials said. "However, we are not a wealthy concern, as our urgent need for the consignment of dust attests. But I don't suppose you could accept a reward in any case; the Pinkertons never do, I'm told."

"Aye, that's true."

Bridgeman said, "Will you explain now how you knew Chadwick was the culprit? And how he accomplished the

37

theft? He refused to confess, you know."

O'Hara nodded. He told them of finding the war-issue coin under the pilothouse stove; his early suspicions of the gambler, Colfax; the reporter's remark that such coins were being used in California to decorate leather goods; his growing certainty that he had seen and heard enough to piece together the truth, and yet his maddening inability to cudgel forth the necessary scraps from his memory.

"It wasn't until this morning that the doors in me mind finally opened," he said. He looked at the newspaperman. "It was this gentleman that gave me the key."

The reporter was surprised. "*I* gave you the key?"

"Ye did," O'Hara told him. "Ye said of the river: *Clear as a mirror, isn't it?* Do ye remember saying that, while we were together at the rail?"

"I do. But I don't see —"

"It was the word *mirror*," O'Hara said. "It caused me to think of reflection, and all at once I was recalling how I'd been able to see me own image in the pilothouse windshield soon after the robbery. Yet Chadwick claimed he was sitting in the pilot's seat when he heard the door open just before he was struck, and that he didn't turn because he thought it was the captain and Mr. Bridgeman returning from supper. But if I was able to see *me* reflection in the glass, Chadwick would sure have been able to see his — and anybody creeping up behind him.

"Then I recalled something else: Chadwick had his coat buttoned when I first entered the pilothouse, on a warm night like the last. Why? And why did his trousers look so baggy, as though they might fall down?

"Well, then, the answer was this: After Chadwick broke open the safe and the strongbox, his problem was what to do with the gold. He couldn't risk a trip to his quarters while he was alone in the pilothouse; he might be seen, and there was also the possibility that the *Delta Star* would run into a bar or snag if she slipped off course. D'ye recall saying it was a miracle such hadn't happened, Captain, thinking as ye were then that Chadwick had been unconscious for some time?"

The captain said he did.

"So Chadwick had to have the gold on his person," O'Hara said, "when you and Mr. Bridgeman found him, and when Hattie and I entered soon afterward. He couldn't have removed it until later, when he claimed to be feeling dizzy and you escorted him to his cabin. That, now, is the significance of the buttoned coat and the baggy trousers.

"What he must have done was to take off his belt, the wide one decorated with war-issue coins that I found in his cabin, and use it to strap the gold pouches above his waist — a makeshift money belt, ye see. He was in such a rush, for fear of being found out, that he failed to notice when one of the coins popped loose and rolled under the stove.

"Once he had the pouches secured, he waited until he heard Mr. Bridgeman and the captain returning, the while tending to his piloting duties; then he lay down on the floor and pretended to've been knocked senseless. He kept his loose coat buttoned for fear someone would notice the thickness about his upper middle, and that he was no longer wearing his belt in its proper place; and he kept hitching up his trousers because he wasn't wearing the belt in its proper place."

Hattie took her husband's arm. "Fergus, what did Chadwick do with the gold afterward? Did he have it hidden in his quarters all along?"

"No, me lady. I expect he was afraid of a search, so first chance he had he put the gold into the calfskin grip and then hung the grip from a metal hook inside the gallows frame."

The Stockton sheriff asked, "How could you possibly have deduced that fact?"

"While in the pilothouse after the robbery," O'Hara said, "I noticed that Chadwick's coat was soiled with dust and soot from his lying on the floor. But it also showed streaks of grease, which couldn't have come from the floor. When the other pieces fell into place this morning, I reasoned that he might have picked up the grease marks while making preparations to hide the gold. My consideration then was that he'd have wanted a place close to his quarters, and the only such place with grease about it was the gallows frame. The hook I discovered inside was new and free of grease; Chadwick, therefore, must have put it there only recently — tonight, in fact, thus accounting for the grease on his coat."

"Amazing detective work," the reporter said, "simply amazing."

Everyone else agreed.

"You really are a fine detective, Fergus O'Hara," Hattie said. "Amazing, indeed."

O'Hara said nothing. Now that they were five minutes parted from the others, walking alone together along Stockton's dusty main street, he had begun scowling and grumbling to himself.

Hattie ventured, "It's a splendid, sunny St. Patrick's Day. Shall we join the festivities in Green Park?"

"We've nothing to celebrate," O'Hara muttered.

"Still thinking about the gold, are you?"

"And what else would I be thinking about?" he said. "Fine detective — faugh! Some consolation *that* is!"

It was Hattie's turn to be silent.

O'Hara wondered sourly what those lads back at the landing would say if they knew the truth of the matter: That he was no more a Pinkerton operative than were the Mulrooney Guards. That he had only been *impersonating* one toward his own ends, in this case and others since he had taken the railroad pass and letter of introduction off the chap in Saint Louis the previous year — the Pinkerton chap who'd foolishly believed he was taking O'Hara to jail. That he had wanted the missing pouches of gold for himself and Hattie. And that he, Fergus O'Hara, was the finest *confidence man* in these sovereign United States, come to Stockton, California, to have for a ride a banker who intended to cheat the government by buying up Indian land.

Well, those lads would never know any of this, because he had duped them all — brilliantly, as always. And for nothing. Nothing!

He moaned aloud, "Forty thousand in gold, Hattie. Forty thousand that I was holding in me hands, clutched fair to me black heart, when that rascal Chadwick burst in on me. Two more minutes, just two more minutes . . ."

"It was Providence," she said. "You were never meant to have that gold, Fergus."

"What d'ye mean? The field was white for the sickle —"

"Not a bit of that," Hattie said. "And if you'll be truthful with yourself, you'll admit you enjoyed every minute of your play-acting of a detective; every minute of the explaining just now of your brilliant deductions."

"I didn't," O'Hara lied weakly. "I hate detectives . . ."

"Bosh. I'm glad the gold went to its rightful owners, and you should be too because your heart is about as black as this sunny morning. You've only stolen from dishonest men in all the time I've known you. Why, if you *had* succeeded in filching the gold, you'd have begun despising yourself sooner than you realize — not only because it belongs to honest citizens but because you would have committed the crime on St. Patrick's Day. If you stop to consider it, you wouldn't commit *any* crime on St. Pat's Day, now would you?"

O'Hara grumbled and glowered, but he was remembering his thoughts in Chadwick's cabin, when he had held the gold in his hands — thoughts of the captain's reputation and possible loss of position, and of the urgent need of the new branch bank in Stockton. He was not at all sure, now, that he would have kept the pouches if Chadwick had not burst in on him. He might well have returned them to the captain. Confound it, that was just what he would have done.

Hattie was right about St. Pat's Day, too. He would not feel decent if he committed a crime on —

Abruptly, he stopped walking. Then he put down their luggage and said, "You wait here, me lady. There's something that needs doing before we set off for Green Park."

Before Hattie could speak, he was on his way through clattering wagons and carriages to where a towheaded boy was scuffling with a mongrel dog. He halted before the boy. "Now then, lad, how would ye like to have a dollar for twenty minutes good work?"

The boy's eyes grew wide. "What do I have to do, mister?"

O'Hara removed from the inside pocket of his coat an expensive gold American Horologe watch, which happened to be in his possession as the result of a momentary lapse in good sense and fingers made nimble during his misspent youth in New Orleans. He extended it to the boy.

"Take this down to the *Delta Star* steamboat and look about for a tall gentleman with a mustache and a fine head of bushy hair, a newspaperman from Nevada. When ye've found him, give him the watch and tell him Mr. Fergus O'Hara came upon it, is returning it, and wishes him a happy St. Patrick's Day."

"What's his name, mister?" the boy asked. "It'll help me find him quicker."

O'Hara could not seem to recall it, if he had ever heard it in the first place. He took the watch again, opened the hunting-style case, and saw that a name had been etched in flowing script on the dustcover. He handed the watch back to the boy.

"Clemens, it is," O'Hara said then. "A Mr. Samuel Langhorne Clemens . . ."

The Desert Limited

Across the aisle and five seats ahead of where Quincannon and Sabina were sitting, Evan Gaunt sat looking out through the day coach's dusty window. There was little enough to see outside the fast-moving Desert Limited except sun-blasted wasteland, but Gaunt seemed to find the emptiness absorbing. He also seemed perfectly comfortable, his expression one of tolerable boredom: a prosperous businessman, for all outward appearances, without a care or worry, much less a past history that included grand larceny, murder, and fugitive warrants in three western states.

"Hell and damn," Quincannon muttered. "He's been lounging there nice as you please for nearly forty minutes. What the devil is he planning?"

Sabina said, "He may not be planning anything, John."

"Faugh. He's trapped on this iron horse and he knows it."

"He does if he recognized you, too. You're positive he did?"

"I am, and no mistake. He caught me by surprise while I was talking to the conductor; I couldn't turn away in time."

"Still, you said it was eight years ago that you had your only run-in with him. And at that, you saw each other for less than two hours."

"He's changed little enough and so have I. A hard case like Gaunt never forgets a lawman's face, any more than I do a felon's. It's one of the reasons he's managed to evade capture as long as he has."

"Well, what *can* he be planning?" Sabina said. She was leaning close, her mouth only a few inches from Quincannon's ear, so their voices wouldn't carry to nearby passengers. Ordinarily the nearness of her fine body and the warmth of her breath on his skin would have been a powerful distraction; such intimacy was all too seldom permitted. But the combination of desert heat, the noisy coach, and Evan Gaunt made him only peripherally aware of her charms. "There are no stops between Needles and Barstow; Gaunt must know that. And if he tries to jump for it while we're traveling at this speed, his chances of survival are slim to none. The only sensible thing he can do is to wait until we slow for Barstow and then jump and run."

"Is it? He can't hope to escape that way. Barstow is too small and the surroundings too open. He saw me talking to Mr. Bridges; it's likely he also saw the Needles station agent running for his office. If so, it's plain to him that a wire has been sent to Barstow and the sheriff and a complement of deputies will be waiting. I was afraid he'd hopped back off then and there, those few minutes I lost track of him shortly afterward, but it would've been a foolish move and he isn't the sort to panic. Even if he'd gotten clear of the train and the Needles yards, there are too many soldiers and Indian trackers at Fort Mojave."

"I don't see that Barstow is a much better choice for him. Unless. . . ."

"Unless what?"

"Is he the kind to take a hostage?"

Quincannon shifted position on his seat. Even though this was October, usually one of the cooler months in the Mojave Desert, it was near-stifling in the coach; sweat oiled his skin, trickled through the brush of his freebooter's beard. It was crowded, too, with nearly every seat occupied in this car and the other coaches. He noted again, as he had earlier, that at least a third of the passengers here were women and children.

He said slowly, "I wouldn't put anything past Evan Gaunt. He might take a hostage, if he believed it was his only hope of freedom. But it's more likely that he'll try some sort of trick first. Tricks are the man's stock-in-trade."

"Does Mr. Bridges know how potentially dangerous he is?"

"There wasn't time to discuss Gaunt or his past in detail. If I'd had my way, the train would've been held in Needles and Gaunt arrested there. Bridges might've agreed to that if the Needles sheriff hadn't been away in Yuma and only a part-time deputy left in charge. When the station agent told him the deputy is an unreliable drunkard, and that it would take more than an hour to summon soldiers from the fort, Bridges balked. He's more concerned about railroad time-tables than he is about the capture of a fugitive."

Sabina said, "Here he comes again. Mr. Bridges. From the look of him, I'd say he's very much concerned about Gaunt."

"It's his own blasted fault."

The conductor was a spare, sallow-faced man in his forties who wore his uniform and cap as if they were badges of honor. The brass buttons shone, as did the heavy gold watch chain and its polished elk's-tooth fob; his tie was tightly knotted and his vest buttoned in spite of the heat. He glanced nervously at Evan Gaunt as he passed, and then mournfully and a little accusingly at Quincannon, as if he and not Gaunt was to blame for this dilemma. Bridges was not a man who dealt well with either a crisis or a disruption of his precise routine.

When he'd left the car again, Sabina said, "You and I

46

could arrest Gaunt ourselves, John. Catch him by surprise, get the drop on him . . .”

"He won't be caught by surprise — not now that he knows we're onto him. You can be sure he has a weapon close to hand and won't hesitate to use it. Bracing him in these surroundings would be risking harm to an innocent bystander.”

"Then what do you suggest we do?”

"Nothing, for the present, except to keep a sharp eye on him. And be ready to act when he does.”

Quincannon dried his forehead and beard with his handkerchief, wishing this was one of Southern Pacific's luxury trains — the Golden State Limited, for instance, on the San Francisco-Chicago run. The Golden State was ventilated by a new process that renewed the air inside several times every hour, instead of having it circulated only slightly and cooled not at all by sluggish fans. It was also brightly lighted by electricity generated from the axles of moving cars, instead of murkily lit by oil lamps; and its seats and berths were more comfortable, its food better by half than the fare served on this southwestern desert run.

He said rhetorically, "Where did Gaunt disappear to after he spied me with Bridges? He gave me the slip on purpose, I'm sure of it. Whatever he's scheming, that's part of the game.”

"It was no more than fifteen minutes before he showed up here and took his seat.”

"Fifteen minutes is plenty of time for mischief. He has more gall than a roomful of senators.” Quincannon consulted his turnip watch; it was nearly two o'clock. "Four, is it, that we're due in Barstow?”

"Four oh five.”

"More than two hours. Damnation!”

"Try not to fret, John. Remember your blood pressure."

Another ten minutes crept away. Sabina sat quietly, repairing one of the grosgrain ribbons that had come undone on her traveling hat. Quincannon fidgeted, not remembering his blood pressure, barely noticing the way light caught Sabina's dark auburn hair and made it shine like burnished copper. And still Evan Gaunt peered out at the unchanging panorama of sagebrush, greasewood, and barren, tawny hills.

No sweat or sign of worry on *his* face, Quincannon thought with rising irritation. A bland and unmemorable countenance it was, too, to the point where Gaunt would all but become invisible in a crowd of more noteworthy men. He was thirty-five, of average height, lean and wiry; and although he had grown a thin mustache and sideburns since their previous encounter, the facial hair did little to individualize him. His lightweight sack suit and derby hat were likewise undistinguished. A human chameleon, by God. That was another reason Gaunt had avoided the law for so long.

There was no telling what had brought him to Needles, a settlement on the Colorado River, or where he was headed from there. Evan Gaunt seldom remained in one place for any length of time — he was a predator constantly on the prowl for any illegal enterprise that required his particular brand of guile. Extortion, confidence swindles, counterfeiting, bank robbery — Gaunt had done them all and more, and served not a day in prison for his transgressions. The closest he'd come was that day eight years ago when Quincannon, still affiliated with the U.S. Secret Service, had led a raid on the headquarters of a Los Angeles-based counterfeiting ring. Gaunt was one of the koniakers taken prisoner after a brief skirmish and personally questioned by

48

Quincannon. Later, while being taken to jail by local authorities, Gaunt had wounded a deputy and made a daring escape in a stolen milk wagon — an act that had fixed the man firmly in Quincannon's memory.

When he'd spied Gaunt on the station platform in Needles, it had been a much-needed uplift to his spirits: he'd been feeling less than pleased with his current lot. He and Sabina had spent a week in Tombstone investigating a bogus mining operation, and the case hadn't turned out as well as they'd hoped. And after more than twenty-four hours on the Desert Limited, they were still two long days from San Francisco. Even in the company of a beautiful woman, train travel was monotonous — unless, of course, you were sequestered with her in the privacy of a drawing room. But there were no drawing rooms to be had on the Desert Limited, and even if there were, he couldn't have had Sabina in one. Not on a train, not in their Tombstone hotel, not in San Francisco — not anywhere, it seemed, past, present, or future. Unrequited desire was a maddening thing, especially when you were in such close proximity to the object of your desire. His passion for his partner was exceeded only by his passion for profitable detective work; Carpenter and Quincannon, Lovers, as an adjunct to Carpenter and Quincannon, Professional Detective Services, would have made him a truly happy man.

Evan Gaunt had taken his mind off that subject by offering a prize almost as inviting. Not only were there fugitive warrants on Gaunt, but two rewards totaling five thousand dollars. See to it that he was taken into custody and the reward money would belong to Carpenter and Quincannon. Simple enough task, on the surface; most of the proper things had been done in Needles and it seemed that Gaunt was indeed trapped on this clattering, swaying iron horse.

And yet the man's audacity, combined with those blasted fifteen minutes —

Quincannon tensed. Gaunt had turned away from the window, was getting slowly to his feet. He yawned, stretched, and then stepped into the aisle; in his right hand was the carpetbag he'd carried on board in Needles. Without hurry, and without so much as an eye flick in their direction, he sauntered past where Quincannon and Sabina were sitting and opened the rear door.

Close to Sabina's ear Quincannon murmured, "I'll shadow him. You wait here." He adjusted the Navy Colt he wore holstered under his coat before he slipped out into the aisle.

The next car back was the second-class Pullman. Gaunt went through it, through the first-class Pullman, through the dining car and the observation lounge, into the smoker. Quincannon paused outside the smoker door; through the glass he watched Gaunt sit down, produce a cigar from his coat pocket, and snip off the end with a pair of gold cutters. Settling in here, evidently as he'd settled into the day coach. Damn the man's coolness! He entered as Gaunt was applying a lucifer's flame to the cigar end. Both pretended the other didn't exist.

In a seat halfway back Quincannon fiddled with pipe and shag-cut tobacco, listening to the steady, throbbing rhythm of steel on steel, while Gaunt smoked his cigar with obvious pleasure. The process took more than ten minutes, at the end of which time the fugitive got leisurely to this feet and started forward again. A return to his seat in the coach? No, not yet. Instead he entered the gentlemen's lavatory and closed himself inside.

Quincannon stayed where he was, waiting, his eye on the lavatory door. His pipe went out; he relighted it. Two more men — a rough-garbed miner and a gaudily outfitted drummer — came into the smoker. Couplings banged and the car lurched slightly as its wheels passed over a rough section of track. Outside the windows a lake shimmered into view on the southern desert flats, then abruptly vanished: heat mirage.

The door to the lavatory remained closed.

A prickly sensation that had nothing to do with the heat formed between Quincannon's shoulder blades. How long had Gaunt been in there? Close to ten minutes. He tamped the dottle from his pipe, stowed the briar in the pocket of his cheviot. The flashily dressed drummer left the car; a fat man with muttonchop whiskers like miniature tumbleweeds came in. The fat man paused, glancing around, then turned to the lavatory door and tried the latch. When he found it locked he rapped on the panel. There was no response.

Quincannon was on his feet by then, with the prickly sensation as hot as a fire-rash. He prodded the fat man aside, ignoring the indignant oath this brought him, and laid an ear against the panel. All he could hear were train sounds: the pound of beating trucks on the fishplates, the creak and groan of axle play, and the whisper of the wheels. He banged on the panel with his fist, much harder than the fat man had. Once, twice, three times. This likewise produced no response.

"Hell and damn!" he growled aloud, startling the fat man, who turned quick for the door and almost collided with another just stepping through. The newcomer, fortuitously enough, was Mr. Bridges.

When the conductor saw Quincannon's scowl, his back stiffened and alarm pinched his sallow features. "What is it?" he demanded. "What's happened?"

"Even Gaunt went in here some minutes ago and he hasn't come out."

"You don't think he — ?"

"Use your master key and we'll soon find out."

Bridges unlocked the door. Quincannon pushed in first, his hand on the butt of his Navy Colt — and immediately blistered the air with a five-jointed oath.

The cubicle was empty.

"Gone, by all the saints!" Bridges said behind him. "The damned fool went through the window and jumped."

The lone window was small, designed for ventilation, but not too small for a man Gaunt's size to wiggle through. It was shut but not latched; Quincannon hoisted the sash, poked his head out. Hot, dust-laden wind made him pull it back in after a few seconds.

"Gone, yes," he said, "but I'll eat my hat if he jumped at the rate of speed we've been traveling."

"But — but he must have. The only other place he could've gone —"

"Up atop the car. That's where he did go."

Bridges didn't want to believe it. His thinking was plain: If Gaunt had jumped, he was rid of the threat to his and his passengers' security. He said, "A climb like that is just as dangerous as jumping."

"Not for a nimble and desperate man."

"He couldn't hide up there. Nor on top of any of the other cars. Do you think he crawled along the roofs and then climbed back down between cars?"

"It's the likeliest explanation."

"Why would he do such a thing? There's nowhere for him to hide *inside,* either. The only possible places are too easily searched. He must know that, if he's ridden a train before."

"We'll search them anyway," Quincannon said darkly. "Every nook and cranny from locomotive to caboose, if necessary. Evan Gaunt is still on the Desert Limited, Mr. Bridges, and we're damned well going to find him."

The first place they went was out onto the platform between the lounge car and the smoker, where Quincannon climbed the iron ladder attached to the smoker's rear wall. From its top he could look along the roofs of the cars, protecting his eyes with an upraised arm: the coal-flavored smoke that rolled back from the locomotive's stack was peppered with hot cinders. As expected, he saw no sign of Gaunt. Except, that was, for marks in the thin layers of grit that coated the tops of both lounge car and smoker.

"There's no doubt now that he climbed up," he said when he rejoined Bridges. "The marks on the grit are fresh."

The conductor's answering nod was reluctant and pained.

Quincannon used his handkerchief on his sweating face. It came away stained from the dirt and coal smoke, and when he saw the streaks, his mouth stretched in a thin smile. "Another fact: No matter how long Gaunt was above or how far he crawled, he had to be filthy when he came down. Someone may have seen him. And he won't have wandered far in that condition. Either he's hiding where he lighted, or he took the time to wash up and change clothes for some reason."

"I still say it makes no sense. Not a lick of sense."

"It does to him. And it will to us when we find him."

They went to the rear of the train and began to work their way forward, Bridges alerting members of the crew and Quincannon asking questions of selected passengers. No one had seen Gaunt. By the time they reached the first-class Pullman, the urgency and frustration both men felt were taking a toll: preoccupied, Quincannon nearly bowled over a pudgy, bonneted matron outside the women's lavatory and Bridges snapped at a white-maned, senatorial gent who objected to having his drawing room searched. It took them ten minutes to comb the compartments there and the berths in the second-class Pullman: another exercise in futility.

In the first of the day coaches, Quincannon beckoned Sabina to join them and quickly explained what had happened. She took the news stoically; unlike him, she met any crisis with a shield of calm. She said only, "He may be full of tricks, but he can't make himself invisible. Hiding is one thing; getting off this train is another. We'll find him."

"He won't be in the other two coaches. That leaves the baggage car, the tender, and the locomotive; he has to be in one of them."

"Shall I go with you and Mr. Bridges?"

"I've another idea. Do you have your derringer with you or packed away in your grip?"

"In here." She patted her reticule.

"Backtrack on us, then; we may have somehow overlooked him. But don't take a moment's chance if he turns up."

"I won't," she said. "And I'll warn you the same."

The baggage master's office was empty. Beyond, the door to the baggage car stood open a few inches.

Scowling, Bridges stepped up to the door. "Dan?" he called. "You in there?"

No answer.

Quincannon drew his revolver, shouldered Bridges aside, and widened the opening. The oil lamps were lighted; most of the interior was visible. Boxes, crates, stacks of luggage, and express parcels — but no sign of human habitation.

"What do you see, Mr. Quincannon?"

"Nothing. No one."

"Oh, Lordy, I don't like this, none of this. Where's Dan? He's almost always here, and he never leaves the door open or unlocked when he isn't. Gaunt? Is he responsible for this? Oh, Lordy, I should've listened to you and held the train in Needles."

Quincannon shut his ears to the conductor's babbling. He eased his body through the doorway, into an immediate crouch behind a packing crate. Peering out, he saw no evidence of disturbance. Three large crates and a pair of trunks were belted into place along the near wall. Against the far wall stood a wheeled luggage cart piled with carpetbags, grips, and war bags. More luggage rested in neat rows nearby; he recognized one of the larger grips, pale blue and floral-patterned, as Sabina's. None of it appeared to have been moved except by the natural motion of the train.

Toward the front was a shadowed area into which he couldn't see clearly. He straightened, eased around and alongside the crate with his Navy at the ready. No sounds, no movement . . . until a brief lurch and shudder as the locomotive nosed into an uphill curve and the engineer used his air. Then something slid into view in the shadowy corner.

A leg. A man's leg, bent and twisted.

Quincannon muttered an oath and closed the gap by another half dozen paces. He could see the rest of the man's body then — a sixtyish gent in a trainman's uniform, lying crumpled, his cap off and a dark blotch staining his gray hair. Quincannon went to one knee beside him, found a thin wrist, and pressed it for a pulse. The beat was there, faint and irregular.

"Mr. Bridges! Be quick!"

The conductor came running inside. When he saw the unconscious crewman he jerked to a halt; a moaning sound vibrated in his throat. "My God, Old Dan! Is he — ?"

"No. Wounded but still alive."

"Shot?"

"Struck with something heavy. A gun butt, like as not."

"Gaunt, damn his eyes."

"He was after something in here. Take a quick look around, Mr. Bridges. Tell me if you notice anything missing or out of place."

"What about Dan? One of the drawing-room passengers is a doctor."

"Fetch him. But look here first."

Bridges took a quick turn through the car. "Nothing missing or misplaced, as far as I can tell. Dan's the only one who'll know for sure."

"Are you carrying weapons of any kind? Boxed rifles, handguns? Or dynamite or black powder?"

"No, no, nothing like that."

When Bridges had gone for the doctor Quincannon pillowed the baggage master's head on one of the smaller bags. He touched a ribbon of blood on the man's cheek, found it nearly dry. The assault hadn't taken place within the past hour, after Gaunt's disappearance from the lavatory. It had happened earlier, during his fifteen-minute absence outside Needles — the very first thing he'd done, evidently, after recognizing Quincannon.

That made the breaching of the baggage car a major part of his escape plan. But what could the purpose be, if nothing here was missing or disturbed?

The doctor was young, brusque, and efficient. Quincannon and Bridges left Old Dan in his care and hurried forward. Gaunt wasn't hiding in the tender; and neither the taciturn engineer nor the sweat-soaked fireman had been bothered by anyone or seen anyone since Needles.

That took care of the entire train, front to back. And where the bloody hell was Evan Gaunt?

Quincannon was beside himself as he led the way back down-train. As he and Bridges passed through the forward day coach, the locomotive's whistle sounded a series of short toots.

"Oh, Lordy," the conductor said. "That's the first signal for Barstow."

"How long before we slow for the yards?"

"Ten minutes."

"Hell and damn!"

They found Sabina waiting at the rear of the second coach. She shook her head as they approached: her back-tracking had also proven fruitless.

The three of them held a huddled conference. Quincannon's latest piece of bad news put ridges in the smoothness of Sabina's forehead, her only outward re-action. "You're certain nothing was taken from the baggage car, Mr. Bridges?"

"Not absolutely, no. Every item in the car would have to be examined and then checked against the baggage mani-fest."

"If Gaunt did steal something," Quincannon said, "he was some careful not to call attention to the fact, in case the baggage master regained consciousness or was found before he could make good his escape."

"Which could mean," Sabina said, "that whatever it was would've been apparent to us at a cursory search."

"Either that, or where it was taken from would've been apparent."

57

Something seemed to be nibbling at her mind; her expression had turned speculative. "I wonder . . ."

"What do you wonder?"

The locomotive's whistle sounded again. There was a rocking and the loud thump of couplings as the engineer began the first slackening of their speed. Bridges said, "Five minutes to Barstow. If Gaunt is still on board —"

"He is."

"— do you think he'll try to get off here?"

"No doubt of it. Wherever he's hiding, he can't hope to avoid being found in a concentrated search. And he knows we'll mount one in Barstow, with the entire train crew and the authorities."

"What do you advise we do?"

"First, tell your porters not to allow anyone off at the station until you give the signal. And when passengers do disembark, they're to do so single file at one exit only. That will prevent Gaunt from slipping off in a crowd."

"The exit between this car and the next behind?"

"Good. Meet me there when you're done."

Bridges hurried away.

Quincannon asked Sabina, "Will you wait with me or take another pass through the cars?"

"Neither," she said. "I noticed something earlier that I thought must be a coincidence. Now I'm not so sure it is."

"Explain that."

"There's no time now. You'll be the first to know if I'm right."

"Sabina . . ." But she had already turned her back and was purposefully heading forward.

He took himself out onto the platform between the coaches. The Limited had slowed to half speed; once more its whistle cut shrilly through the hot desert stillness. He stood holding onto the handbar on the station side, leaning out to where he could look both ways along the cars — a precaution in the event Gaunt tried to jump and run in the yards. But he was thinking that this was another exercise in futility. Gaunt's scheme was surely too clever for such a predictable ending.

Bridges reappeared and stood watch on the offside as the Limited entered the railyards. On Quincannon's side the dun-colored buildings of Barstow swam into view ahead. Thirty years ago, at the close of the Civil War, the town — one of the last stops on the old Mormon Trail between Salt Lake City and San Bernardino — had been a teeming, brawling shipping point for supplies to and high-grade silver ore from the mines in Calico and other camps in the nearby hills. Now, with Calico a near-ghost town and most of the mines shut down, Barstow was a far tamer and less populated settlement. In its lawless days, Evan Gaunt could have found immediate aid and comfort for a price, and for another price, safe passage out of town and state; in the new Barstow he stood little enough chance — and none at all unless he was somehow able to get clear of the Desert Limited and into a hidey-hole.

A diversion of some sort? That was one possible gambit. Quincannon warned himself to remain alert for anything — anything at all — out of the ordinary.

Sabina was on his mind, too. Where the devil had she gone in such a hurry. What sort of coincidence —

Brake shoes squealed on the sun-heated rails as the Limited neared the station platform. Less than a score of men and women waited in the shade of a roof overhang; the knot of four solemn-faced gents standing apart at the near end was bound to be Sheriff Hoover and his deputies.

Quincannon swiveled his head again. Steam and smoke

59

hazed the air, but he could see clearly enough: No one was making an effort to leave the train on this side. Nor on the offside, else Bridges would have cut loose with a shout.

The engineer slid the cars to a rattling stop alongside the platform. Quincannon jumped down with Bridges close behind him, as the four lawmen ran over through a cloud of steam to meet them. Sheriff Hoover was burly and sported a tobacco-stained mustache; on the lapel of his dusty frock coat was a five-pointed star, and in the holster at his belt was a heavy Colt Dragoon. His three deputies were also well-armed.

"Well, Mr. Bridges," the sheriff said. "Where's this man, Evan Gaunt? Point him out and we'll have him in irons before he can blink twice."

Bridges said dolefully, "We don't have any idea where he is."

"You don't — What's this? You mean to say he jumped somewhere along the line?"

"I don't know what to think. Mr. Quincannon believes he's still on board, hiding."

"Does he now." Hoover turned to Quincannon, gave him a quick appraisal. "So you're the flycop, eh? Well, sir? Explain."

Quincannon explained, tersely, with one eye on the sheriff and the other on the rolling stock. Through the grit-streaked windows he could see passengers lining up for departure; Sabina, he was relieved to note, was one of them. A porter stood between the second and third day coaches, waiting for the signal from Bridges to put down the steps.

"Damn strange," Hoover said at the end of Quincannon's recital. "You say you searched everywhere, every possible hiding place. If that's so, how could Gaunt still be on board?"

60

"I can't say yet. But he is — I'll stake my reputation on it."

"Well, then, we'll find him. Mr. Bridges, disembark your passengers. All of 'em, not just those for Barstow."

"Just as you say, Sheriff."

Bridges signaled the porter, who swung the steps down and permitted the exodus to begin. One of the first passengers to alight was Sabina. She came straight to where Quincannon stood, took hold of his arm, and drew him a few paces aside. Her manner was urgent, her eyes bright with triumph.

"John," she said, "I found him."

He had long ago ceased to be surprised at anything Sabina said or did; she was his equal as a detective in every way. He asked, "Where? How?"

She shook her head. "He'll be getting off any second."

"Getting off? How could he — ?"

"There he is!"

Quincannon squinted at the passengers who were just then disembarking: two women, one of whom had a small boy in tow. "Where? I don't see him —"

Sabina was moving again. Quincannon trailed after her, his hand on the Navy Colt inside his coat. The two women and the child were making their way past Sheriff Hoover and his deputies, none of whom was paying any attention to them. The woman towing the little boy was young and pretty, with tightly curled blond hair; the other woman, older and pudgy, powdered and rouged, wore a gray serge traveling dress and a close-fitting Langtry bonnet that covered most of her head and shadowed her face. She was the one, Quincannon realized, that he'd nearly bowled over outside the women's lavatory in the first-class Pullman.

She was also Evan Gaunt.

He found that out five seconds later, when Sabina boldly walked up and tore the bonnet off, revealing the short-haired male head and clean-shaven face hidden beneath.

Her actions so surprised Gaunt that he had no time to do anything but swipe at her with one arm, a blow that she nimbly dodged. Then he fumbled inside the reticule he carried and drew out a small-caliber pistol; at the same time, he commenced to run.

Sabina shouted, Quincannon shouted, someone else let out a thin scream; there was a small scrambling panic on the platform. But it lasted no more than a few seconds, and without a shot being fired. Gaunt was poorly schooled on the mechanics of running while garbed in women's clothing: the traveling dress's long skirt tripped him before he reached the station office. He went down in a tangle of arms, legs, petticoats, and assorted other garments that he had padded up and tied around his torso to create the illusion of pudginess. He still clutched the pistol when Quincannon reached him, but one well-placed kick and it went flying. Quincannon then dropped down on Gaunt's chest with both knees, driving the wind out of him in a grunting hiss. Another well-placed blow, this one to the jaw with Quincannon's meaty fist, put an end to the skirmish.

Sheriff Hoover, his deputies, Mr. Bridges, and the Limited's passengers stood gawping down at the now half-disguised and unconscious fugitive. Hoover was the first to speak. He said in tones of utter amazement, "Well, I'll be damned."

Which were Quincannon's sentiments exactly.

"So that's why he assaulted Old Dan in the baggage car," Bridges said a short while later. Evan Gaunt had been carted off in steel bracelets to the Barstow jail, and Sabina,

Quincannon, Hoover, and the conductor were grouped together in the station office for final words before the Desert
Limited continued on its way. "He was after a change of
women's clothing."

Sabina nodded. "He devised his plan as soon as he recognized John and realized his predicament. A quick thinker,
our Mr. Gaunt."

"The stolen clothing was hidden inside the carpetbag he
carried into the lavatory?"

"It was. He climbed out the window and over the tops of
the smoker and the lounge car to the first-class Pullman,
waited until the women's lavatory was empty, climbed down
through that window, locked the door, washed and shaved
off his mustache and sideburns, dressed in the stolen clothing, put on rouge and powder that he'd also pilfered, and
then disposed of his own clothes and carpetbag through the
lavatory window."

"And when he came out to take a seat in the forward day
coach," Quincannon said ruefully, "I nearly knocked him
down. If only I had. It would've saved us all considerable
difficulty."

Hoover said, "Don't chastise yourself, Mr. Quincannon.
You had no way of suspecting Gaunt had disguised himself
as a woman."

"That's not quite true," Sabina said. "Actually, John did
have a way of knowing — the same way I discovered the
masquerade, though at first notice I considered it a coincidence. Through simple familiarity."

"Familiarity with what?" Quincannon asked.

"John, you're one of the best detectives I've known, but
honestly, there are times when you're also one of the least
observant. Tell me, what did I wear on the trip out to Ari-
zona? What color and style of outfit? What type of hat?"

63

"I don't see what that has to do with —" Then, as the light dawned, he said in a small voice, "Oh."

"That's right," Sabina said, smiling. "Mr. Gaunt plundered the wrong woman's grip in the baggage car. The gray serge traveling dress and Langtry bonnet he was wearing are mine."

Medium Rare

The night was dark, cold; most of San Francisco was swaddled in a cloak of fog and low-hanging clouds that turned streetlights and house lights into ghostly smears. The bay, close by this residential district along lower Van Ness Avenue, was invisible and the foghorns that moaned on it had a lonely, lost-soul sound. Bittersharp, the wind nipped at Quincannon's cheeks, fluttered his thick piratical beard as he stepped down from the hansom. A sudden gust almost tore off his derby before he could clamp it down.

A fine night for spirits, he thought wryly. The liquid kind, to be sure — except that he had been a temperance man for several years now. And the supernatural kind, in which he believed not one whit.

He helped Sabina alight from the coach, turned to survey the house at which they were about to call. It was a modest gingerbread affair, its slender front yard enclosed by a black-iron picket fence. Rented, not purchased, as he had discovered earlier in the day. Gaslight flickered behind its lace-curtained front windows. No surprise there. Professor Vargas would have been careful to select a house that had not been wired for electricity; the sometimes spectral trembles produced by gas flame were much more suited to his purposes.

On the gate was a discreet bronze sign whose raised letters gleamed faintly in the outspill from a nearby streetlamp. Sabina went to peer at the sign as Quincannon paid and dismissed the hack driver. When he joined her he, too, bent for a look.

UNIFIED COLLEGE OF THE ATTUNED IMPULSES
Prof. A. Vargas
Spirit Medium and Counselor

"Bah. Hogwash," Quincannon said grumpily, straightening. "How can any sane person believe in such hokum?"

"Self-deception is the most powerful kind."

He made a derisive noise in his throat, a sound Sabina had once likened to the rumbling snarl of a mastiff.

She said, "If you enter growling and wearing that ferocious glare, you'll give the game away. We're here as potential devotees, not ardent sceptics."

"Devotees of claptrap."

"John, Mr. Buckley is paying us handsomely for this evening's work. Very handsomely, if you recall."

Quincannon recalled; his scowl faded and was replaced by a smile only those who knew him well would recognize as greed-based. Money, especially in large sums, was what soothed his savage breast. In fact, it was second only in his admiration to Sabina herself.

He glanced sideways at her. She looked even more fetching than usual this evening, dressed as she was in an outfit of black silk brocade, her raven hair topped by a stylish hat trimmed in white China silk. His mouth watered. A fine figure of a woman, Sabina Carpenter. A man engaged in the time-honored profession of detective couldn't ask for a more decorous — or a more intelligent and capable — partner. He could, however, ask for more than a straightforward business arrangement and an occasional night on the town followed by a chaste handshake at her door. Not getting it, not even coming close to getting it, was his greatest defeat, his greatest frustration. Why, he had never even been inside Sabina's Russian Hill flat. . . .

"John."

"Mmm?"

"Will you please stop staring at me that way."

"What way, my dear?"

"Like a cat at a bowl of cream. We've no time for dallying, we're late as it is. Mr. Buckley and the others will be waiting to begin the seance."

Quincannon took her arm, chastely, and led her through the gate. As they mounted the front stairs, he had a clear vision of Cyrus Buckley's bank check and a clear auditory recollection of the financier's promise of the check's twin should they successfully debunk Professor Vargas and his Unified College of the Attuned Impulses.

Buckley was a reluctant follower of spiritualism, in deference to his wife, who believed wholeheartedly in communication with the disembodied essences of the dead and such mediumistic double-talk as "spiritual vibrations of the positive and negative forces of material and astral planes." She continually sought audiences with their daughter, Bernice, the childhood victim of diphtheria, a quest which had led them to a succession of mediums and cost her husband "a goodly sum." Professor Vargas was the latest and by far the most financially threatening of these paranormal spirit-summoners. A recent arrival in San Francisco — from Chicago, he claimed — Vargas evidently had a more clever, extensive, and convincing repertoire of "spirit wonders" than any other medium Buckley had encountered, and of course his fees were exorbitant as a result.

The Buckleys had attended one of Vargas's sittings a few days ago — a dark seance in a locked room in his rented house. The professor had ordered himself securely tied to his chair and then proceeded to invoke a dazzling array of bell-ringing, table-tipping, spirit lights, automatic writings, ectoplasmic manifestations, and other phenomena. As his finale, he announced that he was being unfettered by his friendly spirit guide and guardian, Angkar, and the rope that had bound him was heard to fly through the air just before the lights were turned up; the rope, when examined, was completely free of the more than ten knots which had been tied into it. This supernatural flimflam had so impressed Margaret Buckley that she had returned the next day without her husband's knowledge and arranged for another sitting — tonight — and a series of private audiences at which Vargas promised to establish and maintain contact with the shade of the long-gone Bernice. Mrs. Buckley, in turn and in gratitude, was prepared to place unlimited funds in the medium's eager hands. "Endow the whole damned Unified College of the Attuned Impulses," was the way Buckley put it. Nothing he'd said or done could change his wife's mind. The only thing that would, he was convinced, was a public unmasking of the professor as the knave and charlatan he surely was. Hence, his visit to the Market Street offices of Carpenter & Quincannon, Professional Detective Services.

Quincannon had no doubt he and Sabina could accomplish the task. They had both had dealings with phony psychics before, Sabina when she was with the Pinkertons in Denver and on two occasions since they had opened their joint agency here. But Cyrus Buckley wasn't half so sanguine. "You'll not have an easy time of it," he'd warned them. "Professor Vargas is a rare bird and rare birds are not easily plucked. A medium among mediums."

Medium rare, is he? Quincannon thought as he twisted the doorbell handle. Not for long. He'll not only be plucked but done to a turn before this night is over.

The door was opened by a tiny woman of indeterminate age, dressed in a flowing ebon robe. Her skin was very white, her lips a bloody crimson in contrast; sleek brown hair was pulled tight around her head and fastened with a jeweled barette. Around her neck hung a silver amulet embossed with some sort of cabalistic design. "I am Annabelle," she said in sepulchral tones. "You are Mr. and Mrs. John Quinn?"

"We are," Quincannon said, wishing wistfully that it were true. Mr. and Mrs. John Quincannon, not Quinn. But Sabina had refused even to adopt his name for the evening's play-acting, insisting on the shortened version instead.

Annabelle took his greatcoat and Sabina's cape, hung them on a coat tree. According to Buckley, she was Professor Vargas's "psychic assistant." If she lived here with him, Quincannon mused, she was likely also his wife or mistress. Seeking communion with the afterworld did not preclude indulging in the pleasure of the earthly sphere, evidently; he had never met a medium who professed to be celibate and meant it.

"Follow me, please."

They trailed her down a murky hallway into a somewhat more brightly lighted parlor. Here they found two men dressed as Quincannon was, in broadcloth and fresh linen, and two women in long fashionable dresses; one of the men was Cyrus Buckley. But it was the room's fifth occupant who commanded immediate attention.

Even Quincannon, who was seldom impressed by physical stature, had to grudgingly admit that Professor A. Vargas was a rather imposing gent. Tall, dark-complected, with a curling black moustache and piercing, almost hypnotic eyes. Like his psychic assistant, he wore a long flowing black robe and a silver amulet. On the middle fingers of each hand were two enormous glittering rings of intricate design, both of which bore hieroglyphics similar to those which adorned the amulets.

He greeted his new guests effusively, pressing his lips to the back of Sabina's hand and then pumping Quincannon's in an iron grip. "I am Professor Vargas. Welcome, New Ones, welcome to the Unified College of the Attuned Impulses." His voice was rich, stentorian. "Mr. and Mrs. Quinn, is it not? Friends of the good Mr. Buckley? Your first sitting but I pray not your last. You are surrounded by many anxious friends in spirit-life who desire to communicate with you once you have learned more of the laws which govern their actions. Allow your impulses to attune with theirs and your spirit friends will soon identify themselves and speak with you as in earth-life. . . ."

There was more, but Quincannon shut his ears to it.

More introductions followed the medium's windy come-on. Quincannon shook hands with red-faced, mutton-chopped Cyrus Buckley and his portly, gray-haired wife, Margaret; with Oliver Cobb, a prominent Oakland physician who bore a rather startling resemblance to the "literary hangman," Ambrose Bierce; and with Grace Cobb, the doctor's much younger and attractive wife. Attractive, that is, if a man preferred an overly buxom and overly rouged blonde to a svelte brunette of Sabina's cunning dimensions. The Cobbs, like the Buckleys, had attended the professor's previous seance.

Margaret Buckley looked upon Vargas with the rapt gaze of a supplicant in the presence of a saint. Dr. Cobb was also a true believer, judging from the look of eager anticipation he wore. The blond Mrs. Cobb seemed to find the medium fascinating as well, but the glint in her eye was much more

70

predatory than devout. Buckley appeared ill at ease, as if he wished the evening's business was already finished; he kept casting glances at Quincannon which the detective studiously ignored.

Vargas asked Quincannon and Sabina if they would care for a refreshment — coffee, tea, perhaps a glass of sherry. They both declined. This seemed to relieve Buckley; he asked Vargas, "Isn't it about time to begin the seance?"

"Soon, Mr. Buckley. The spirits must not be hurried."

"Are they friendly tonight?" Mrs. Buckley asked. "Can you tell, dear Professor Vargas?"

"The auras are uncertain. I perceive antagonistic waves among the benign."

"Oh, Professor!"

"Do not fear," Vargas said. "Even if a malevolent spirit should cross the border, no harm will come to you or to any of us. Angkar will protect us."

"But will my Bernice's spirit be allowed through if there is a malevolent force present?"

Vargas patted her arm reassuringly. "It is my belief that she will, though I cannot be certain until the veil has been lifted. Have faith, dear Mrs. Buckley."

Sabina asked him, "Isn't there anything you can do to prevent a malevolent spirit from crossing over?"

"Alas, no. I am merely a teacher of the light and truth of theocratic unity, merely an operator between the Beyond and this mortal sphere."

Merely a purveyor of pap, Quincannon thought.

Grace Cobb touched Vargas's sleeve; her fingers lingered almost caressingly. "We have faith in you, Professor."

"In Angkar, dear lady," Vargas told her, but his fingers caressed hers in return and the look he bestowed upon her had a smouldering quality — the same sort of cat-at-cream look, Quincannon thought, that Sabina had accused him earlier of directing at her. "Place your faith in Angkar and the spirit world."

Quincannon asked him, "Angkar is your spirit guide and guardian angel?"

"Yes. He lived more than a thousand years past and his spirit has ascended to one of the highest planes in the Afterworld."

"A Hindu, was he?"

Vargas seemed mildly offended. "Not at all, my dear sir. Angkar was an Egyptian nobleman in the court of Nebuchadnezzar."

Quincannon managed to refrain from pointing out that Nebuchadnezzar was not an Egyptian but the king of Babylon and conqueror of Jerusalem some six centuries B.C. Not that any real harm would have been done if he had mentioned the fact; Vargas would have covered by claiming he had meant Nefertiti or some such. None of the others, except Sabina perhaps, seemed to notice the error.

Sabina said, "Those rings are most impressive, Professor. Are they Egyptian?"

"This one is." Vargas presented his left hand. "An Egyptian Signet and Seal Talisman Ring, made from virgin gold. It preserves its wearer against ill luck and wicked influences." He offered his right hand. "This is the Ring of King Solomon. Its Chaldaic inscription stands as a reminder to the wearer that no matter what his troubles may be, they shall soon be gone. The inscription — here — translates as 'This shall also pass.' "

"Oh, Professor Vargas," Mrs. Buckley gushed, "you're so knowledgeable, so wise in so many ways."

Quincannon's dinner stirred ominously under his breastbone.

He was spared further discomfort, at least for the present, by the entrance of the psychic assistant, Annabelle. She announced, "All is in readiness, Professor," and without waiting for a response, glided out again.

"Good ladies and gentlemen," Vargas said, "before we enter the spirit room may I accept your most kind and welcome donations to the Unified College of the Attuned Impulses, so that we may continue in our humble efforts to bring the psychic and material planes into closer harmony?"

Quincannon paid for himself and Sabina — the outrageous "New Ones" donation of fifty dollars each. If he had not been assured of reimbursement from their client, he would have been much more grudging than he was in handing over the greenbacks. Buckley was tight-lipped as he paid, and sweat oiled his neck and the lower of his two chins; the look he gave Quincannon was a mute plea not to botch the job he and Sabina had been hired to do. Only Dr. Cobb ponied up with what appeared to be genuine enthusiasm.

The medium casually dropped the wad of bills onto a table, as if money mattered not in the slightest to him personally, and led them out of the parlor, down the gloomy hallway, and then into a large chamber at the rear. The "spirit room" contained quite a few more accoutrements than the parlor, of greater variety and a more unusual nature. The floor was covered by a thick Oriental carpet of dark blue and black design. Curtains made of the same ebon material as the professor's and Annabelle's robes blotted the windows, and the gaslight had been turned low enough so that shadows crouched in all four corners. The overheated air was permeated with the smell of incense; Quincannon, who hated the stuff, immediately began to breathe through his mouth. The incense came from a burner on the mantel of a small fireplace — a horsey-looking bronze monstrosity with tusks as well as equine teeth and a shaggy mane and beard.

The room's centerpiece was an oval, highly polished table around which six straight-backed chairs were arranged; a seventh chair, larger than the others, with a high seat and arms raised on a level with that of the tabletop, was placed at the head. Along the walls were a short, narrow sideboard of Oriental design, made of teak, with an intricately inlayed center top; a tall-backed rococo love seat; and an alabaster pedestal atop which sat a hideous bronze statue of an Egyptian male in full headdress — a representation, evidently, of the mythical Angkar. In the middle of the table was a clear-glass jar, a tiny silver bell suspended inside. On the sideboard were a silver tray containing several bottles of various sizes and shapes, a tambourine, and a stack of children's school slates with black wooden frames. Propped against the wall nearby was an ordinary-looking three-stringed guitar. And on the high seat of the armchair lay a coil of sturdy rope Quincannon estimated as some three yards in length.

When the sitters were all inside and loosely grouped near the table, Vargas closed the door, produced a large brass key from a pocket in his robe, and proceeded with a flourish to turn the key in the latch. After which he brought the key to the sideboard and set it beside the tray in plain sight. While this was being done, Quincannon eased over in front of the door and tested it behind his back to determine if it was in fact locked. It was.

Still at the sideboard, Vargas announced that before they formed the "mystic circle" two final preparations were necessary. Would one of the good believers be so kind as to assist him in the first of these? Quincannon stepped forward just ahead of Dr. Cobb.

The medium said, "Mr. Quinn, will you kindly examine each of the slates you see before you and tell us if they are as they seem — ordinary writing slates?"

Quincannon examined them more carefully than any of the devotees would have. "Quite ordinary," he said.

"Select two, if you please, write your name on each with this slate pencil, and then place them together and tie them securely with your handkerchief."

When Quincannon had complied, Vargas took the bound slates and placed them in the middle of the stack. "If the spirits are willing," he said, "a message will be left for you beneath the signatures. Perhaps from a loved one who has passed beyond the pale, perhaps from a friendly spirit who may be in tune with your particular psychic impulses. Diacarnate forces are never predictable, you understand."

Quincannon nodded and smiled with his teeth.

"We may now be seated and form the mystic circle."

When each of the sitters had selected and was standing behind a chair, Sabina to the medium's immediate left and Quincannon directly across from him, both by prearrangement, Vargas again called for a volunteer. This time it was Dr. Cobb who stepped up first. Vargas handed him the coiled rope and seated himself in the high chair, his forearms flat on the chair arms with only his wrists and hands extended beyond the edges. He then instructed Cobb to bind him securely — arms, legs, and chest — to the chair, using as many knots as possible. Quincannon watched closely as this was done. He caught Sabina's eye when the doctor finished; she dipped her chin to acknowledge that she too had spotted the gaff in this phase of the professor's game.

Cobb, with Buckley's help, moved Vargas's chair closer

to the table, so that his hands and wrists rested on the surface. Smiling, the medium asked the others to take their seats. As Quincannon sat down he bumped against the table, then reached down to feel one of its legs. As he'd expected, the table was much less heavy than it appeared to be at a glance. He stretched out a leg and with the toe of his shoe explored the carpet. The floor beneath seemed to be solid, but the nap was thick enough so that he couldn't be certain.

Vargas instructed everyone to spread their hands, the fingers of the left to grasp the wrist of the person on that side; thus one hand of each person was holding and the other was being held. "Once we begin," he said, "attempt to empty your minds of all thought, to keep them as blank as the table's surface throughout. And remember, you must not move either hands or feet during the seance — you must not under any circumstances break the mystic circle. To do so could have grave consequences. There have been instances where inattention and disobedience have been fatal to sensitives such as myself."

The professor closed his eyes, let his chin lower slowly to his chest. After a few seconds he commenced a whispering chant, a mixture of English and simulated Egyptian in which he called for the door to the spirit world to open and the shades of the departed to pass through and reveal their presence. While this was going on, the lights began to dim as if in phantasmical response to Vargas's exhortations. The phenomenon elicited a shivery gasp from Margaret Buckley, but Quincannon was unimpressed. Gaslight in one room was easily controlled from another — in this case by the assistant, Annabelle, at a prearranged time or on some sort of signal.

The shadows congealed until the room was in utter darkness. Vargas's chanting ceased abruptly; the silence deepened as it lengthened. Long minutes passed with no sounds except for the somewhat asthmatic breathing of Cyrus Buckley, the rustle of a dress or shuffle of a foot on the carpet. A palpable tension began to build. Sweat formed on Quincannon's face, not from any tension but from the overheated air. He was not a man given to fancies, but he was forced to admit that there was an eerie quality to sitting in total blackness this way, waiting for something to happen. Spiritualist mediums counted on this reaction, of course. The more keyed up their dupes became, the more eager they were to believe in the incredible things they were about to witness; and the more eager they were, the more easily they could be fooled by their own senses.

Someone coughed, a sudden sharp sound that made even Quincannon twitch involuntarily. He thought the cough had come from Vargas, but in such stifling darkness you couldn't be certain of the direction of any sound. Even when the medium spoke again, the words might have come from anywhere in the room.

"Angkar is with us. I feel his presence."

On Quincannon's left, Dr. Cobb stirred and their knees bumped together; Mrs. Buckley, on his right, brought forth another of her shivery gasps.

"Will you speak to us tonight, Angkar? Will you answer our questions in the language of the dead and guide us among your fellow spirits? Please grant our humble request. Please answer yes."

The silver bell inside the jar rang once, muted but clear.

"Angkar has consented. He will speak, he will lead us. He will ring the bell once for yes to each question he is asked, twice for no, for that is the language of the dead. Will someone ask him a question? Doctor Cobb?"

77

"I will," Cobb's voice answered. "Angkar, is my brother Philip well and happy on the Other Side?"

The bell tinkled once.

"Will he appear to us in his spirit form?"

Yes.

"Will it be tonight?"

Silence.

Vargas said, "Angkar is unable to answer that question yet. Please ask another."

There was a good deal more of this, with questions from Cobb, his wife, and Mrs. Buckley. Then Vargas called on Sabina to ask the spirit guide a question.

She obliged by saying, "Angkar, tell me please, is my little boy John with you? He was always such a bad little boy that I fear for his poor troubled soul."

Yes, he is one of us.

No, he is not here tonight.

"Has he learned humility and common sense, two qualities which he lacked on this earthly sphere?"

Yes.

"And has he learned to take no for an answer?"

Yes.

Quincannon scowled in the darkness. Although Sabina had been married once, she had no children. The "little boy John" was her doting partner, of course. Having a bit of teasing fun at his expense while at the same time establishing proof of Vargas's deceit.

"Mr. Quinn?" the professor said. "Will you ask Angkar a question?"

He might not have responded as he did if the heat and the sickly sweet incense hadn't given him a headache. But his head throbbed, and Sabina's playfulness rankled, and the words were out of his mouth before he could bite them back. "Oh yes, indeed," he said. "Angkar, will my dear wife ever consent to share my cold and lonely bed?"

Shocked murmurs, a muffled choking sound that might have come from Sabina, rose around him. The bell was silent. And then, without warning, the table seemed to stir and tremble beneath Quincannon's outstretched hands. Its smooth surface rippled; a faint creak sounded from somewhere underneath. In the next instant the table tilted sideways, turned and rocked and wobbled as if it had been injected with a life of its own. The agitated movements continued for several seconds, stopped altogether — and then the table lifted completely off the floor, seemed to float in the air for another two or three heartbeats before finally thudding back onto the carpet. Throughout all of this, the silver bell inside the jar remained conspicuously silent.

"Mr. Quinn, you have angered Angkar." The medium's voice was sharply reproachful. "He finds your question inappropriate, frivolous, even mocking. He may deny us further communication and return to the Afterworld."

Mrs. Buckley cried, "Oh no, please, he mustn't go!"

Cobb said angrily, "Damn your eyes, Quinn —"

"Silence!" Vargas, in a sibilant whisper. "We must do nothing more to disturb the spirits or the consequences may be dire. Do not move or speak. Do not break the circle."

The stuffy blackness closed down again. It was an effort for Quincannon to hold still. He regretted his question, though not because of any effect on Angkar and his discarnate legion; he was sure that the table-tipping and levitation would have taken place in any event. His regret was that he had allowed Sabina to glimpse the depth of his frustration, and into the bargain added weight to her already erroneous idea of the nature of his passion. Seduction wasn't his game; his affection for her was genuine, abiding. Hell and damn! Now it might take him days, even weeks, to undo the damage done by his profligate tongue —

A sound burst the heavy stillness, a jingling that was not of the silver bell in the jar. The tambourine that had been on the sideboard. Its jingling continued, steady, almost musical in an eerily discordant way.

Vargas's whisper was fervent. "Angkar is still present. He has forgiven Mr. Quinn, permitted us one more chance to communicate with the spirits he has brought with him."

Mrs. Buckley: "Praise Angkar! Praise the spirits!"

The shaking of the tambourine ended. And all at once a ghostly light, pale and vaporous, appeared at a distance overhead, hovered, and then commenced a swirling motion that created faint luminous streaks on the wall of dead black. One of the sitters made an ecstatic throat noise. The swirls slowed, the light stilled again for a moment; then it began to rise until it seemed to hover just below the ceiling, and at last it faded away entirely. Other lights, mere pinpricks, flicked on and off, moving this way and that as if a handful of fireflies had been released in the room.

A thin, moaning wail erupted.

The pinpricks of light vanished.

Quincannon, listening intently, heard a faint ratchety noise followed by a strumming chord. The vaporous light reappeared, now in a different location closer to the floor; at the edge of its glow the guitar could be seen to leap into the air, to gyrate this way and that with no hand upon it. The strumming chord replayed and was joined by others — strange music that sounded and yet did not sound as though it were being made by the strings.

For three, four, five seconds the guitar continued its levitating dance, seemingly playing a tune upon itself. Then the glow once more faded, and when it was gone the music ceased and the guitar twanged to rest on the carpet.

Nearly a minute passed in electric silence.

Grace Cobb shrieked, "A hand! I felt a hand brush against my cheek!"

Vargas warned, "Do not move, do not break the circle."

Something touched Quincannon's neck, a velvety caress that lifted the short hairs there and bristled them like a cat's fur. If the fingers — they felt exactly like cold, lifeless fingers — had lingered he would have ignored the professor's remonstration and made an attempt to grab and hold onto them. But the hand or whatever it was slid away almost immediately.

Moments later it materialized long enough for it to be identifiable as just that — a disembodied hand. Then it was gone as if it had never been there at all.

Another period of silence.

The unearthly moan again.

And a glowing face appeared, as disembodied as the hand, above where Dr. Cobb sat.

The face was a man's, shrouded as if in a kind of whitish drapery that ran right around it and was cut off at a straight line on the lower part. The eyes were enormous black-rimmed holes. The mouth moved, formed words in a deep-throated rumble.

"Oliver? It's Philip, Oliver."

"Philip! I'm so glad you've come at long last." Cobb's words were choked with feeling. "Are you well?"

"I am well. But I cannot stay long. The Auras have allowed me to make contact but now I must return."

"Yes . . . yes, I understand."

"I will come again. For a longer visit next time, Oliver. Next time . . ."

The face was swallowed by darkness.

More minutes crept away. Quincannon couldn't tell how many; he had lost all sense of time and space in the suffocating dark.

A second phantomlike countenance materialized, this one high above Margaret Buckley's chair. It was shimmery, indistinct behind a hazy substance like a luminous veil. The words that issued from it were an otherworldly, childlike quaver — the voice of a little girl.

"Mommy? Is that you Mommy?"

"Oh, thank God! Bernice!" Margaret Buckley's cry was rapturous. "Cyrus, it's our darling Bernice!"

Her husband made no response.

"I love you, Mommy. Do you love me?"

"Oh yes! Bernice, dearest, I prayed and prayed you'd come. Are you happy in the Afterworld? Tell Mommy."

"Yes, I'm very happy. But I must go back now."

"No, not so soon! Bernice, wait —"

"Will you come again, Mommy? Promise me you'll come again. Then the Auras will let me come too."

"I'll come, darling, I promise!"

The radiant image vanished.

Mrs. Buckley began to weep softly.

Quincannon was fed up with this hokum. Good and angry, too. It was despicable enough for fake mediums to dupe the gullible, but when they resorted to the exploitation of a middle-aged woman's yearning for her long-dead child the game became intolerable. The sooner he and Sabina put a finish to it, the better for all concerned. If there was even one more materialization . . .

There wasn't. He heard scratchings, the unmistakable sound of the slate pencil writing on a slate. This was followed by yet another protracted silence, broken only by the faintest of scraping and clicking sounds that Quincannon couldn't identify.

Vargas said abruptly, "The spirits have grown restless. All except Angkar are returning now to the land beyond the Border. Angkar will leave too, but first he will free me from my bonds, just as one day we will all be freed from our mortal ties —"

The last word was chopped off in a meaty smacking noise and an explosive grunt of pain. Another smack, a gurgling moan. Sabina called out in alarm, "John! Something's happened to Vargas!" Other voices rose in frightened confusion. Quincannon pushed up from the table, fumbling in his pocket for a lucifer. His thumbnail scratched it alight.

In the smoky flare he saw the others scrambling to their feet around the table, all except Professor Vargas. The medium, still roped to his chair, was slumped forward with his chin on his chest, unmoving. Quincannon kicked his own chair out of the way, carried the lucifer across to the nearest wall sconce. The gas was off; he turned it, and applied the flame. Flickery light burst forth, chasing shadows back into the room's corners.

Outside in the hallway, hands began to beat on the door panel. Annabelle's voice rose shrilly: "Let me in! I heard a cry . . . let me in!"

"Dear Lord, he's been stabbed!"

The exclamation came from Cyrus Buckley. There were other cries overridden by a shriek from Mrs. Buckley; Quincannon turned in time to see her swoon in her husband's arms. He ran to where Sabina stood staring down at the medium's slumped body.

Stabbed, for a fact. The weapon, a dagger whose ornate hilt bore a series of hieroglyphics, jutted from the back of his neck. Another wound, the first one struck for it still oozed blood, showed through a rent in Vargas's robe lower down, between the shoulder blades.

Ashen-faced, Dr. Cobb bent to feel for a pulse in the professor's neck. He shook his head and said, "Expired," a few moments later.

"It isn't possible," his wife whispered. "How could he have been stabbed?"

Buckley had lowered his wife onto one of the chairs and was fanning her flushed face with his hand. He said shakily, "How — and by whom?"

Quincannon caught Sabina's eye. She wagged her head to tell him, she didn't know, or couldn't be sure, what had happened in those last few seconds of darkness.

The psychic assistant, Annabelle, was still beating on the door, clamoring for admittance. Quincannon went to the sideboard. The brass key lay where Vargas had set it down before the seance began; he used it to unlock the door. Annabelle rushed in from the dark hallway, her eyes wide and fearful. She gave a little moan when she saw Vargas and ran to his side, knelt to peer into his dead face.

When she straightened again her own face was as white as milk. She said tremulously, "One of you did this?"

"No," Dr. Cobb told her. "It couldn't have been one of us. No one broke the circle until after the professor was stabbed."

"Then . . . it was the spirits."

"He did perceive antagonistic waves tonight. But why would a malevolent spirit — ?"

"He made all the Auras angry. I warned him but he didn't listen."

Sabina said, "How did he make the Auras angry, Annabelle?"

The woman shuddered and shook her head. Then her

eyes shifted into a long stare across the room. "The slates," she said.

"What about the slates?"

"Did the spirits leave a message? Have you looked?"

Quincannon swung around to the sideboard; the others, except for Margaret Buckley, crowded close behind him. The tied slates were in the center of the stack where Vargas had placed them. He pulled those two out, undid the knot in his handkerchief, parted them for his eyes and the eyes of the others.

Murmurs and a mildly blasphemous exclamation from Buckley.

In a ghostlike hand beneath the "John Quinn" signatures on each, one message upside down and backwards as if it were a mirror image of the other, was written: I Angkar destroyed the evil one.

"Angkar!" Dr. Cobb said. "Why would the professor's guide and guardian turn on him that way?"

"The spirits are not mocked," Annabelle said. "They know evil when it is done in their name and guardian becomes avenger."

"Madam, what are you saying?"

"I warned him," she said again. "He would not listen and now he has paid the price. His torment will continue on the Other Side, until his essence has been cleansed of wickedness."

Quincannon said, "Enough talk and speculation," in authoritarian tones that swiveled all heads in his direction. "There'll be time for that later. Now there's work to be done."

"Quite right," Cobb agreed. "The police —"

"Not the police, Doctor. Not yet."

"Here Quinn, who are you to take charge?"

"The name isn't Quinn, it's Quincannon. John Quincannon. Of Carpenter and Quincannon, Professional Detective Services."

Cobb gaped at him. "A detective? You?"

"Two detectives." He gestured to Sabina. "My partner, Mrs. Carpenter."

"A woman?" Grace Cobb said. She sounded as shocked as if Sabina had been revealed as a soiled dove.

Sabina, testily: "And why not, pray tell?"

Dr. Cobb: "Who hired you? Who brought you here under false pretenses?"

Quincannon and Sabina both looked at Buckley. To his credit, the financier wasted no time in admitting he was their client.

"You, Cyrus?" Margaret Buckley had revived and was regarding them dazedly. "I don't understand. Why would you engage detectives?"

Before her husband could reply, Quincannon said, "Mr Buckley will explain in the parlor. Be so good, all of you, as to go there and wait."

"For what?" Cobb demanded.

"For Mrs. Carpenter and me to do what no other detective, police officer, or private citizen can do half so well." False modesty was not one of Quincannon's character flaws, despite Sabina's occasional attempts to convince him otherwise. "Solve a baffling crime."

No one protested, although Dr. Cobb wore an expression of disapproval and Annabelle said, "What good are earthly detectives when it is the spirits who have taken vengeance?" as they left the room. Within a minute Quincannon and Sabina were alone with the dead man.

Quincannon turned the key in the lock to ensure their privacy. He said then, "Well, my dear, a pretty puzzle, eh?"

Instead of answering, Sabina fetched him a stinging slap that rattled his eyelids. "That," she said, "is for the rude remark about sharing your bed."

For once, he was speechless. He might have argued that she had precipitated the remark with her own sly comments, but this was neither the time nor the place. Besides, he could not recall ever having won an argument with Sabina over anything of consequence. There had been numerous draws, yes, but never a clear-cut victory. At times he felt downright impotent in her presence. Impotent in the figurative sense of the word, of course.

"Now then," she said briskly, "shall we see if we can make good on your boast?"

They proceeded first to extinguish the incense burner and to open a window so that cold night air could refresh the room, and then with an examination of the walls, fireplace, and floor. All were solid; there were no secret openings, crawlspaces, hidey holes, or trapdoors. Quincannon then went to inspect the corpse, while Sabina examined the jar-encased bell on the table.

The first thing he noticed was that although the rope still bound Professor Vargas to his chair, it was somewhat loose across forearms and sternum. When he lifted the limp left hand he found that it had been freed of the bonds. Vargas's right foot had also been freed. Confirmation of his suspicions in both cases. He had also more or less expected his next discovery, the two items concealed inside the sleeve of the medium's robe.

He was studying the items when Sabina said, "Just as I thought. The jar was fastened to the table with gum adhesive."

"Can you pry it loose?"

"I already have. The clapper on the bell —"

"— is either missing or frozen. Eh?"

"Frozen. Vargas used another bell to produce his spirit rings, obviously."

"This one." Quincannon held up the tiny handbell with its gauze-muffled clapper. "Made and struck so as to produce a hollow ring, as if it were coming from the bell inside the jar. The directionless quality of sounds in total darkness, and the power of suggestion, completed the deception."

"What else have you got there?"

He showed her the second item from Vargas's sleeve.

"A reaching rod," she said. "Mmm, yes."

Quincannon said, "His left hand was holding yours on the table. Could you tell when he freed it?"

"No, and I was waiting for just that. I think he may have done it when he coughed. You recall?"

"I do."

"He was really quite cunning," Sabina said. "A charlatan among charlatans, to paraphrase Mr. Buckley."

Medium rare, Quincannon thought again, and now medium dead. Plucked and done to a turn, for a fact, though not at all in the way anticipated. "Have you a suggestion as to who stabbed him?"

"None yet, except that it wasn't Angkar or any other supernatural agency. Annabelle may believe in spirits who wield daggers, but I don't."

"Nor I."

"One of the others at the table. A person clever enough to break the circle in the same way Vargas did and then to stand up, commit the deed, and return to his chair — all in utter darkness."

"Doesn't seem possible, does it?"

"No more impossible than any of the other humbug we

witnessed tonight. We've encountered such enigmas before, John."

"Too often for my liking. Well, we already have some of the answers to the evening's queer show. Find the rest and we'll solve the riddle of Vargas's death as well."

One of the missing answers came from an examination of the professor's mystic rings. The one on his left hand that he had referred to as an Egyptian Signet and Seal Talisman Ring had a hidden fingernail catch; when it was flipped, the entire top hinged upward to reveal a small sturdy hook within. Quincannon had no doubt that were he to get down on all fours and peer under the table where the medium sat, he would find a tiny metal eye screwed to the wood.

The miraculous self-playing guitar, which of course was nothing of the kind, drew him next. He already knew how its dancing levitation had been managed; a close scrutiny of the instrument revealed the rest of the gaff.

"John, look at this."

Sabina was at the sideboard, fingering a small bottle. When he'd set the guitar down and joined her he saw that she had removed the bottle's glass stopper. "This was among the others on the tray," she told him, and held it up for him to sniff its contents.

"Ah," he said. "Almond oil."

"Mixed with white phosphorous, surely."

He nodded. "The contents of the other bottles?"

"Liquor and incense oils. Nothing more than window dressing."

Quincannon stood looking at the sideboard. At length he knelt and ran his hands over its smooth front, its fancily inlayed center top. There seemed to be neither doors nor a way to lift open the top, as if the sideboard might be a sealed wooden box. This proved not to be the case, however. It took him several minutes to locate the secret spring catch, cleverly concealed as it was among the dark-squared inlays. As soon as he pressed it, the catch released noiselessly and the entire top slid up and back on oiled hinges.

The interior was a narrow, hollow space — a box, in fact, that seemed more like a child's toy chest than a sideboard. A clutch of items were pushed into one corner. Quincannon lifted them out one by one.

A yard or two of white silk.

Another yard of fine white netting, so fine that it could be wadded into a ball no larger than a walnut.

A two-foot-square piece of black cloth.

A small container of safety matches.

A theatrical mask.

And a pair of rubber gloves almost but not quite identical, both of which had been stuffed with cotton and dipped in melted paraffin.

He returned each item to the sideboard, finally closed the lid. He said with satisfaction, "That leaves only the writing on the slates. And we know now how that was done, don't we, my dear?"

"And how Professor Vargas was murdered."

"And by whom."

They smiled at each other. Smiles that gleamed wolfishly in the trembling gaslight.

Neither the Buckleys nor the Cobbs took kindly to being ushered back into the seance room, even though Quincannon had moved both Vargas's body and chair away from the table and draped them with a cloth Sabina had found in another room. There was some grumbling when he asked them to assume their former positions around the table, but they all complied. A seventh chair had been

90

added at Vargas's place; he invited Annabelle to sit there. She, too, complied, maintaining a stoic silence.

Buckley asked, "Will this take long, Quincannon? My wife has borne the worst of this ordeal. She isn't well."

"Not long, Mr. Buckley, I assure you."

"Is it absolutely necessary for us to be in here?"

"It is." Quincannon looked around at the others. "We have nothing to fear from the dead, past or present. The spirits were not responsible for what took place here tonight. Not any of it."

Grace Cobb: "Are you saying one of us stabbed Professor Vargas?"

Annabelle: "No. It was Angkar. You mustn't deny the spirits. The penalties —"

"A pox on the penalties," Quincannon said. "Professor Vargas was murdered by a living, flesh-and-blood individual."

Dr. Cobb: "Who? If you're so all-fired certain it was one of us, name him."

"Perhaps it was you, Doctor."

"See here — ! What motive could I possibly have?"

"Any one of several. Such as a discovery prior to tonight that Vargas was a fake —"

"A fake!"

"— and you were so enraged by his duplicity that you determined to put a stop to it once and for all."

"Preposterous."

Quincannon was enjoying himself now. Dramatic situations appealed to his nature; he was, as Sabina had more than once pointed out, a bit of a ham. He turned his gaze on Grace Cobb. "Or you, Mrs. Cobb. Perhaps you're the guilty party."

She regarded him haughtily. "If that is an accusation —"

"Not at all. Merely a suggestion of possibility, of hidden motives of your own." Such as an interest in the medium that had gone beyond the spiritual and ended in a spurned lover's — or even a blackmail victim's — murderous rage.

"Or it could be you, Mr. Buckley, and your hiring of Carpenter and Quincannon but a smokescreen to hide your lethal intentions for this evening."

The financier's eyes glittered with anger. Sabina said warningly, "That'll do, John."

"It had better do," Buckley said, "if you entertain any hope of receiving the balance of your fee. You know full well neither I nor my wife ended that scoundrel's life."

Dr. Cobb: "I don't see how it could have been any of us. We were all seated here — all except Annabelle, and she was on the other side of the locked door. And none of us broke the circle."

"Are you certain of that, Doctor?" Quincannon asked.

"Of course I'm certain."

"But you're wrong. Vargas himself broke it."

"That's impossible."

"Not at all. Neither impossible nor difficult to manage."

"Why would he do such a thing? For a medium to break the mystic circle is to risk the wrath of the spirits, endanger his own life. He told us so himself."

"He had already incurred the wrath of the Auras," Annabelle said fervidly. "It was Angkar, I tell you. Angkar who plunged the dagger into his body —"

Quincannon ignored her. He said to no one in particular, "You don't seem to have grasped my words to you a minute ago. Professor Vargas was a fake. The Unified College of the Attuned Impulses is a fake. He was no more sensitive to the spirit world than you or I or President Cleveland."

"That . . . that can't be true!" Margaret Buckley's face

92

was strained, her eyes feverish. "Everything we saw and heard tonight . . . the visitations . . . my daughter . . ."

"Sham and illusion, the lot of it," Sabina said gently. "I'm sorry, Mrs. Buckley."

"But . . . but how . . ."

"We'll explain," Quincannon told her, "all of Vargas's tricks during the seance. To begin with, the way in which he freed his left hand while seeming to maintain an unbroken clasp of hands.

"The essence of that trick lies in the fact that the hand consists of both a wrist and fingers and the wrist is able to bend in different directions. The fingers of Vargas's left hand, you remember, were holding Mrs. Carpenter's wrist, while Mrs. Cobb's fingers were gripping his right wrist. By maneuvering his hands closer and closer together as he talked, in a series of small spasmodic movements, he also brought the ladies' hands closer together. When they were near enough for his own thumbs to touch, he freed his left hand in one quick movement and immediately reestablished control with his right — the same hand's fingers holding Mrs. Carpenter while its wrist was being gripped by Mrs. Cobb."

Buckley: "But how could he manage that when we were all concentrating on tight control?"

"He coughed once, rather loudly, if you recall. The sound was a calculated aural distraction. In that instant — and an instant was all it took — he completed the maneuver. He also relied on the fact that a person's senses become unreliable after a protracted period of sitting in total darkness. What you think you see, hear, feel at any given moment may in fact be partly or completely erroneous."

There was a brief silence while the others digested this. Dr. Cobb said then, "Even with one hand free, how could he have rung the spirit bell? I bound him myself, Quincannon, and I am morally certain the loops and knots were tight."

"You may be certain in your own mind, Doctor, but the facts are otherwise. It is a near impossibility for anyone, even a professional detective, to securely tie a man to a chair with a single length of rope. And you were flurried, self-conscious, anxious to acquit yourself well of the business, and you are a gentleman besides. You would hardly bind a man such as Professor Vargas, whom you admired and respected, with enough constriction of the rope to cut into his flesh. A fraction of an inch of slack is all a man who has been tied many times before, who is skilled in muscular control, requires in order to free one hand."

Cobb was unable to refute the logic of this. He lapsed into a somewhat daunted silence as Quincannon went on to explain and demonstrate the bell-ringing trick.

"Next we have the table-tipping and levitation. Vargas accomplished this phenomenon with but one hand and one foot, the right lower extremity having been freed with the aid of the upper left." Quincannon had removed the Egyptian talisman ring from the medium's finger; he held it up, released the fingernail catch to reveal the hook within. "He attached this hook to a small eye screwed beneath the table, after which he gave a sharp upward jerk. The table legs on his end were lifted off the carpet just far enough for him to slip the toe of his shoe under one of them, thus creating a 'human clamp' which gave him full control of the table. By lifting with his ring and elevating his toe while the heel remained on the carpet, he was able to make the table tilt, rock, gyrate at will."

Sabina added, "And when he was ready for the table to appear to levitate, he simply unhooked his ring and thrust upward with his foot, withdrawing it immediately afterward. The illusion of the table seeming to float under our hands for a second or two before it fell was enhanced by both the circumstances and the darkness."

Buckley, with some bitterness: "Seems so blasted obvious when explained."

"Such flummery always is, Mr. Buckley. It's the trappings and manipulation that make it mystifying. The so-called spirit lights is another example." Sabina placed the stoppered glass bottle on the table and described where she'd found it and what it contained. "Mix white phosphorous with any fatty oil, and the result is a bottle filled with hidden light. As long as the bottle remains stoppered the phosphorous gives off no glow, but as soon as the cork is removed and air is permitted to reach the phosphorous, a faint unearthly shine results. Wave the bottle in the air and the light seems to dart about. Replace the stopper and the light fades away as the air inside is used up."

"The little winking lights were more of the same, I suppose?"

"Not quite," Quincannon said. "Match-heads were their source. Hold a match-head between the moistened forefinger and thumb of each hand, wiggle the forefinger enough to expose and then once more quickly conceal the match-head, and you have flitting fireflies."

Grace Cobb asked, "The guitar that seemed to dance and play itself — how was that done?"

Quincannon fetched the guitar, brought it back to the table.

Beside it he set the reaching rod from Vargas's sleeve. The rod was only a few inches in length when closed, but when he opened out each of its sections after the fashion of a telescope, it extended the full length of the table and beyond — more than six feet overall. "Vargas extended this rod in his left hand," he said, "inserted it in the hole in the neck of the instrument, raised and slowly turned the guitar this way and that to create the illusion of air-dancing. As for the music . . ."

He reached into the hole under the strings, gave a quick twist. The weird strumming they had heard during the seance began to emanate from within.

Mrs. Cobb: "A music box!"

"A one-tune music box, to be precise, affixed to the wood inside with gum adhesive."

Buckley: "The hand that touched Mrs. Cobb's cheek? The manifestations? The spirit writing on the slate?"

"All part and parcel of the same flummery," Quincannon told him. Again he went to the sideboard, where he pressed the hidden release to raise its top. From inside he took out the two stuffed and wax-coated rubber gloves, held them up for the others to view.

"These are the ghostly fingers that touched Mrs. Cobb and my neck as well. The smoothness of the paraffin gives them the feel of human flesh. One 'hand' has been treated with luminous paint; it was kept covered under this" — he showed them the black cloth — "until the time came to reveal it as a glowing disembodied entity."

He lifted out the silk drapery and theatrical mask. "The mask has been treated in the same way. The combination of these two items was used to create the manifestation alleged to be Philip Cobb."

He raised the fine white netting. "Likewise made phosphorescent and draped over the head to create the manifestation purported to be the Buckleys' daughter."

"But . . . I heard Bernice speak," Margaret Buckley said weakly. "It was her voice, I'm sure it was. . . ."

Her husband took her hand in both of his. "No, Margaret, it wasn't. You only imagined it to be."

"An imitation of a child's voice," Quincannon said, "just as the other voice was an imitation of a man's deep articulation."

He picked up the two slates which bore the "spirit message" under his false signatures. " 'I Angkar destroyed the evil one.' Vargas's murderer wrote those words, in sequence on one slate and upside down and backwards on the other to heighten the illusion of spirit writing. Before the murder was done, in anticipation of it."

"Who?" Buckley demanded. "Name the person, Quincannon."

"Professor Vargas's accomplice, of course."

"Accomplice?"

"Certainly. No one individual, no matter how skilled in supernatural fakery, could have arranged and carried out all the tricks we were subjected to, even if he hadn't been roped to his chair. Someone else had to direct the reaching rod to the guitar and then turn the spring on the music box. Someone else had to jangle the tambourine, make the wailing noises, carry the phosphorous bottle to different parts of the room and up onto the love seat there so as to make the light seem to float near the ceiling. Someone else had to manipulate the waxed gloves, don the mask and drapery and netting, imitate the spirit voices."

"Annabelle? Are you saying it was Annabelle?"

"None other."

They all stared at the pale, silent woman at the head of the table. Her expression remained frozen, but her gaze burned with a zealot's fire.

Dr. Cobb said, "But she wasn't in the room with us . . ."

"Ah, but she was, Doctor. At first I believed her to have

been in another part of the house — not because of the locked door but because of the way in which the lights dimmed and extinguished to begin the seance. It seemed she must have turned the gas off at a prearranged time. Not so. Some type of automatic timing mechanism was used for that purpose. Annabelle, you see, was already present here before the rest of us entered and Vargas locked the door."

"Before, you say?"

"She disappeared from the parlor, you'll recall, as soon as she announced that all was in readiness. While Vargas detained us with his call for 'donations,' Annabelle slipped into this room and hid herself."

"Where? There are no hiding places . . . unless you expect us to believe she crawled up inside the fireplace chimney."

"Not there, no. Nor are there any secret closets or passages or any other such hocus-pocus. She was hidden —"

"— in the same place as her spirit props," Sabina interrupted, "within the sideboard." Her testy glance at Quincannon said he'd hogged center stage long enough; she wasn't above a bit of a flare for the dramatic herself, he thought fondly. "The interior is hollow, and she is both tiny and enough of a contortionist to fold her body into such a short, narrow space. The catch that releases the hinged top can be operated from within as well. Once the room was in total darkness and Vargas began invoking the spirits, she climbed out to commence her preparations. Under her robe, I'll warrant, is an all-black, close-fitting garment. Black gloves and a mask of some sort to cover her white face completed the costume. And her familiarity with the room allowed her to move about in silence."

"All well and good," Buckley said, "but the woman was outside the locked door, pounding on it, less than a minute after Vargas was stabbed. Explain that."

"Simple misdirection, Mr. Buckley. Before the stabbing she replaced all props in the sideboard and closed the top, then unlocked the door, the key made a faint scraping and the bolt clicked, sounds which John and I both heard. Then she crossed the room, plunged her dagger into Vargas, recrossed the room immediately after the second thrust, let herself out into the darkened hallway, and relocked the door from that side. Not with Vargas's key, which remained on the sideboard, but with a duplicate key of her own."

No one spoke for a cluster of seconds. In hushed tones, then, Grace Cobb asked, "Why did you do it, Annabelle?"

The psychic assistant's mouth twisted. Her voice, when it came, was with passion. "He was an evil unbeliever. He mocked the spirits with his schemes, laughed and derided them and those of us who truly believe. I did his bidding because I loved him, I obeyed him until the spirits came in the night and told me I must obey no longer. They said I must destroy him. Angkar guided my hand tonight. Angkar showed me the path to the truth and light of the Afterworld. . . ."

Her words trailed off; she sat staring fixedly. Looking at no one there with her blazing eyes, Quincannon thought, but at whatever she believed waited for her beyond the pale.

It was after midnight before the bumbling constabulary (Quincannon considered all city policemen to be bumbling) finished with their questions, took Annabelle away, and permitted the others to depart. On the mist-wet walk in front, while they waited for hansoms, Cyrus Buckley drew Quincannon aside.

"You and Mrs. Carpenter are competent detectives, sir, I'll grant you that even though I don't wholly approve of your methods. You'll have my check for the balance of our arrangement tomorrow morning."

Quincannon bowed and accepted the financier's hand. "If you should find yourself in need of our services again . . ."

"I trust I won't." Buckley paused to unwrap a long-nine seegar. "One question before we part. As I told you in your offices, the first seance Mrs. Buckley and I attended here was concluded by Vargas's claim that Angkar had untied him. We heard the rope flung through the air, and when the gas was turned up we saw it lying unknotted on the floor. He couldn't have untied all those knots himself, with only one free hand."

"Hardly. Annabelle assisted in that trick, too."

"I don't quite see how it was worked. Can you make a guess?"

"I can. The unknotted rope, which he himself hurled across the room, was not the same one with which he was tied. Annabelle slipped up behind him and cut the knotted rope into pieces with her dagger, then hid the pieces in the sideboard. The second rope was concealed there with the props and given to Vargas after she'd severed the first."

"His planned finale for tonight's seance too, I fancy."

"No doubt. Instead, Annabelle improvised a far more shocking finish."

"Made him pay dearly for mocking the spirits, eh?"

"If you like, Mr. Buckley. If you like."

Quincannon had time to smoke a bowlful of shag to-bacco before a hansom arrived for him and Sabina. Settled in the darkened coach on the way to Russian Hill, he said, "All's well that ends well. But I must say I'm glad this case is closed. Psychic phenomena, theocratic unity . . . bah. The lot of it is —"

"— horsefeathers," Sabina said. "Yes, I know. But are you

100

quite sure there's no truth in it?"

"Spiritualism? None whatsoever."

"Not spiritualism. The existence of a spirit afterlife."

"Don't tell me you give a whit of credence to such folly?"

"I have an open mind."

"So do I, my dear, on most matters."

"But not the paranormal."

"Not a bit of it."

For a time they sat in companionable stillness broken only by the jangle of the horses' bit chains, the clatter of the iron wheels on rough cobblestones. Then there was a faint stirring in the heavy darkness, and to Quincannon's utter amazement, a pair of soft, sweet lips brushed his, clung passionately for an instant, then withdrew.

He sat stunned for several beats. At which point his lusty natural instincts took over; he twisted on the seat, reached out to Sabina with eager hands and mouth. Both found yielding flesh. He kissed her soundly.

In the next second he found himself embracing a struggling, squirming spitfire. She pulled free, and the crack of her hand on his cheek was twice as hard as the slap in Vargas's spirit room. "What makes you think you can take such liberties, John Quincannon!" she demanded indignantly.

"But . . . I was only returning your affection. . . ."

"My affection?"

"You kissed me first. Why, if you didn't care to have it reciprocated?"

"What are you gabbling about? I didn't kiss you."

"Of course you did. A few moments ago."

"Faugh! I did no such thing and you know it." Her dress rustled as she slid farther away from him. "Now I'll thank you to keep your distance and behave yourself."

He sat and behaved, not happily. Had he imagined the kiss? No, he wasn't that moonstruck. She had kissed him, for a fact; he could still feel her lips against his. Some sort of woman's game to devil him. He imagined her smiling secretly in the dark — but then the hack passed close to a streetlamp and he saw that she was leaning against the far door with her arms folded, unsmiling and wearing an injured look.

The only other explanation for the kiss . . . but that was sheer lunacy, not worth a moment's consideration. It must have been Sabina. Of course it was Sabina. And yet . . .

The hansom clattered on into the cold, damp night.

Jade

La Croix had not changed much in the three years since I had last seen him. He still had a nervous twitch, still wore the same ingratiating smile. We sat together in a booth in the Seaman's Bar, on Singapore River's South Quay. It was eleven-thirty in the morning.

He brushed at an imaginary speck on the sleeve of his white tropical suit. "You will do it, *mon ami?*"

"No," I said.

His smile went away. "But I have offered you a great deal of money."

"That has nothing to do with it."

"I do not understand."

"I'm not in the business anymore."

The smile came back. "You are joking, of course."

"Do you see me laughing?"

Again, the smile vanished. "But you *must* help me. Perhaps if I were to tell you the reason —"

"I don't want to hear about it. There are plenty of others in Singapore. Why don't you hunt up one of them?"

"You and I, we have done much business together," La Croix said. "You are the only one I would trust. I will double my offer. Triple it."

"I told you, the money has nothing to do with it. I'm not the same man I was before you went away to Manila or Kuala Lumpur or wherever the hell you've been."

"*Mon ami*, I beg of you!" Sweat had broken out on his forehead.

"No." I stood abruptly. "I can't do anything for you, La Croix. Find somebody else."

I walked away from him, through the beaded curtains into the bar proper. La Croix hurried after me, pushed in next to me as I ordered another iced beer. When the bartender moved away La Croix said urgently, "I beg of you to reconsider, *M'sieu* Connell. I . . . as long as I remain in Singapore my life is in grave danger . . ."

"La Croix, how many times do I have to say it? I'm not in the business anymore. There's nothing I can do."

"But I have already —" He broke off, his eyes staring into mine, and then he swung around and was gone.

I finished my beer and went out into what the Malays call the *roote hond,* the oppressive, prickly heat that was Singapore at midday. There were a few European tourists about — talking animatedly, taking pictures the way they do — but the natives had sense enough to stay in where it was cool.

I walked down to the river. The water was a dark, oily bluish-green. Its narrow expanse, as always, was crowded with sampans, *prahus,* small bamboo-awninged Chinese junks, and the heavily laden, almost flat-decked lighters called *tongkangs.* There was the smell of rotting garbage, intermingled with that of salt water, spices, rubber, gasoline, and the sweet, cloying scent of frangipani. The rust-colored roofs that cap most of Singapore's buildings shone dully through thick heat haze on both sides of the river.

I followed the line of the waterfront for a short way until I came to one of the smaller *godowns* or storage warehouses. Harry Rutledge, the big, florid-faced Englishman who ran the place, was there, supervising the unloading of a shipment of copra from one of the lighters.

"Can you use me today, Harry?" I asked him.

"Sorry, lad. Plenty of coolies on this one."

"Tomorrow?"

He rubbed his peeling red nose. "Cargo of palm oil due in," he said musingly. "Holdover, awaiting transshipment. Could use you, at that."

"What time will it be in?"

"By eleven, likely."

"I'll be here at ten."

"Right-o."

I moved on along the river. I had never really gotten used to the heat, even after fifteen years in the South China Seas, and I was sweaty and dry-mouthed and I wanted another iced beer. But not in the Seaman's Bar, and it would be better if I had something to eat first. I had not eaten all day.

Here and there along the waterfront are small eating stalls. I stopped at the first one I saw and sat on one of the foot-high wooden stools, under a white canvas awning. I ordered shashlick and rice and a fresh mangosteen. I was working on the thick, pulpy fruit when the three men walked up.

The two on either side were copper-skinned, flat-eyed, and stoic. Both were dressed in white linen jackets and matching slacks. The man in the middle was about fifty, short and plump; his skin had the odd look of kneaded pink dough. He was probably Dutch or Belgian, I thought. He wore white also, but that was the only similarity between his clothes and those of the other two. The suit was impeccably tailored, the shirt of silk; the leather shoes were handmade and polished to a gloss. On the little finger of his left hand he wore a gold ring with a jade stone in the shape of a lion's head — symbolic, probably, of the Lion City.

He sat down carefully on the stool next to me. The other two remained standing. The plump man smiled as if he had

105

just found a missing relative. "You are Daniel Connell?" he asked.

"That's right."

"I am Jorge Van Rijk."

I went on eating the mangosteen.

"You were at the Seaman's Bar a short while ago. In the company of an acquaintance of mine."

"Is that so?"

"*M'sieu* La Croix."

"The name's not familiar."

"Come now, Mr. Connell. What did he want of you?"

"I don't see that it's any of your business."

"Ah, but it is. It is very much my business."

"Then go ask La Croix."

"An excellent suggestion," Van Rijk said. "However, he seems to have temporarily eluded us."

"Too bad for you."

"Necessarily, then, I must ask you. What did he want?"

"He wanted to sell me something," I said. "But I wasn't buying."

"No?" Van Rijk smiled again, but his eyes were as cold as dry ice. "You are a pilot, are you not?"

"Not anymore."

"A pilot for hire, I'm told. La Croix wished you to fly him somewhere."

"You think so? You weren't there."

"To what destination?"

"I didn't let him get that far."

"What destination, Mr. Connell? When and from where?"

"Ask as many questions as you want. I don't have any answers for you."

Van Rijk was losing patience; his eyes said so and so did

the threatening tone when he said, "You would be wise not to play games with me, Mr. Connell."

"I'm not playing games. Why should I? I don't know who you are or what your connection is to La Croix and I don't much care."

"Then tell me what you know of La Croix's plans, or —"

"Or what, Van Rijk?" My patience was gone, too. I laid my hands flat on the table, leaning toward him. That brought the other two in closer; one of them put his hand inside his jacket. "Or you sic your two bodyguards or whatever they are on me? I'm sure they're armed to the teeth, but I doubt you'd have them shoot me in a crowded bazaar. Or try to kidnap me, either. In fact I doubt you'll make any trouble at all, unless you want to spend some time in a city *penjara* for street brawling."

Anger blotched his pink cheeks. The other two were poised on the balls of their feet, watching me, waiting for orders from Van Rijk. But I'd read him right; he didn't want anything to do with the Singapore *polis*. He got slowly and stiffly to his feet.

"There will be another time, Mr. Connell," he said. "When the streets are not so crowded." Then he stalked off, threading his way between the tables, his two *orang séwaan-séwaan* at his heels. The three of them disappeared into the waterfront confusion.

I sat there for a time. Van Rijk and his threats didn't worry me much. There had been a time when they might have, but that time was two years dead; his type didn't bother me anymore. I wasn't even curious about his relationship with La Croix.

I drank a couple of iced Anchor beers in a nearby bar, then took a taxi to my flat on Punyang Street in Chinatown. A forty-minute nap, a tepid shower, and a fresh change of clothes put me in a better frame of mind. And by then I was thirsty again.

On Jalan Barat, not far away, there was a bar called the Malaysian Gardens — a gross misnomer. No flower, shrub or plant has ever been cultivated within a radius of one hundred yards of the place. Its facade was reminiscent of a Chinatown tenement and its barnlike interior was scruffy, bare, and redolent of the sweat, blood, and tears of its equally scruffy clientele. A dive the Malaysian Gardens may be, catering to the Caucasian, Eurasian, and Asian dregs, but the beer was cheap and nobody cared who or what you were. You could do your drinking alone or in the company of friendly and sympathetic — for the right price — bar girls. Mostly I did mine alone.

I had been there for perhaps three hours, sitting by myself at a rear table and thinking a lot of old and useless thoughts, when I realized I was being stared at. I was still fairly sober and it wasn't much of an effort to get my eyes focused. The starer was a woman. Not one of the bar girls — a young Caucasian woman who didn't belong in the Malaysian Gardens.

She was standing about fifteen feet away, tall and dark-haired and well-dressed. In the smoky dimness of the Gardens it was difficult to determine her age, but she couldn't have been older than thirty. She had eyes for me alone, no question of that, but not for the usual reason women stare at men in bars. She seemed nervous and uncomfortable and maybe a little scared.

My being aware of her seemed to make up her mind about something. She came forward jerkily and stopped in front of my table. "You're . . . Mr. Connell? Dan Connell?" American, I thought. Or possibly Canadian.

"That's me."

"My name is Tina Kellogg. I'd like to talk to you. It's . . . it's very important to me."

I indicated an empty chair and invited her to sit down.

"I don't know quite how to say this," she said. "I'm . . . I have no experience with this sort of thing."

"What sort of thing is that?"

She hesitated. "Well, *intrigue*, I guess you'd call it."

"That's a pretty melodramatic word."

"Yes, I know." She hesitated again. Then, in a rush, as if she needed to relieve herself of the pressure of the words: "Mr. Connell, I'm told that you fly people out of Singapore, people who can't leave any other way."

Christ, I thought. First La Croix, then Van Rijk, and now this woman. Some damn day this had been. "Who told you that?" I asked her.

"I don't know his name. A man I talked to on the waterfront. I spent most of the day asking around and this man said the person I should see was Dan Connell and that I could find him here most nights, so I . . ." Her voice trailed off.

"I can't help you," I told her.

"But . . . the man said . . ."

"I don't care what he said. I can't help you."

"It isn't very far, where I want to . . . where I *have* to go." Desperation put a tremble in her voice. "Just the Philippines. Anywhere near Luzon."

I drank from my glass. I thought she might go away if I ignored her, but she didn't.

"It's my father," she said. "The reason I have to get home so quickly. There was a telegram this morning, from the Luzon police. My father has been arrested. There have been terrorist attacks recently and they think he's involved with the Communist guerillas responsible." She took a deep, shuddery breath. "It's not true! I know my father. He's . . . we're Canadian. He owns a small import-export business, his sympathies are all with the present government. He would never become mixed up with the Communists — he'd have nothing to gain and everything to lose. It's all a mistake, a terrible mistake."

I sighed. "Why don't you just take one of the scheduled flights?"

"I haven't enough money. Nor any credit cards — my father doesn't believe in them."

"Can't someone in your family make the arrangements?"

"There's no one but my father and me."

"His business associates? Personal friends?"

She shook her head. "There's no one. I suppose I might be able to arrange something with his bank, but that might take days. And he has no close friends in Luzon. Even if he had, they'd be afraid to help me — afraid of being implicated with the Communists."

"What about people here? You have a job or just on holiday?"

"I've been working here four months," she said. "In a department store near Raffles Square. But it doesn't pay much and the owners won't help me. I've already asked them."

"Uh-huh. You could try the Canadian consulate, or have you already thought of that?"

"Yes. They wouldn't help, either, at least not to get me home quickly so I can be with my father."

I finished my beer. "So you think your only option is somebody like me. That's too bad because there's nothing I can do for you. I don't fly anymore. I haven't flown a plane in two years."

"But I can pay you, really I can. After we arrive I'll arrange with my father's bank —"

"You could lay a fortune in cash on this table and it wouldn't make any difference," I said. "It's not a matter of money. There's no way I can help you."

"Then . . . then what am I going to do?" She seemed on the verge of tears.

"Find somebody else." I'd had enough of this. I shoved my chair back and got on my feet. "Good night, Miss Kellogg. And good luck."

"No, wait . . ."

But I was already leaving. Without looking at her again I threaded my way through the crowded bar and went outside.

The night was dark — street lamps are few and far between on Jalan Barat. No wind and still muggy, but the fresh air cleared my head. I started away along the deserted street. Behind me I heard Tina Kellogg's voice calling my name; she'd followed me out. I didn't turn or slow my pace, then or when I heard her steps hurrying after me. It wasn't until I heard the sound of the car speeding down Jalan Barat past the Gardens, traveling much too fast from the whiny roar of the engine, that I swiveled my head for a backward look.

The car, its headlights glaring, was less than fifty yards away. There was the pig squeal of brakes locking and tires biting into pavement as the driver swung the car in at an angle to the curb close behind me. Both front doors opened at the same time, and two men came out in a hurry. I saw their faces clearly as they ran through the headlight spill: the two flat-eyed *orang séwaan-séwaan* who had been with Van Rijk earlier.

I had enough time to turn and set myself before the driver reached me. His right arm was raised across his body; he brought it down in a backward, chopping motion, karate-style. I got my left arm up and blocked his descending forearm with my own. The force of his rush threw him off balance, made him vulnerable. I jabbed the stiffened fingers of my right hand into his stomach, just below the breastbone. All the air went out of him. He stumbled backward, retching, and sat down hard on the sidewalk.

The other one had got there by then, but when he saw the driver fall he came up short and fumbled beneath his white linen jacket. I took three quick steps and laid the hard edge of my hand across his wrist. He made a pained noise deep in his throat and there was a metallic clatter as the gun or knife dropped to the pavement. I hit him twice in the face with quick jabs, turning him, then drove the point of my elbow into his kidneys. The blow sent him staggering blindly forward; he collided with the side of a building, slid down along it and lay still.

I looked at the driver again, but he was still sitting on the sidewalk, holding his stomach with both hands. I let my body relax, breathing raggedly, and scanned the street behind the stalled car. There was no sign of Tina Kellogg.

Other people came running toward me, shouting. I started toward them, thinking that I could decide later what to do, if anything, about Van Rijk. The thing to do right now was to avoid any contact with the *polis*. My reputation being what it was, the less I had to do with them, the better. Even though it had been two years since the trouble on Penang, memories are long in the South China Seas.

Somebody came up and asked me what had happened. "An accident," I said, and kept right on going. No one tried to stop me. And I did not look back.

Somebody was pounding on the door.

I rolled over on the sweat-slick sheets and opened my

eyes. It was morning; the sun lay outside the bedroom window of my flat like a red-orange ball suspended on glowing wires. I closed my eyes again and lay there listening to the now-impatient knocking. Whoever it was did not give up and go away.

"All right," I called finally. "All right."

I threw back the mosquito netting, got up and went to where my clothes were strewn on the rattan settee. The fan on the bureau had quit working sometime during the night, which accounted for the hot, stale air. I opened a window, then put on my trousers and crossed to unlock the door.

Standing there was a little, wiry, dark-skinned man wearing a pith-style helmet, white shorts, knee-high white socks, and a short-sleeved bush jacket. The outfit was a uniform, and he wore it proudly as native Malayans in an official capacity often do.

"I am Inspector Kok Chin Tiong of the Singapore *polis*," he said. "I would like to speak with you, please."

"What about?"

"May I come in, Mr. Connell?"

"If you don't make any comments about my housekeeping."

I stood aside to let him walk in past me. He stood in the middle of the room, looking around, then turned to confront me as I shut the door. His face and eyes were expressionless.

"You are acquainted with a French national named La Croix," Tiong said. It wasn't a question.

"I know him, yes."

"When did you last see him?"

He already knew the answer to that or he wouldn't be here. I said, "Yesterday. He looked me up. First time I'd seen him in three years."

113

"Why did he look you up, as you say?"

"He wanted me to do something for him."

"And that was?"

"Fly him out of Singapore."

"To what destination?"

"He didn't get around to telling me."

"You didn't ask?"

"I wasn't interested enough to ask."

"Did you agree to his request?"

"No. I don't fly anymore."

"Ah, yes," Tiong said. "There was an accident two years ago on Penang island. Involving an aircraft belonging to you and a Mr. Lawrence Falco."

"Yeah," I said. "An accident."

"You and Mr. Falco were co-owners of an air cargo company. The plane, piloted by you, crashed late one night in the jungle near a remote airstrip. You escaped serious injury but your partner was killed."

I didn't say anything.

"Explain, please, what you and Mr. Falco were doing in such a place at such a late hour. No flight plan was filed for the trip."

"There was a full investigation at the time. I gave a statement. Look up the records."

He smiled faintly. "I have already done so. There was strong suspicion that you and Mr. Falco were involved in the smuggling of contraband."

"Nothing was proven."

"Yes, both the plane and its cargo were destroyed in the explosion following the crash. But your commercial license was revoked."

My head had begun to ache. "Listen," I said, "I don't know why you're here, Inspector, but what I was or wasn't

114

doing two years ago is a dead issue, just like Larry Falco. I haven't been up in a plane since, and I never will again. Now if you don't mind, I'd like to wash up and get dressed."

His black eyes searched my face for a few seconds, then he put his hands behind his back and walked to the window. He stood looking down at noisy activity on Punyang Street. After a time, as I finished putting on my pants, he turned and said, "I would like to know your whereabouts last evening, Mr. Connell."

I told him, leaving out Tina Kellogg and the incident with Van Rijk's toughs.

He rubbed at his upper lip with the tip of one finger. "You are familiar with the East Coast Road, near Bedok?"

"A little."

"The French national was found there early this morning," Tiong said. "He had been dead for several hours. Quite badly used and then shot through the temple with a small caliber weapon."

I went to the bureau, shook a cigarette out of my pack and lit it. "How do you mean, badly used?"

"Tortured. With lighted cigarettes," he added pointedly.

I stubbed mine out; it had tasted foul anyway. "So you think I had something to do with it."

"Did you?"

"I told you where I was last night."

"Do you own a gun, please?"

"No."

"Would you object to a search of your room?"

"Be my guest," I said. "But you're wasting your time, Inspector. I didn't kill La Croix. I didn't have any reason to kill him."

"Have you any idea who did?"

"As a matter of fact, I do. Look up a guy named Van Rijk, Jorge Van Rijk, and ask him the same questions you've asked me."

Tiong's eyes narrowed. "What do you know of Van Rijk?"

"He looked me up yesterday, too, after I saw La Croix. Wanted to know where La Croix was and what his plans were. I brushed him off. He didn't like it, made a few veiled threats — and last night, when I left the Gardens, the two men he'd had with him jumped me. They didn't have any better luck."

"I see," Tiong said slowly. "Most interesting."

"I take it you're familiar with Van Rijk. Who is he?"

"A Dutch merchant currently living in Johore Bahru. But we have reason to believe he has other interests — illegal and quite profitable interests. He is also known to be an avid collector of rare jade." Tiong paused. "You are aware, of course, of the recent theft from the Museum of Oriental Art?"

"No," I said.

"It has been prominent in the newspapers."

"I'm not much of a reader."

"Early last week," Tiong said, "a valuable white jade figurine, the *Burong Chabak,* was taken from an exhibit at the museum. The robbery was cleverly planned and executed."

"You think Van Rijk was involved in it?"

"We do. We believe the French national was involved as well."

"It wouldn't surprise me. La Croix would do just about anything for the right price . . . but then I guess you know that."

Tiong nodded.

"If you're right," I said, "La Croix must have double-crossed Van Rijk and tried to keep the figurine for himself. That's why he was in such a sweat to have me fly him out of Singapore."

"So it would seem."

"Van Rijk and his boys must've caught up with him last night. Which means that now they have the figurine."

"Possibly."

"Have you picked up Van Rijk yet?"

"No. But we will. Everyone involved in the theft of the *Burong Chabak* will be taken into custody eventually."

"If you've got some idea that I'm mixed up in it, you're dead wrong. Everything I've told you is the truth."

"I hope so, Mr. Connell. Is there any more information you can give me?"

"No."

"Very well. I will take up no more of your time. You will, of course, keep yourself available in the event I need to speak with you again."

"I hadn't planned on going anywhere."

He nodded curtly. "Then, *selamat jalan*, Mr. Connell," and he went away and left me alone. For now.

The sun bore down mercilessly on the bared upper half of my body. My khakis were soaked through with a viscid sweat; the back of my neck was blotched and raw from the *roote hond*.

I rolled another barrel of palm oil from the deck of the *tongkang* across the plank and onto the dock. One of the Chinese coolies took it there and muscled it onto a wooden skid. An ancient forklift waited nearby.

I paused for a breather, rubbing the back of my forearm across my eyes. I was thinking how good an iced Anchor beer would taste once we were done for the day, when

117

Harry Rutledge came walking over to me.

"How's it going, lad?"

"Another hour or so should do it."

"Well, you have a visitor. An impatient one, at that."

"Visitor?"

"Bit of a pip, too," Harry said. "You Americans have all the luck."

"A woman? She tell you her name?"

"Tina Kellogg."

I frowned. "Where is she?"

"My office. You know where it is."

I put my shirt on, then went inside the huge, high-raftered *godown* and threaded my way through the stacked barrels and crates and skids to Harry's cluttered office. Tina Kellog was sitting in the bamboo armchair near the window, wearing a tailored white suit with a skirt short enough to reveal long, slender legs. She stood as I entered, smiling hesitantly. Her eyes were green and full of pleading.

"Mr. Connell, I . . . I'm sorry to bother you like this, but I wanted to make sure you're all right. Those men last night . . ."

"Uh-huh. Muggers are a hazard in that district."

She nodded. "I shouldn't have run away as I did. But I was frightened. It all happened so quickly."

"You did the right thing."

She sat in the armchair again, began twisting her hands nervously in her lap.

"Okay," I said. "Now you can tell me the real reason you're here. As if I didn't already know."

Color came into her cheeks. "I . . . I went back to the consulate this morning. They still won't help me. I have nowhere else to turn . . ." Abruptly she began to cry.

I stood there in the heat and watched her. Then, as the

tears slowed and became a series of snuffles, I moved over to Harry's desk and cocked a hip against it and lit a cigarette.

She looked up at me, her face wet, her eyes shining. "Please, Mr. Connell, please help me. I'll pay or do anything you ask . . ."

"I told you last night, I don't fly anymore. I don't own a plane anymore, don't have access to one because my license was revoked two years ago."

"But . . . the man I talked with yesterday, the one who gave me your name, he said you keep a DC-3 hidden at an abandoned airstrip here on the island." She snuffled, brushed at her eyes. "Isn't it still there?"

I didn't say anything for a time. The smoke from the cigarette burned my throat; I butted it in Harry's overflowing ashtray. "Yes," I said then. "It's still there."

"Then . . . ?"

"I'm treading on thin ice with the government," I said. "One more mark against me, I'll be declared *persona non grata* and deported. I don't have any other home to go to."

"No one will ever know," she said. "You'll be very careful, I know you will. And I'll pay you whatever you ask, any amount, as soon as I can make arrangements with my father's bank . . ."

I was silent again, thinking. Not liking what I was thinking, but there it was just the same.

"Mr. Connell?"

"All right," I said.

"You'll help me?"

"I'll help you."

She came up out of the chair, threw her arms around my neck. "Oh, thank you, thank you! You won't regret this, I promise you."

I pushed her away gently. "I sure as hell hope not."

"When can we leave?"

"Tonight. It'll have to be late, around eleven."

"We couldn't go sooner?"

"No. Do you know the Esplanade on Cecil Street?"

"Yes. Yes, I know it."

"Meet me there at ten o'clock," I said, and left her and Harry's hot, cramped office and went back to work. Telling myself I was a damn fool and knowing I was going to go through with it anyway.

It rained the early part of the evening, a torrential tropical downpour that lasted for more than an hour and left the air, as the daily rains always did, smelling clean and sweet. But by then, when I left my flat, it had grown oppressively hot and humid again.

Tina Kellogg was waiting in the shadows near the Esplanade when I arrived at Cecil Street. Tonight she wore men's khakis and a gray bush jacket — her traveling outfit.

"No luggage?" I asked her.

"No. I didn't want to bother with it. I can send for it later."

"All right. Let's get started."

I hailed one of the H.C.S. taxis that roam the streets of Singapore in droves. The driver, a bearded Sikh, did not ask any questions when I told him where we wanted to go, even though he wouldn't get many fares to the remote Jurong section of the island that I named. There was nothing much out there but mangrove swamps and a few native fishing *kampongs*.

It was nearly eleven when he turned onto Kelang Bahru Road, leading toward the abandoned airstrip, Mikko Field. The moon was up and nearly full, lighting the road brightly

120

enough so that you could have driven it without headlights.

When we neared the access road to the strip, the Sikh slowed and asked, "Do you wish me to drive to the field, sahib? The road is very bad."

"Go in as far as you can," I told him. "We'll walk the rest of the way."

He made the turn onto the access road. It was chuckholed and choked with tall grass and tangled vegetation. We crawled along for about a quarter mile. Finally, in the bright moonshine, I could see the long, rough runway, raised some ten feet on steep earth mounds from the mangrove jungle on both sides. At its upper end, to our left, were the decaying wooden outbuildings, and farther behind them, the broken-domed hangar. The airstrip had been deserted since the end of the Second World War. Few people remembered, or cared, that it hadn't yet rotted into extinction.

The Sikh brought the taxi to a stop. The road was mostly impassable from this point; the marsh grass was tall and thick, and parasitic vines and creepers and thornbushes had encroached thickly in places.

I paid the Sikh, and Tina Kellogg and I stepped out. The night was alive with the buzzing hum of mosquitoes, midges, the big Malaysian cicadas. There was the heavy smell of decaying vegetation, of dampness from the rain.

The taxi backed around a jog in the road, its lights making filtered splashes through the mangroves. I stood looking toward the airstrip, listening to the throb of the engine as the Sikh got turned around and headed away.

Tina Kellogg had not spoken during the ride out. Now she said, "The runway doesn't seem very well maintained. Are you sure it'll be safe to take off?"

"You let me worry about that."

121

I took her arm and pushed ahead through the grass. We hadn't gone far when I heard the engine sound. Not the taxi's; that one had faded to silence. This was a new, different sound — the unmistakable whine of a four-cylinder engine held in low gear — and it was coming this way. Coming fast and without headlights; when I turned to look back, all I could see was moonlight and thick shadow.

"That's not the taxi," Tina Kellogg said. Her fingers bit urgently into my arm. "Who — ?"

"I don't know, but I've got a good idea."

We both started to run. We had to stay on what was left of the road; the mangroves were a dense snarl of roots and underbrush, home of a hundred dangers including poisonous snakes. The oncoming car was very close now, and even though the grass was thick here, it wasn't tall enough to hide us. We were clearly visible in the bright moonglow.

Headlights stabbed on behind us; I heard the familiar pig squeal of brakes. A vine or creeper caught Tina's leg and she stumbled and fell. I hauled her up again, pulled her along to the left where the grass was thinner and there were more bushes to cast shadow. A hoarse shout cut through the insect hum. I half-expected a gun to start popping, too, but that didn't happen yet.

Ahead the road curled to the left, paralleling the airstrip and leading to the hangar and outbuildings. Vines and wildly tangled shrubs clogged it completely after forty or fifty yards. If we couldn't get through, we wouldn't stand a chance. And even if we could, needle-sharp thorns would shred clothing and skin, slow us down.

The only other way to the buildings was the runway. We'd be exposed up there, but no more than down here. And it was a straight line to the buildings, no more than seventy-five yards to the first of them. Find a hiding place over there and we'd have a better chance than floundering around in the jungle.

I plowed through underbrush and ground cover, half-dragging Tina along with me. Something ripped at my bare arms; something else brushed my face, whispering, cold. Then we were out of the bushes and at the base of the embankment. The mounded earth was a quagmire from the evening rain, but we managed to fight our way up onto the strip without losing balance. A gun cracked somewhere close behind us, but neither of us was hit.

"Run" I said to Tina. "Off to the left!"

We ran. Our muddied boots slapped wetly on the rough concrete. There was another shout, another pistol crack. I glanced back. Two men were scrambling up the embankment. A third stood in the headlamp beams of a small car slewed on the road where the taxi had let us off. He was doing the shouting. I couldn't see his face clearly, but I knew it was Van Rijk.

I turned my head, just in time to avoid stepping into a pothole and maybe breaking a leg. We were almost to the first of the outbuildings now. There were no more shots. They'd finally figured out that you can't shoot accurately while you're on the run.

The closest building was a long, low-roofed affair that had been used to quarter duty personnel. All the glass had been broken out of its windows years ago, and some of the side boarding had rotted or pulled away, leaving shadowed gaps like missing teeth. Off to one side was a smaller, ramshackle shed of some kind.

I steered Tina that way. We ran around the corner of the low-roofed building, along the side of the shed. At its rear, a jagged-edged hole above the foundation yawned black, like a small cave opening.

I pulled up, fighting breath into my lungs. "Through there!"

She obeyed instantly, dropping to her knees and scuttling through the hole. I followed close behind her.

Thin shafts of moonlight made a pale, irregular pattern on the debris-ridden floor inside. The shed was empty. It was close, humid in there — a pervasive heat like that in an orchid hothouse.

Tina's breath came in thick gasps. She crouched on her knees with her head lowered. I left her and crawled to the front of the shed. When I peered through one of the smaller gaps there, I had a full view of the airstrip and part of the access road beyond.

Two sets of headlights, one tight behind the other, were coming fast along the road. Seeing them eased a little of the tension in me. I could not see the portion of the road where Van Rijk and his car were, but the two *orang séwaan-séwaan*, on the runway and pounding toward the low-roofed building, had a good sidewise look at both Van Rijk and the oncoming cars. They pulled up and danced around some, then began running back the way they'd come.

"What is it?" Tina asked. She was beside me now, trying to peer out. "What's happening?"

The sounds of jamming brakes, doors slamming, men shouting carried to us on the still night air. I said, "The *polis* are here."

"The *polis?*"

Van Rijk's men were dancing around again, over at the edge of the strip. One of them went into a crouch and fired a round toward the glaring headlights. In response I heard a short, sharp burst from an automatic weapon. The man fell sprawling. The other one veered to his right and disappeared onto the embankment. A few seconds later there was another chattering burst, two pistol shots, a third burst. After that, silence.

I turned away from the opening. "It's all over now," I said.

Tina's fingers bit into my arm. "The plane!" she breathed. "There might still be time to reach the plane, get away . . ."

"There isn't any plane."

"What? I . . . I don't understand . . ."

"There's no plane here. Hasn't been one here in a long time."

She stared at me. Her face was shadowed and I couldn't see her eyes. I didn't see the movement of her hand, either, until it was too late to stop her from reaching under her bush jacket and drawing the automatic she'd had tucked into her belt. A shaft of pale moonlight glinted off the surface of its barrel. Small caliber automatic aimed right at my belly.

I said, "Is that the gun you shot La Croix with? After you tortured him?"

She leaned forward slightly, and I could see her face then. It was as cold and hard as white jade. "All right," she said. "So you know."

"I've known since this afternoon," I said. "It was a nice little act you put on, but I didn't believe it last night and I saw all the way through it at the *godown*. You said your mythical informant told you I keep a DC-3 out here. But damn few people knew it when I did keep one, for obvious reasons. My former partner was one and he's dead. Another is a German named Heinrich and he's serving ten years in a Djakarta prison. The only man you could've gotten the information from was La Croix."

Nothing from her. The gun was steady in her hand.

125

"After I finished work this afternoon, I went down to the government precinct and talked to a *polis* inspector Tiong. He did some checking with the Canadian consulate. They never heard of a Luzon import-export dealer named Kellogg, or a Tina Kellogg. But the American consulate has a record of one Tanya Kasten. So does Interpol, because of the art theft you were implicated in last year in Amsterdam. Is that where you met or got put in touch with Van Rijk, Tanya?"

"A trap. All a damn trap."

"That's right. To catch you with the *Burong Chabak*. Tiong figured you were in on the theft, found La Croix before Van Rijk did, and got it from him. But I don't think you did get it. No luggage, no figurine. What happened? You lose your temper and kill him too soon?"

"Shut up," she spat at me.

"I think La Croix hid the figurine out here. You think so, too. And you think I know where. If Van Rijk hadn't been trailing me tonight and started his boys shooting at us, you'd have thrown down on me as soon as we reached the hangar."

"You do know where he hid it, don't you? All right. You're going to take me to it, right now."

"Don't be a fool. Tiong and his men will be here pretty quick. You can't get past them."

"*We'll* get past them," she said. "With the figurine."

"If you're thinking about using me as a hostage, you can forget it. The law doesn't give a damn about me."

"We'll see about that."

"No," I said, "we won't."

She made an impatient gesture with the gun — just what I wanted her to do. I swept my left hand out and up, palm open and driving against her hand and the auto-

126

matic's barrel, knocking them upward. There was a crack and a flash as the gun went off; I felt heat along my forearm, but the bullet thudded somewhere into the shed's roof. I caught her wrist with my right hand, pressured it until she cried out in pain. The weapon fell thudding to the floor.

I picked it up, sliding back away from her. She stayed put, holding her wrist and cursing me steadily and bitterly. I tucked the automatic into my belt, moved to the jagged wall opening, and squeezed through it backward. Outside I stood and went to where I could see the airstrip.

Half a dozen men were fanned out and closing in on the runway, one of them brandishing an automatic weapon, the others with drawn pistols. Inspector Kok Chin Tiong was in the lead. I stepped out of the shadows into the moonlight, my hands up in plain sight.

Tiong was out of breath as he came running up. "You are all right, Mr. Connell?"

"Yeah."

"The woman?"

"In the shed. I don't think she'll give you any trouble."

Tiong said something in Malay and two of his officers went to take Tanya Kasten into custody.

I asked, "What about Van Rijk?"

"Shackled and under guard," Tiong said. "The other two are dead."

"You could've been saying the same about me. You took your sweet time getting here."

He smiled faintly. "At the Esplanade we saw that Van Rijk was following you."

"So you decided to nab him along with the woman. But did you have to give him such a bloody big lead?"

"We did not wish him to realize that he, too, was being

followed," Tiong said. "Now, Mr. Connell. The *Burong Chabak*."

I'd told him that I had a pretty good idea where La Croix had stashed it — a drop point we'd used in my black market days, where he'd leave cash for me when I brought in a shipment of contraband. I led Tiong to the rear of the hangar, between its back wall and two big, corroded tanks that had once been used for the storage of airplane fuel. Set into the ground there was a wooden box housing regulator valves for the airstrip's water supply.

The *Burong Chabak* was inside the box, all right, wrapped in chamois and canvas and tied with string.

I had my first clear look at the figurine later that night, in Tiong's office. It was very old and beautifully carved in intricate detail, depicting a nightbird — a *burong chabak* — in full flight, wings spread, head extended as if into the wind. The bird itself was of white jade, the purest, most valuable of all jade; the squarish pedestal upon which it rested was of the dark green variety.

"Is it not beautiful?" Tiong asked.

I didn't agree with him. It looked and felt cold to me — as cold as Tanya Kasten's face in the moonlit shed.

"It is said to be worth a minimum of four hundred thousand Straits dollars. A hundred and fifty thousand dollars, American. Tanya Kasten's buyer in Luzon, whoever he is, may even have been willing to pay more. To some men, such a rarity is worth any price."

"I suppose so."

"The money, too, would tempt many men. Particularly one with a past such as yours. Yet you chose to come to the *polis*, to help us recover the figurine, instead of attempting to keep it for yourself. Why, Mr. Connell?"

128

"Does it really matter?"

"I would like to know."

"All right, then. The main reason is Larry Falco."

"Your former partner?"

"My *dead* former partner," I said. "A nice guy, with a lot of ideas about making an honest living from an air cargo company, who died because I had other ideas — like transporting a load of contraband silk to a treacherous jungle airstrip at midnight. He tried to talk me out of it, but I wouldn't listen. I could land a plane anywhere, I told him, under any conditions. Well, I was wrong and it cost him his life instead of mine."

Tiong nodded slowly and said, "I see."

Maybe he did, maybe he didn't. I did not really care one way or the other.

Vanishing Act
(with Michael Kurland)

The three of us — Ardis, Cedric Clute and I — were sitting at a quiet corner table, halfway between the Magic Cellar's bar and stage, when the contingent of uniformed policemen made their entrance. There were about thirty of them, all dressed in neatly pressed uniforms and gleaming accessories, and they came down the near aisle two abreast like a platoon of marching soldiers. Most of the tables that front the stage were already occupied, so the cops took over the stack of carpet- covered trunks which comprise a kind of bleacher section directly behind the tables.

I cocked an eyebrow. "Most saloon owners would object to such an influx of fuzz," I said to Cedric. He owns the Cellar, San Francisco's only nightclub devoted to the sadly vanishing art of magic.

"Policemen have a right to be entertained," he said, smiling.

"Their lot, I understand, is not a happy one."

Ardis said speculatively, "They look very young."

"That's because they're most of the graduation class of the Police Academy," Cedric told her. "Their graduation ceremony was this afternoon, and I invited them down as a group. Actually, it was Captain Dickensheet's idea." He indicated a tall, angular, graying man, also in uniform, who was about to appropriate a table for himself and two other elder officers. "I've known him casually for a couple of years, and he thought his men would enjoy the show."

"With Christopher Steele and The Amazing Boltan on the same bill," Ardis said, "they can't help but enjoy it."

I started to add an agreement to that — and there was Steele himself standing over the table, having appeared with that finely developed knack he has of seeming to come from nowhere.

Christopher Steele is the Cellar's main attraction and one of the greatest of the modern illusionists. I don't say that because I happen to be his manager and publicist. He's also something of a secretive type, given to quirks like an inordinate fascination for puzzles and challenges, the more bizarre the better. Working for and with him the past five years has been anything but dull.

Steele usually dresses in black, both on stage and off, and I think he does it because he knows it gives him, with his thick black hair and dark skin and eyes, a vaguely sinister air. He looked sinister now as he said, "The most amazing thing about Phil Boltan, you know, is that he's still alive. He does a fine job on stage, but he has the personal habits and morals of a Yahoo."

Ardis' eyes shone as they always did when Steele was around; she's his assistant and confidante and lives in a wing of his house across the Bay, although if there is anything of a more intimate nature to their relationship neither of them has ever hinted at it to me. She said, "You sound as though Boltan is not one of your favorite people, Christopher."

"He isn't — not in the least."

Cedric frowned, "If you'd told me you felt that way, I wouldn't have booked you both for the same night."

"It doesn't matter. As I said, he is a fine performer."

"Just what is it that you find so objectionable about Boltan?" I asked as Steele sat down.

131

"He's a ruthless egomaniac," Steele said. "Those in the psychological professions would call him a sociopath. If you stand in his way, he'll walk over you without hesitation."

"A fairly common trait among performers."

"Not in Boltan's case. Back in the 40s, for example, he worked with a man named Granger —"

"The Four-Men-in-a-Trunk Illusion," Ardis said immediately.

"Right. The Granger Four-Men-in-a-Trunk Illusion premiered at the Palladium before George the Fifth. That was before Boltan's time, of course. At any rate, Granger was getting old, but he had a beautiful young wife named Cecily and an infant son; he also had Phil Boltan as an assistant.

"So one morning Granger awoke to find that Boltan had run off with Cecily and several trunks of his effects. He was left with the infant son and a load of bitterness he wasn't able to handle. As a result, he put his head in a plastic bag one evening and suffocated himself. Tragic — very tragic."

"What happened to the son?" Cedric asked.

"I don't know. Granger had no close relatives, so I imagine the boy went to a foster home."

Ardis asked, "Did Boltan marry Cecily?"

"No. Of course not. He's never married any of his conquests."

"Nice guy," I said.

Steele nodded and leaned back in his chair. "Enough about Phil Boltan," he said. "Matthew, did you have any problem setting up for my show?"

"No," I told him. "All your properties are ready in the wings."

"Sound equipment?"

"In place."

"Ultraviolet bulbs?"

"Check," I said. The u.v. bulbs were to illuminate the special paint on the gauze and balloons and other "spook" effects for Steele's midnight seance show. "It's a good thing I did a precheck; one of the Carter posters fluoresced blue around the border, and I had to take it down. Otherwise it would have been a conspicuous distraction."

Cedric looked at me reproachfully. "I suppose you'd have removed the Iron Maiden if that had fluoresced," he said, meaning the half-ton iron torture box in one corner.

"Sure," I said. "Dedication is dedication."

We made small talk for a time, and then Cedric excused himself to take his usual place behind the bar; it was twenty past ten. I sipped my drink and looked idly around the Cellar. It was stuffed with the paraphernalia and memorabilia of Carter the Great, a world-famous illusionist in the '20s and '30s. His gaudy posters covered the walls.

The stage was rather small, but of professional quality; it even had a trapdoor, which led to a small tunnel, which in turn came up in the coatroom adjacent to the bar. The only other exits from the stage, aside from the proscenium, were curtains on the right and left sides, leading to small dressing rooms. Both rooms had curtained second exits to the house, on the right beyond the Davenport Brothers Spirit Cabinet — a privy-sized cubicle in which a tarot reader now did her thing — and on the left behind a half-moon table used for close-up card tricks.

At 10:30 the voice of Cedric's wife Jan came over the loud-speaker, announcing the beginning of Boltan's act. The lights dimmed, and the conversational roar died to a murmur. Steele swiveled his chair to face the stage, the glass of brandy he had ordered in one hand. He cupped the glass like a fragile relic, staring over its lip at the stage as the curtain went up.

"Oh, for a muse of fire . . ." he said softly, when The Amazing Boltan made his entrance.

"What was that?" I whispered, but Steele merely gave me one of his amused looks and waved me to silence.

The Amazing Boltan was an impressive man. Something over six feet tall and ever so slightly portly, he had the impeccable grooming and manners of what would have been described fifty years ago as a "born gentleman." His tuxedo didn't seem like a stage costume, but like a part of his personality. It went with the gold cuff-links and cigar case, and the carefully tonsured, white-striped black hair. He looked elegant, but to my eyes it was the elegance of a con man or a head waiter.

Boltan's act was showy, designed to impress you with his power and control. He put a rabbit into a box, then waved his hands and collapsed the box, and the rabbit was gone. He took two empty bowls and produced rice from them until it overran the little table he was working on and spilled in heaps onto the stage floor. He did a beautiful version of an effect called the Miser's Dream. Gold coins were plucked out of the air and thrown into a bucket until it rattled with them; then he switched to paper money and filled the rest of the bucket with fives and tens. All the while he kept up a steady flow of patter about "The Gold of Genies" and "The Transmutations of the Ancients of Lhassa."

When he was finished with this effect, Boltan said to the audience, "I shall now require an assistant. A young lady, perhaps. What about you, miss? That's it — don't be afraid. Step right up here on stage with me." He helped a young, winsome-looking blonde across the footlights, and proceeded to amaze her and the rest of the audience by causing sponge balls to multiply in her closed hand and appear

134

and disappear from his.

He excused the girl finally and asked for another volunteer: "A young man, perhaps, this time." I could tell by the pacing of the act that he was headed toward some impressive finale.

A bulky bearded man who had just pushed himself to a table at the front, and was therefore still standing, allowed himself to be talked into climbing onto the stage. He was dressed somewhere between college casual and sloppy: a denim jacket, jeans, and glossy black shoes. He appeared to be in his late twenties, though it wasn't easy to tell through his medium-length facial hair.

"Thank you for coming up to help me," Boltan said in his deep stage voice. "Don't be nervous. Now, if you'll just hold your two hands outstretched in front of you, palms up . . ."

The bearded man, instead of complying with this request, took a sudden step backward and pulled a small automatic from his jacket pocket.

The audience leaned forward expectantly, thinking that this was part of the act; but Steele, who apparently felt that it wasn't, jumped to his feet and started toward the stage. I pushed my own chair back, frowning, and went after him.

Boltan retreated a couple of steps, a look of bewilderment crossing his elegant features. The bearded man leveled the gun at him, and I heard him say distinctly, "I'm going to kill you, Boltan, just as someone should have done years ago."

Steele shouted something, but his words were lost in the deafening explosion of three shots.

Boltan, staggering, put a hand to his chest. Blood welled through his fingers, and he slowly crumpled. A woman screamed. The uniformed police cadets and their officers were on their feet, some of them starting for the stage. Steele had reached the first row of tables, and was trying to push between two chairs to get to the stage. The bearded man dropped his weapon and ran off stage right, disappearing behind the curtain leading to the dressing room on that side.

The entire audience knew now that the shooting wasn't part of the show; another woman screamed, and people began milling about, several of them rushing in panic toward the Cellar's two street exits. Blue uniforms converged on the stage, shoving tables and civilians out of the way, leaping up onto it. Steele had made it up the steps by this time, with me at his heels, but his path to the stage right curtain was hampered by the cadets. Over the bedlam I heard a voice shout authoritatively, "Everyone remain calm and stay where you are! Don't try to leave these premises!"

Another voice, just as authoritative, yelled, "Jordan, Bently, Cullen — cover the exits! Let no one out of here!"

I could see the stage area exit beyond the Spirit Cabinet, the one from the dressing room area stage right to the club floor; in fact, I had kept my eyes on it from the moment the bearded man had run off, because that was the only other way out of that dressing room. But no one appeared there. Steele and the cops pushed their way through the stage right curtain just as several other cadets reached the exit I was watching. Any second now they would drag the bearded man out, I thought, and we could start to make sense out of what had just happened.

Only they didn't emerge, and I heard shouts of surprise and confusion instead.

"He's got to be in here somewhere."

"He's not here, damn it, you can see that."

"Another exit . . ."

"There isn't any other exit," Steele's voice said.

"Well, he's hiding in here somewhere."

"Where? There's no place for a man to hide."

"Those costume trunks —"

"They're too small to hold a man, as you can plainly see."

"Then where the hell is he? He can't have vanished into thin air!"

Subsequently, however, it appeared that the man who had shot The Amazing Boltan in full view of more than thirty cops had done just that.

Half an hour later I was again sitting at the corner table, along with Steele, Ardis, a harassed looking Cedric, and Ced's slender and attractive wife Jan. The contingent of police had managed to quiet the frightened patrons, who were now all sitting at the tables or in the grandstand, or clustered along the walls, or bellied up to the bar for liquid fortification; they looked nervous and were mostly silent. Blue uniforms and business suits — the cadets and their officers, and several regular patrolmen and Homicide people — stood guard or moved about the room examining things and asking questions and doing whatever else it is cops do at the scene of a violent crime.

A number of things had occurred in that half hour.

Item: Boltan had died of the gunshot wounds, probably instantaneously.

Item: The gun which the murderer had dropped, a Smith & Wesson M39, had been turned over to the forensic lab men. If they had found any fingerprints on it, we hadn't heard of it yet.

Item: The police cadets who had covered the Cellar's

137

two street exits immediately after the shooting swore that no one had left.

Item: The entire stage area and the remainder of the club had been thoroughly searched without turning up any sign of the bearded killer.

Conclusions: The Amazing Boltan had been shot to death by a man who could not have left the Magic Cellar, was therefore still here, and yet, seemingly, was not here at all.

All of us were baffled, as we had said to each other several times in the past few minutes. Or, rather, Ardis and Cedric and Jan and I had said so; Steele sat in silence, which was unusual for him, and seemed to be brooding. When I asked him how he thought it had been done, since after all he was a master illusionist and a positive fanatic when it came to "impossible challenges," he gave me a meditative look and declined comment.

We had considered, of course, the trapdoor in the stage, and had instantly ruled it out. For one thing, it was located in the middle of the stage itself — right behind where Boltan had fallen, as a matter of fact — and all of us had seen the killer exit stage right through the side curtain; there was no trap in that dressing room area. The tunnel leading from under the stage trap to the coatroom had been searched anyway, but had been empty.

I dredged my memory for possible illusions which would explain the bearded man's vanishing act, but they all seemed to demand a piece of apparatus or specific condition which just wasn't present. Houdini once vanished an elephant off the stage of the Hippodrome, but he had a large, specially made cage to do it. What did seem clear was that the murderer knew, and had applied, the principles of stage magic to come up with a brilliant new effect, and then had used it to commit a cold-blooded homicide on the stage of the Magic Cellar.

Captain Dickensheet approached our table and leaned across it, his palms hard on the edge. "Everybody," he said pointedly to Cedric, "has to be somewhere. Don't you have *any* ideas where the killer got to — and how?"

Cedric shook his head wearily. "There's just no other way out of that dressing room besides the curtain onto the stage and the curtain next to the Spirit Cabinet," he said. "The Cabinet is solid down to the floor, and the other walls are brick."

"No gimmick or gizmo to open that Cabinet's back wall?"

"No, none."

"Even if there were," Steele said, "it would merely propel the killer into the audience. The fact is, Captain, he could not have gotten out of the dressing room unseen. You have my professional word on that."

Dickensheet straightened up, glaring. "Are you telling me, then, that what we all saw couldn't have happened?"

"Not at all." Steele stood abruptly and squeezed past my chair to the aisle. "I can assure you that what you saw is exactly what happened. Exactly." Then, nodding to the table, he headed back to the stage left dressing room.

Dickensheet lowered his lanky frame into the aisle chair and stared across at the Carter the Great poster on the wall facing him. It depicted Carter astride a camel, surrounded by devils and imps, on his way to "steal" the secrets of the Sphinx and the marvels of the tomb of old King Tut. "Magicians!" the captain said, with feeling.

Cedric asked, "How much longer will you be holding everyone here?"

"I don't know yet."

139

"Well, can't you just take all their names and addresses, and let them go home?"

"That's not up to me," Dickensheet said sourly. "You'll have to talk to Lupoff, the homicide inspector in charge of the investigation."

"All right." Cedric sighed, and got up to do that.

I decided to leave the table too, because I was wondering what Steele was up to backstage. I excused myself and went into the left dressing room where I found Steele sitting in front of the mirror, carefully applying his stage makeup.

"What are you doing?" I demanded.

"It's twenty till twelve, Matthew," he said. "I'm on at midnight."

"You don't think they're going to let you do your show *now*, do you?"

"Why not?"

"Well, they just took Boltan's body off the stage fifteen minutes ago."

"Ah yes," Steele said. "Life and death, the eternal mysteries. My audience is still here, I note, and I'm sure they'd like to be entertained. Not that watching the police poking and prying into all the comers big enough to conceal a man isn't entertaining."

"I don't understand why you'd even *want* to go on tonight," I said. "There's no way you can top the last performance. Besides, a spook show would hardly be in good taste right now."

"On the contrary, it would be in perfect taste. Because during the course of it, I intend to reveal the identity of the murderer of Philip Boltan."

"What!" I stared at him. "Do you mean you know how the whole thing was done?"

"I do."

140

"Well — how? How did the killer disappear?"

"The midnight show, Matthew," he said firmly.

I looked at him with sufferance, and then nodded. Steele never does anything the easy way. As well, here was an opportunity to put on a kind of show of shows, and Steele is first and foremost a showman. Not that I objected to this, you understand. My business is publicity and public relations, and Steele's flair for drama is the best kind of both. If he named the killer during his midnight show, and brought about the capture of the bearded man, the publicity would be fantastic.

"All right," I said, "I'll use my wiles to convince the cops to allow you to go ahead. But I hope you know what you're doing."

"I always know what I'm doing."

"Ninety percent of the time, anyway."

"Ask Ardis to come in here," Steele said. "I'll have to tell her what effects we're doing now, and in what order."

"You wouldn't want to give me some idea of what's going on, would you?"

Steele smiled a gentle, enigmatic smile. "It is now quarter to twelve, Matthew. I would like the show to begin at exactly midnight."

Which meant that he had said all he intended to say for the time being, and I was therefore dismissed. So I went back out into the club where Captain Dickensheet was still sitting at our table with Jan and Ardis; Cedric had also returned, and had brought with him the dark, intense-looking inspector-in-charge, Lupoff.

When I got to the table I told Ardis that Steele wanted to see her. Immediately, she hurried to the stage left dressing room. I sat down and put on my best PR smile for Lupoff and Dickensheet.

"I have a request from Christopher Steele," I said formally. "He wants to be allowed to do his midnight show."

Both cops frowned, and Lupoff said, "I'm in no mood for levity."

"Neither is Steele. He wants to do the show, he says, in order to name the murderer and explain how the vanishing act was done."

Everyone at the table stared at me, Cedric and Jan looking relieved. Lupoff and Dickensheet, on the other hand, looked angrily disbelieving. The inspector said, "If Steele knows how and who, why the hell doesn't he just come out here and say so?"

"You have to understand him," I said. "He's an artist, a showman. He thinks only in theatrical terms." I went on to tell them about Steele's idiosyncrasies, making it sound as though he were a genius who had to be treated with kid gloves — which was true enough. "Besides, if he solves the case for you, what can it hurt to let him unmask the killer in his own way?"

"The murderer *is* still here, then?" Cedric asked.

"I think so," I said. "Steele didn't really tell me much of anything, but that's what I would assume." I returned my gaze to the two cops. "You've got the Cellar sealed off, right? The killer can't possibly escape."

"I don't like it," Lupoff said. "It's not the way things are done."

I had to sell them quickly; it was nearing midnight. I decided to temporize. "Steele needs the show in order to expose the guilty man," I said. "He's not sure of the killer's identity, but something he has planned in the show will pin it down."

"How does he know it will work?" Dickensheet asked. Then he scowled. "He wouldn't be wanting to do this show of his just for publicity, would he?"

"Listen, Captain," I said, "the publicity won't be very good if he blows it. I'd say Steele's pretty sure of himself."

Cedric nodded eagerly; he knew, as I did, that if Steele came through as usual, it would turn a possibly harmful blow to the Cellar's image into a potential drawing card. He said, "I've known Christopher Steele for a long time, and I'll vouch for what Mr. Booth says. If Steele claims to know what happened here tonight, then he does know. I think you ought to go along with him."

Lupoff and Dickensheet held a whispered conference. Then they both got up, told us to wait, and went backstage, no doubt to confront Steele. Three minutes later they came out again, still looking dubious — but knowing Steele as I did, I could tell even before Dickensheet confirmed it that they had given him the go-ahead.

Midnight.

The civilian audience had been fidgeting in their seats for a couple of minutes, since Cedric had announced to them over the loudspeaker that Steele was going to do his midnight show. The contingent of police were also fidgeting, owing to the fact that none of them had any idea, either, of what was about to happen. I was alone at the table, Jan having gone back to the bar and Cedric off to work the light board.

The house lights dimmed, and the curtain rolled up. Steele stood motionless at center stage, the rose-gelled spots bathing him in soft light; his work clothes, a black suit over a dark turtleneck, gave him a sinister-somber look. He bowed slightly and said, "Good evening."

The last murmur died away among the audience, and two hundred people silently watched for whatever miracle Chris-

143

topher Steele, Master of Illusion, was about to perform.

"We have, all of us," he said, "just witnessed a murder, and a murder is a horrible thing. It is the one irremediable act, terrible in its finality and inexcusable in any sane society. No matter how foul the deeds or repugnant the actions of another human being, no one has the right to take from him that which cannot be given back: his life.

"But the murder itself has been overshadowed by the miraculous disappearance of the killer, seemingly before our very eyes. He ran into that dressing room —" Steele gestured to his left, "— which has only two exits, and apparently never came out. The room has been thoroughly searched, and no human being could possibly remain concealed therein. A vanishing act worthy of a Houdini."

Steele's eyes peered keenly around at the audience. "I am something of an authority on vanishing —"

Suddenly the lights went out.

There was an immediate reaction from the audience, already edgy from the past hour-and-a-half's happenings; no screams, but a nervous titter in the dark and the sound of chairs being pushed back and people standing.

Then the lights came back on, and Steele was still there, center stage, facing the audience. "Accept my apologies," he said. "Please, all of you be seated. As you can see —" he indicated the two police officers standing one on each side of the stage, "— there is nowhere I could go. As well, the lights were off then for a full five seconds, which is much too long for an effective disappearance. A mere flicker of darkness, or a sudden burst of flame, is all that is needed.

"I shall now attempt to solve this mystery, which has so baffled my friends on the police and the rest of us. I'm sure you will forgive me if, in so doing, I create a small mystery of my own."

Steele clapped his hands together three times, and on the third clap there was a blinding flash of light — and the stage lights went out again — and came back on almost instantly.

Steele was gone.

In his place stood the beautiful Ardis, in her long white stage gown, her arms outstretched and a smile on her lips. "Hello," she said.

The audience gasped. The thing was done so neatly, and so quickly; Steele had turned into Ardis before their eyes. Someone tentatively applauded, as much in a release of tension as anything else, but there was no doubt that the audience was impressed.

Ardis held up her hands for silence. "What you have just seen is called a transference," she said when the room grew still again. "Christopher Steele is gone, and I am here. And now I, too, in my turn, shall leave. I shall go into the fourth dimension, and you shall all observe the manner of my going. Yet none of you will know where I have gone. Thus — farewell."

There was another bright flash, and the lights once more went out; but we could still see Ardis before us as a kind of ghostly radiance, her white dress almost glowing in the dark. Then she dwindled before our eyes, as though receding to a great distance. Finally, the lights came on to stay, and the stage was empty, and she was gone.

There was a shocked silence, as though the audience was collectively holding its breath. In that silence, a deep, imperious voice said, "I am here!"

Everybody turned in their seats, including me, for the voice had come from the rear of the room.

Incredibly, there stood the murderer — beard, denim jacket, and all.

145

Several of the policemen started toward him, and one woman shrieked. At the same time, the bearded man extended his arm and pointed a long finger. "I," he said, "am you."

He was pointing at one of the young police cadets standing near the Iron Maiden.

The cadet backed away, startled, looking trapped. Immediately, the bearded man hunched in on himself and pulled the denim jacket over his head. When he stood up again, he was Steele — and the apparition that had been the murderer was a small bundle of clothing in his hand. Even the jeans had been replaced by Steele's black suit trousers.

"You are the murderer of Philip Boltan," Steele said to the cadet. "You —"

The cadet didn't wait for any more; he turned and made a wild run for the nearest exit. He didn't make it, but it took three other cops a full minute to subdue him.

Some time later, Steele, Ardis, Cedric, Jan, and I were sitting around the half-moon table waiting for Inspector Lupoff and Captain Dickensheet to return from questioning the murderer of Philip Boltan. The Cellar had been cleared of patrons and police, and we were alone in the large, dark room.

Steele occupied the seat of honor: an old wooden rocking chair in the dealer's spot in the center of the half-moon. He had said little since the finale of his special midnight show. All of us had wanted to ask him how he knew the identity of the killer, and exactly how the vanishing act had been worked, but we knew him well enough to realize that he wouldn't say anything until he had the proper audience. He just sat there smiling in his enigmatic way.

When the two officers finally came back, they looked disgruntled and morose. They sat down in the two empty chairs, and Dickensheet said grimly, "Well, we've just had an unpleasant talk with Spellman — or the man I knew as Spellman, anyway. He's made a full confession."

"The man you knew as Spellman?" I said.

"His real name is Granger. Robert Granger."

Cedric frowned, looking at Steele. "Isn't that the name of Boltan's former partner, the one you told us committed suicide?"

"It is," Steele told him. "I had an idea that might be who the young cadet was."

"You mean he killed Boltan because of what happened to his father?" I asked.

"Yes," Lupoff said. "He decided years ago that the perfect revenge was to kill Boltan on stage, in full view of an audience, and then disappear. He's been planning it ever since, mainly by studying and mastering the principles of magic."

"Then he intended from the beginning to murder Boltan in circumstances such as those tonight?"

"More or less," Dickensheet said. "He wanted to do the job during one of Boltan's regular performances, and the invitation to the Academy graduating class tonight convinced him that now was the time. It was only fitting, according to Granger, that Boltan die on stage under an aura of mystery."

Jan said bewilderedly, "But why would a potential murderer join the *police* force?"

"Spellman, or Granger, is mentally unstable. We try to weed them out, but every once in a while one slips by. He believes in meting out punishment to those who would 'do evil,' in his own words just now. God only knows what he might have done if he'd gotten away with this murder and gone on to become an officer in the field." Dickensheet shuddered at the possibility. "As if we don't have enough problems . . ."

"I don't understand how Granger could join the force under an assumed name," Cedric said. "I mean, if his real name is Granger and you knew him as Spellman —"

"Spellman is the name of the family who adopted him out of the orphanage he ended up in after his father died. As far as our people knew, that was his real name. I mean, you usually don't check back past a kid's sixth birthday. We might never have known he was Boltan's partner's son if he hadn't admitted it himself tonight."

"What else did he say?" I asked.

"Not much. He talked freely enough about who he was and his motives, but when we started asking him about the details of the murder, he closed up tight."

So we all looked at Steele, who continued to sit there smiling to himself.

"All right, Steele," Lupoff said, "you're on again. How did Spellman-Granger commit the murder?"

"With a gun," Steele told him.

"Now look —"

Steele held up a placating hand. "Very well," he said, "although you must realize that I dislike explaining any illusion." He began to rock gently in the chair. "Granger used a clever variant on an illusion first employed by Houdini. As Houdini did it, the magician rode into an arena — this was a major effect done only in stadiums and arenas — on a white horse, dressed in flowing Arabian robes. His several assistants, clad in red work suits, would grab the horse. Houdini would then stand up in the saddle and fire a gun in the air, at which second a previously arranged action of some type would direct all eyes to another part of the arena.

148

During that instant, Houdini would vanish; and his assistants would then lead the horse out."

Dickensheet asked, "So how did he do it?"

"By a costume change. He would be wearing, underneath the Arabian robes, a red work suit like his assistants; the robes were specially-made breakaway garments, which he could get out of in a second, roll into a ball, and hide beneath his work suit. So he became one of the assistants and went out with them and the horse.

"Spellman's vanishing act was worked in much the same way. He probably donned his breakaway costume and false beard in the men's room just prior to Boltan's act, *over* his police uniform, and made sure he was picked from the audience by being there standing up when Boltan did the selecting. After he shot Boltan and ran into the dressing room through the curtain, he pulled off his breakaway costume and false hair, rolled them into a bundle and stuffed them into one of the costume trunks. Then he backed against the side of the curtain, so that when the first cadets dashed through, he immediately became one of them."

"But we looked in all of the trunks . . ."

"Yes, but you were looking for a man hiding, not for a small bundle of denim and hair stuffed in toward the bottom."

Lupoff shook his head. "It sounds so simple," he said.

"Much magic works that way," Steele said. "You could never in a lifetime guess how it's done, but if it's explained it sounds so easy you wonder how you were fooled. Which is one reason magicians do not like to explain their effects."

Ardis said, "You knew all along it had to be one of the cadets, Christopher?"

"By the logic of the situation," Steele agreed. "But I had further confirmation when I remembered that, despite his somewhat scruffy appearance, the murderer was wearing well-shined black shoes — the one item he wouldn't have time to change — just as were all the other graduating cadets."

"But how did you know which of the cadets it was?"

"I didn't until I was on stage. I had found the costume and the beard right before that, and I saw that the guilty man had fastened his face hair on with spirit gum, as most professionals do. It must have been very lightly tacked on so he could rip it off effectively, but the spirit gum would leave a residue nonetheless."

"Of course!" I said. "Spirit gum fluoresces under ultraviolet light."

Steele smiled. "Not very much, but enough for me to have detected the outline of a chin and upper lip when I looked for them in the darkness."

Lupoff and Dickensheet seemed baffled, so I explained that there were u.v. bulbs in some of the spots because they were necessary for Steele's spook show effects.

They nodded. Lupoff asked Steele, "How did you manage *your* disappearance?"

"The stage trap. I dropped into it, and Ardis popped out of it. Then she kept the audience's attention long enough for me to crawl to the coatroom, put on the breakaway costume, and approach the audience from the rear. When the lights went out again and she disappeared, I looked again for the outline of chin and upper lip, to make sure I would be confronting exactly the right man."

"And now your disappearance, young lady?" Dickensheet asked Ardis.

She laughed. "I walked off the stage in the dark."

"But we saw you, ah, dwindle away . . ."

"That wasn't me. It was a picture painted on an inflated

balloon which was held over the stage for our show. I pulled it down with a concealed string while the lights were out, and allowed it to deflate. So you saw the picture getting smaller and seeming to recede. The method's been used for many years," Ardis explained.

Dickensheet and Lupoff exchanged glances. The inspector said, "All of this really is obvious. But now that we know how obvious magic tricks are, we'd never fall for anything like them again."

"Absolutely not," the captain agreed.

"So you say," Steele said. "But perhaps —"

Suddenly Ardis jumped up, backed off two steps, and made a startled cry. Naturally, we all looked around at her — and she was pointing across the table to Steele's chair.

When we looked back there again, after no more than a second, the chair was rocking gently and Steele had vanished.

Dickensheet's mouth hung open by several inches. Lupoff said in a surprised voice, "He didn't have time to duck through the curtain there. Then — where did he go?"

I know most of Steele's talents and effects, but not all of them by any means. So I closed my own mouth, because I had no answer to Lupoff's question.

The Desperate Ones

Carmody had never liked Algiers. It was hot, overcrowded, dirty, and seemed saturated with a permanent sweet-sour stink. But the main reason was that it was full of people you couldn't trust, people who would cut your throat for a couple of dinars and smile while they were doing it.

In his room at the St. George, on the Boulevard Salah Bouakouir, he stood sourly looking out over the harbor and the Mediterranean beyond. It was washday, and every grill-work balcony on every stark-white, tile-roofed building was draped with laundry: a gigantic open-air drycleaning plant. In the hotel garden below, the palms and the olive and acacia trees had a wilted, strangulated look. Like Algiers itself, even on its best days.

Carmody turned from the window, began to pace the room — a lean, predatory man, thirty-seven years old, with flat green eyes and shaggy graying-black hair. A sardonic mouth made him appear faintly satanic. There was a vague air of brittleness about him, as if you could hurt him physically without too much effort; but his eyes told you this was a lie, that he was as hard as a block of forged steel inside.

The room was air-conditioned but he was sweating inside a thin yellow shirt and white ducks. A rum collins would have gone good about now, but he was supposed to go to work soon and he seldom drank when he worked. He glanced again at his watch. Almost four-thirty. The woman, Nicole, was late. He didn't care for people who weren't punctual, especially where business was concerned. He was not a patient man.

Carmody was a freelance bodyguard, a supplier of legal and extra-legal services and material, with connections that reached into nearly every country in the world; he dealt with desperate men and desperate women, with profiteers and black marketeers, with thieves and smugglers and murderers — on his terms, according to his own brand of ethics; and he thrived on the action, adventure, danger in each of the jobs he undertook. He worked inside the law and outside it, whichever suited the occasion, and had never failed a client or been arrested for even the most minor of offenses. It wasn't cheap, going to him, but you were guaranteed results. He was good, so good that in the shadow world in which he operated his reputation commanded the highest respect.

The job that had brought him to North Africa had to do with a quarter of a million dollars in assorted raw gems. The day before, at his villa on the island of Majorca, he had received a call from one of his contacts, an Algierian black marketeer named Achmed. Achmed had been approached by a Frenchman calling himself Paul Tobiere, the man with the gems. Tobiere had come to Algiers from the Sudan, where he had lived for several years; come by way of the Libyan Desert, Tripoli, and the coast of Tunisia. Twice en route he'd nearly been killed by former associates who wanted the stones and their ex-partner's skin as a bonus. How Tobiere had come by the gems, who the former associates were, didn't concern Carmody. What concerned him was that Tobiere was so anxious to get out of North Africa, he was willing to pay one-tenth of the gems' worth for safe passage to France and a new identity when he got there.

Contact with the Frenchman was not to be made through Achmed, as Carmody would have preferred, but through a woman Tobiere had known in the Sudan named Nicole Moreau, now a resident of Algiers. Apparently Nicole was the one providing Tobiere with his hidey-hole here. He hadn't told Achmed where that was; he was too frightened to trust anyone with that knowledge, he'd said, except Carmody himself.

The meeting with Nicole had been arranged for four o'clock, but there was still no sign of the woman. Carmody would give her until five o'clock. If she hadn't showed by then, the deal was off. He didn't need $25,000 that badly. It was the work that energized him anyway, not the money he got from it.

It didn't come down to a call-off; Nicole Moreau beat the deadline by ten minutes. She was in her late twenties, tall, broad-hipped, with thick blue-black hair cropped short. Dark brooding eyes appraised him coolly as he let her into the room.

He said, "What's the idea of keeping me waiting so long?"

"I apologize, *m'sieu*. I was detained."

"Detained how?"

"With my profession."

"What profession is that?"

"I am a dancer at the Café Bulbul."

"Yes? Why didn't you call?"

"There was not time to use the telephone."

"What's more important, your dancing or Tobiere's life?" She made a pouting face. "You are not very pleasant, *m'sieu*."

"I'm not paid to be pleasant. Where's Tobiere?"

"A house on the Rue Kaddour Bourkika."

"Where's that?"

"The Casbah."

154

"That figures," Carmody said. "He have the gems with him?"

"No."

"Did he tell you where they are?"

"No. He will tell only you."

Carmody went to the wardrobe, strapped on his Beretta in its belt half-holster. The woman watched him without expression. He donned a lightweight cotton jacket; with the bottom button fastened, the gun didn't show at all.

He said, "You drive here or come in a taxi?"

"A taxi," Nicole answered.

"Then we'll use my car."

It was in the hotel garage, a small Fiat he'd rented at the Dar-el-Beida Airport. He knew the steep, twisting streets of Algiers only slightly, so he let Nicole direct him through the congested midday traffic. They climbed one of the hills on which the city had been built, toward the basilica of Notre Dame d'Afrique on Mt. Bouzarea high above. Two-thirds of the way up Nicole veered them to the left and into the fringes of the Casbah.

It had a romantic image, the Casbah, thanks to the Pepé LeMoko nonsense, but the reality of it was anything but romantic. It was a vast, squalid slum in which eighty thousand Arabs were packed like cattle into ancient buildings sprawled along a labyrinth of narrow streets and blind alleys. It teemed with flies, heat, garbage, and vermin both animal and human. Europeans and Americans were safe enough there in the daytime, as long as they didn't venture too deep into the maze of back alleys. At night, not even Carmody would have gone there alone.

The Arabs had a saying: *Tawakkul' al' Allah*. Rely on God. If you lived in the Casbah, Carmody thought, and you weren't a thief or a cutthroat, you'd have to rely on God;

155

you wouldn't have another choice.

The woman directed him into a bare cement plaza crowded with dark-skinned children, veiled women, old men in burnooses and striped *gallabiyyas*. It was the nearest place where a car could be parked, she said. They went on foot down the Street of Many Steps, into the bowels of the district. On the way a rag-clad beggar accosted them, asking *baksheesh;* Nicole brushed by him roughly but Carmody gave him a dinar. He reserved his cruelty for those who deserved it.

Half a dozen turns brought them into Rue Kaddour Bourkika. It was no more than three feet wide, the rough stucco walls on either side chalked and crayoned in Arabic and English, in one place marred with old bullet scars — mementoes of the French-Algerian War. They passed beneath balconies supported by wooden poles cemented in stone in the old Turkish manner — some of the buildings in the Casbah dated back to the Second Century — and went down more littered steps and finally stopped before an archway.

"Through here," Nicole said.

Carmody followed her through a tunnellike passageway adorned with mosaic tile, walking hunched over to keep from cracking his head on the low stone roof. The passage opened into a small courtyard with a waterless fountain and a half-dead pomegranate tree in its middle. Doorways opened off the courtyard, off an encircling balcony above. The air here was filled with tinny Arab music, the cries of children; the hot, sweet-sour stink, sharp in this enclosed space, made Carmody's head ache.

Nicole rapped on one of the doors beneath the balcony — three times, a five-second wait, and another three times. The man who opened up was in his late thirties, muscled, dry-faced in spite of the heat. He had long blond hair and pale features, the eyes of glacial blue. His white suit was rumpled but not unclean.

He said in English, "What took you so long?"

"Ask your friend here," Carmody said. "Are you Tobiere?"

"I am."

Carmody prodded the woman ahead of him, inside. A weak ceiling light let him see old square-cut furnishings covered with handwoven blankets. A window was open but there was no breeze and the air in there was stifling.

He said, "Let's have a look at the gems."

"I don't have them here," Tobiere said.

"No? Where are they?"

"In a safe place. Outside the city."

"How soon can you get them?"

"Tonight."

"What's wrong with right now?"

"Tonight," Nicole said. "Late tonight."

Carmody turned to her. "Are you his partner?"

"Not exactly that, *m'sieu* . . ."

"Then let him talk for himself."

"She's going with us to France," Tobiere said. "She won't —"

"Oh, she is?"

"Yes. She won't be ready to leave until later."

"The arrangement was for you alone."

"I know, but my plans have changed. Nicole will go with me."

"She will if you pay me another ten thousand."

"Another ten thousand — !"

"Two people are twice as much trouble as one," Carmody said. "Plus I'll have to make arrangements for a

157

second set of papers. I should charge you double, fifty thousand."

Tobiere started to argue, but Nicole put a hand on his arm to silence him. She said, "He will pay what you ask. Thirty-five thousand American dollars."

"Is that right, Tobiere?"

"Yes. As you wish."

"What time will you be ready?" Carmody asked Nicole.

"Midnight, perhaps a little sooner."

"All right. We don't leave from here, though. I'm not coming back here after dark. Pick another place."

"Your hotel?" Nicole said.

"Too public. This place where you dance — the Café Bulbul. How about there?"

"Yes, good. I live nearby."

"What's the address?"

"Rue de Marbruk. Number Eleven."

"I'll find it," Carmody said. He shifted his gaze back to Tobiere. "You'd better have the gems with you. We don't go anywhere until I get a look at them."

"I will have them," Tobiere promised.

Carmody went to the door. "You coming with me or staying here?" he asked the woman.

"I will stay."

"Suit yourself."

He left them, returned to the Rue Kaddour Bourkika. But instead of turning upward toward the plaza, he hurried down several more steps to the Street of the Slipper Makers. There were several open-air markets here, swarming with activity, and doorless shops of all types set into tiny niches no larger than coat closets; there was also a small open-front native bar, its tables occupied by Arabs drinking glasses of mint tea. Carmody took a chair at one of the tables, positioning himself so he could look up along Rue Kaddour Bourkika; he had a clear angled view of the entrance to the courtyard. He ordered a glass of mint tea, closed his ears to the din around him, and waited.

He didn't have to wait long.

Inside of ten minutes Tobiere and Nicole Moreau came out through the passage, began to climb upward. Carmody dropped a couple of dinars on the table and glided after them. When they reached the upper plaza they crossed to where a dark green Citröen was parked at some distance from Carmody's Fiat. Carmody stayed hidden inside the Street of Many Steps until Nicole, who was driving the Citröen, circled past him; then he ran for the Fiat. There was only one street out of the plaza, so he had no trouble locating them and then following at a measured distance.

No trouble keeping the Citröen in sight, either, as they descended toward the harbor. The heavy traffic made speed impossible. The way Nicole drove told him she had no idea they were being tailed.

They proceeded past the Place des Martyrs to the harbor, turned west, and followed the shoreline crescent out of the city. Traffic thinned considerably then, and Nicole began driving at a hurry-up pace. Carmody dropped farther back, adjusting his speed to match hers.

The Citröen stayed on the coastal road for some thirty-five kilometers, until the village of Bou-Ismail took shape in the distance. Then the woman swung right toward the Mediterranean on a badly paved secondary road that slanted in among fields of vegetables. Carmody slowed, made the turn, fell back even farther. After another three kilometers, the Citröen swung off again and disappeared. Narrow sandy lane, Carmody saw when he reached the place, leading to an ancient farmhouse set at the foot of high, reddish dunes; the sea shimmered in the hot glow of the setting sun just beyond. The Citröen was drawn up near the farmhouse porch, Nicole and the man just emerging from it.

Carmody continued past the intersection by a hundred yards, to where a line of scruffy palms blocked out his vision of the farmhouse. Then he parked, got out into the humid, early-evening stillness.

There were no other cars in sight, no signs of life. He trotted across the road, climbed a fence into one of the fields, made his way toward the farmhouse. The vegetables were laid out in squared patches, separated by woven straw fences that acted as windbreaks. By moving in a low crouch, he was able to make good time without worrying about being spotted.

When he could see the farmhouse through chinks in the woven straw he stopped and gave it a long scan. Nothing moved over there, at least nothing outside. He worked his way in a wide loop, coming in from the rear, until a small barnlike outbuilding again cut off his view of the house. Then he ran across to a sagging wooden fence that enclosed the yard, climbed it, went to the wall of the barn and peered around the corner. Still no activity at the house.

He was sweating; he dried his face and cleared his eyes with the sleeve of his jacket. He drew the Beretta, ran in a low weave to the house's side wall, flattened back against it. Again he waited, listening. Quiet, except for the murmur of the sea beyond.

Carmody eased ahead to a closed window of dirt-streaked glass. As he leaned up close to it he could hear voices, but what they were saying to each other was unclear. A drawn shade kept him from seeing inside.

He went to the front corner, looked around it at the

160

porch. Empty, the house door shut. He leaned back against the wall, the Beretta held down along his right leg, trying to make up his mind whether or not to break in on them. He didn't like the idea of that because he didn't know what the situation was in there. But he didn't like the idea of waiting around out here, either.

As it turned out, he didn't have to make a decision either way. The door opened abruptly and the blond man stepped out onto the porch. Carmody tensed. From inside he heard Nicole's sultry voice call out in French, "Hurry, *cherie*. It's getting late."

"We have plenty of time," the blond man answered. He turned to shut the door.

Carmody stepped around the corner, caught the porch rail, vaulted it. He landed running. The blond man spun toward him, confused, his hand fumbling at the pocket of his jacket. Carmody hit him in the face with the Beretta, a blow that sent him reeling, then veered to his left, kicked the door wide open, and went in low and fast with his gaze and the Beretta sweeping the room.

Nicole cried out, *"Zut alors merde!"* and a heavy gun crashed. She wasn't much of a shot; the bullet came nowhere near Carmody. He might have had to shoot her if she'd kept on potting at him but she didn't; she tried to run away through a rear doorway. There was a straight-backed chair on his immediate left, and he caught it up and threw it at her in one motion. She shrieked as it smacked into her backside, knocked her sideways against the door jamb; she went down hard to her knees. She still had the gun in her hand, a big Luger, but only for another couple of seconds. He was on her by then and he yanked it out of her hand before she could bring it to bear.

The fat sun-darkened man who had been sitting in one

161

of the other chairs, and who had thrown himself to the floor when the shooting started, now yelled at Carmody from behind an ancient daybed, "Look out! The front door!"

Carmody's reaction was instantaneous: he whirled to his left, down and around into a shooter's crouch. The blond man stood in the doorway, the mate to Nicole's Luger in his hand, blood streaming down from a cut on his forehead. He fired once, wildly, just before Carmody shot him in the upper body. This time, when he fell back onto the porch, he stayed down and didn't move.

Carmody straightened slowly, letting breath out between his teeth, and looked over at Nicole. She was crouched against the wall, hating him with her eyes. He put her gun into one jacket pocket, went onto the porch and picked up the blond man's weapon and put that into the other jacket pocket.

The fat man came out from behind the daybed as Carmody walked back inside. His moonface was slick with sweat. He said, "He's dead? You killed him?"

"No. He'll live if he gets medical attention."

That disappointed the fat man. With good reason, Carmody thought. There were marks on his face, arms, neck: beaten on and burned with cigarettes, among other indignities. Carmody watched him turn blazing eyes on the woman, call her a vicious name in French, take a step toward her with his hands clenched. He stopped him halfway by catching hold of his shoulder.

"She's not worth the trouble. Leave her alone."

The fat man took a shuddering breath, relaxed a little. His pained eyes focused on Carmody without recognition. "Who are you?"

"Carmody."

"*Mon Dieu!* But how — ?"

162

"We'll get to that. You're Tobiere, right? The real Paul Tobiere?"

Convulsive nod. "They were going to kill me. Nicole and that . . . that *fils de putain*."

"I figured as much. Who is he — the blond?"

"His name is Chagal," Tobiere said. "One of Nicole's filthy lovers."

Carmody said, "They were trying to pass him off as you, to take advantage of your arrangement with me." He didn't add that they must have known of his particular code of ethics, that he couldn't be bought off and that any kind of double-dealing was anathema to him. One hint that the real Tobiere had been robbed and murdered and he'd have called off the deal immediately.

"I was a fool to trust her," Tobiere said. "But I believed she cared for me; I believed —"

"Cochon! Je t'emmerge, à pied, à cheval et en voiture!"

Carmody said, "Shut up, Nicole." His tone said he didn't want any arguments. She didn't give him any.

"How did you know to come here?" the fat man asked.

Carmody told him how he'd followed Nicole and Chagal from the Casbah.

"But what made you suspect Chagal was not me?"

"Several things. She seemed to be running the show, not him; that didn't jibe with what Achmed told me. Neither did the way he acted. Achmed said you were frightened and anxious after what happened to you en route from the Sudan. Chagal wasn't either one. Then there was the fact that you lived in the Sudan for years, came here through the Libyan Desert. No man can spend time in that kind of desert country without picking up a black tan like you have, or at least some sun color. Chagal is pale — no tan, no burn. He's been nowhere near Sudan or the Libyan Desert.

163

Not long out of France, probably."

Tobiere nodded. "I owe you my life, *m'sieu*."

"I'll settle for ten percent of those gems," Carmody said. "Where are they? You didn't tell Nicole and Chagal or you'd be dead already."

"No, but I . . . I think I would have." He shuddered. "The things they did to me . . . the things they threatened to do . . ."

"Never mind that. The gems, Tobiere. Are they here?"

"Nearby. Shall I get them?"

"We'll both go get them. If they're as advertised, you'll be on a boat for France by midnight."

"Nicole? You will kill her before we leave here?"

"I'm not an assassin," Carmody said.

"But they were going to kill me . . ."

"They've got each other, her and Chagal, and they've got Algiers. That's worse than being dead. That's a living hell."

He took Tobiere's arm and prodded him out into the breathless North African twilight.

Blood Money

Carmody spent the morning at Bacino di Borechi, checking out the boat and captain Della Robbia had hired for the run south to Sardinia. The boat was forty-two feet and twenty years old — the *Piraeus*, flying a Greek flag. She was scabrous and salt-scarred, her fittings flecked with rust, but she seemed seaworthy and she had an immaculate power-plant: a twin-screw GMC diesel, well-tuned and shiny clean.

The captain looked all right too. He was an Australian named Vickers, who had been in Venice for a couple of years and who had handled some other smuggling jobs for Della Robbia, one involving a boatload of illegal aliens from Albania. Della Robbia said he was the best man available and he probably was. Sardinia would be a piece of cake compared to getting into Albanian waters and then out again safely with forty-three passengers.

From the *bacino* Carmody took a water taxi to St. Mark's Square. Della Robbia hadn't shown up yet at the open-air cafe on the Piazzeta. Carmody took a table, ordered a cup of cappucino. It was a warm, windy September day, and the square was jammed with tourists, vendors, freelance artists, the ever-present pigeons. On the wide fronting basin, into which emptied Venice's two major canals, the Grand and the Giudecca, gondolas and water taxis, passenger ferries and small commercial craft maneuvered in bright confusion. The sun turned the placid water a glinting silver, gave it a mercurial aspect.

Cities were just cities to Carmody — places to be and to

work in and to leave again — but Venice intruded on his consciousness more than most. For one thing, you didn't have to worry about traffic problems because it had no automobiles. It was built on a hundred little islands interconnected by a hundred and fifty bridges, and you got from place to place on foot through narrow, winding interior streets or by water taxi and ferry. The pocked, sagging look of most of the ancient buildings was due to the fact that the city was sinking at the rate of five inches per century; the look and smell of the four hundred canals was the result of pollution. It was a seedy, charming, ugly, beautiful, dangerous, amiable city — one Carmody understood, and felt at ease in, and worked well in.

He had been sitting there for fifteen minutes when Della Robbia came hurrying between the two red granite obelisks that marked the beginning of the Piazzeta. Dark, craggy-featured, in his middle thirties, wearing a light gray suit and a pair of fat sunglasses, Della Robbia looked exactly like what he was: a minor Italian gangster. That worked in his favor more often than not. Because he looked like a thug, a lot of people figured he wasn't one.

When Della Robbia sat down Carmody said, "You make the arrangements for the launch?"

"Just as you instructed, Signor Carmody."

"What did you tell the driver?"

"Only that he is to pick up a passenger, transport him to an address he will be given, pick up additional passengers, and then proceed to a boat in the Lagoon."

"Does he speak English?"

"Enough to understand simple directions."

"You're sure he can be trusted?"

"*Assolutamente, signor.*"

"He'll be ready to go tonight?"

"Any time you wish."

"The way it looks now," Carmody said, "we can do it to-night. I went to see Vickers and his boat this morning. I'm satisfied."

"I was certain you would be."

Carmody lit one of his thin, black cigars. "I'll call you later and let you know what time the launch driver is to pick me up. Where do I meet him?"

"The Rio de Fontego, at the foot of Via Giordano," Della Robbia said. "A quiet place without much water traffic, so you can be sure you are not followed."

"How far is the Rio de Fontego from my hotel?"

"Ten minutes by water taxi."

"All right, good."

"There are other arrangements to be made?"

"No. I'll handle the rest of it. But stay where I can reach you the rest of the day."

Della Robbia said, *Va bene,* and got to his feet. "A safe journey, Signor Carmody." He lifted his hand in a salute and moved off across the Piazzeta, disappeared into the crowd of tourists and pigeons in front of the Ducal Palace.

Carmody finished his cigar, walked away from St. Marks along the Grand Canal quay. He found a stop for water taxis, rode in one to the Rio de Fontego. It turned out to be near the arched Rialto Bridge, in the approximate center of the city. Via Giordano was a quiet street lined with old houses and a few small shops that would be shuttered after dark. From the seawall at the foot of the street he could see for some distance both ways along the canal and back along Via Giordano. Della Robbia had chosen well. Carmody hadn't expected otherwise, but he hadn't had any prior dealings with the Italian and he was a careful man besides.

He got back into the water taxi and went to keep his appointment with Renzo Lucarelli.

Lucarelli was forty-two years old, thick-necked and wolf-eyed. Until recently he'd sported a luxuriant black military mustache that made him look more like an Italian Army colonel than a criminal on the run. Carmody had had him shave it off for his new identity and passport photo. Lucarelli missed the mustache; he kept fingering his upper lip self-consciously, as if he felt conspicuous without it.

He peered at the map spread open on the table, laid a thick forefinger on an X marked on the Venice Lagoon. "This boat, this *Piraeus*, will meet the launch here?" he asked.

Carmody said, "That's right."

"But we can be seen from the Quartiere."

"Who's going to see us?"

"Gambresca has many eyes. So does the *carabinieri* —"

"Gambresca can't have any idea when or how you're leaving Venice; neither can the government. And there's nothing along the Quartiere except warehouses and anchored freighters. Even if we're seen, nobody's going to question the transfer. Launches take passengers out to private vessels all the time. I know, I checked it."

"But a little farther out on the Lagoon . . ."

"Listen," Carmody said, "we want to stay in the shipping roads. Any farther out and we're inviting the attention you're so worried about. Besides, the quicker we get onto the *Piraeus* and out of the Lagoon, the better."

Lucarelli stroked his barren upper lip. "You are certain of this man Vickers?"

"Della Robbia vouches for him. And I'll be along to see that he's no problem."

"I do not like putting my life in the hands of men I have never met."

"Yes? You've only known me four days."

"I have known of your great reputation for many years," Lucarelli said, and fingered his naked lip again. "The *Piraeus* is old and rusty, you said. Suppose something happens to her engines before we reach Sardinia? She might even sink in a sudden squall —"

"For Christ's sake, Lucarelli, I told you the boat was all right. Don't you think I know what I'm doing? How do you figure I got that reputation of mine? Now stop fussing like an old woman and quit asking questions I've already answered."

Lucarelli gestured apologetically. "It is only that I am nervous, Signor Carmody. I meant no offense." He lifted the glass at his elbow, drank off the last of the red wine it contained. Then he glanced over to where his woman sat paging through a magazine. "Rita, another glass of wine."

She stood immediately, came to the table. She was tall and plump and huge-breasted, with thick black hair pulled back tight from her forehead and fastened with a jeweled barette; Carmody thought she'd have made a fine Rueben's nude. He preferred slender, less top-heavy women himself. Her expression was neutral but her eyes betrayed her unease. She was not bearing up under the waiting any better than Lucarelli.

Lucarelli gave her his glass, then said to Carmody, "You will have some wine now, Signor Carmody?"

"No. And you'd better go easy on that stuff yourself. If we go tonight I don't want you drunk or anywhere near it."

"Then it *will* be tonight?"

"Everything's set for it. I don't see any reason for holding off another day."

"Good. Ah, good."

169

Rita poured Lucarelli's glass full of Chianti, brought it back to him, went over and sat down again with her magazine. She hadn't said a word since Carmody's arrival twenty minutes ago.

The room they were in was the main parlor of a crumbling building perched on the edge of Rio San Spirito, in a northeastern sector not far from Laguna Morta and the island that served as the city cemetery. A poor neighborhood; and a poor house that had water-stained wallpaper, rococo lighting fixtures tarnished by age, and a lingering odor of damp decay mixed with the fish-and-garbage reek of the canal outside. It was a long way from the walled palace-house Lucarelli claimed to have occupied on Lido Island before the fat little world he'd created for himself had collapsed.

Lucarelli was, or had been, a smuggler and black-marketeer who dealt in the lucrative commodity of cigarettes. The Italian government owned a monopoly on the manufacture and sale of all tobacco products, and imposed a high duty on the import of American and English brands. Since most Italians preferred the imported to the raw homemade variety, and the demand grew greater every year, tons of contraband cigarettes were smuggled annually into the country. Lucarelli's operation, independent of syndicate ties, had been one of the largest in the northern provinces. He'd had cigarettes coming into Venice across the gulf from Trieste and down from Switzerland, and a fleet of trucks and men to distribute them throughout Italy.

But then the Guardia de Finanza, the agents of the ministry that ran the monopoly for the government, had made a series of raids that left Lucarelli's operation hurting and vulnerable. And one of the other cigarette smugglers in the city, a long-time rival of Lucarelli's named Gambresca, had seen his chance and ordered two unsuccessful attempts on Lucarelli's life. With the Guardia de Finanza and the local *carabinieri* preparing to make an arrest on one side, and Gambresca and his group devouring what was left of Lucarelli's empire on the other, Lucarelli had been forced to abandon his palace-house and most of his possessions and to go into hiding. The woman, Rita, his mistress of several years, was the only person he'd taken with him.

If he hadn't waited so long he would have been able to get out of Italy on his own; he'd amassed a fortune in smuggling profits, most of which he'd brought with him in cash. But with the heat on from both sides, he'd been afraid to trust former friends and allies and afraid to chance any known escape routes. So, out of desperation, he'd gotten word to Guiseppe Piombo, Carmody's Italian contact in Rome. It was costing him $25,000 for Carmody's services, and it was cheap at the price. Lucarelli knew it too. If Carmody had been a gouger, he could have asked and gotten twice as much.

It was Piombo who had brought in Gino Della Robbia. Carmody needed a man in Venice who knew the city, knew people both reliable and close-mouthed, and Piombo said Della Robbia was that man. The recommendation was good enough for Carmody, but he still hadn't entrusted Della Robbia with Lucarelli's name, the location of the San Spirito house, or any except essential details. No one other than Piombo had that information. The fewer people who knew, the less chance there was of something screwing up.

Della Robbia had proved capable, and now all the details were set. They would take Vickers' boat straight down the Adriatic and into the Mediterranean, then swing around Sicily and go up to the southern coast of Sardinia to the port of Cagliari. Lucarelli wanted to live in an Italian-

171

speaking area, and the rich man's playground of Sardinia was a good place to get lost if you had enough money, a new name, and a new background that would stand up to any but the sharpest scrutiny. Carmody had made arrangements for a villa outside Cagliari and a set of forged papers that included a marriage license and new passports. After they reached Sicily, what happened to Lucarelli and his mistress was up to them.

Lucarelli drank from his fresh glass of wine, worked his upper lip over, looked at the map again. "What time do we leave tonight?" he asked.

"I'll meet the launch at ten," Carmody told him. "It shouldn't take more than half an hour to get here, so we'll figure on ten-thirty as the pick-up time. Another half-hour to get to the *Piraeus*. We'll be on our way out of the Lagoon not much after eleven."

"We wear dark clothing?"

"That's right. But keep it simple — and not all black. We don't want to look like a commando team."

"Just as you say, *signor.*"

Carmody got to his feet, refolded the map, put it away inside his jacket. "If anything comes up that you should know about, I'll notify you. Otherwise be ready at ten thirty."

Lucarelli nodded.

From the chair across the room, Rita spoke for the first time. "I cannot stay in this house another night. This waiting . . . it makes me crazy."

"Tonight, *dulce mia,*" Lucarelli said to her. "The plans will not change. Tonight we leave, Saturday we are on Sardinia. Yes, Signor Carmody?"

"That's how it shapes up," Carmody said. "Just hang loose. And remember what I said about the wine. If you're even half-drunk when I get here, we don't go."

In his room at the Saviola, a renovated sixteenth-century palace that was one of the more comfortable hotels along the Grand Canal, Carmody called Della Robbia. "It's tonight," he said. "Get in touch with Vickers, tell him to be three hundred yards off the Quartieri Vergini, opposite the clock tower, at least twenty minutes before eleven."

"*Si,* Signor Carmody."

"And tell your launch driver to pick me up at ten sharp, just where you told him. Make sure he understands ten sharp."

"It will be done."

"Call me if there are any problems."

"There will be no problems."

"I hope not. As soon as I'm paid in full, I'll wire your money to you care of Piombo."

"*Bene,*" Della Robbia said.

Carmody lay back on the bed with one of his cigars and waited for it to be time to move out.

In the shadows at the foot of Via Giordano, Carmody stood looking for the launch. The night was dark, moonless, hushed except for the faint pulsing sounds of water traffic on the Grand Canal. An occasional black gondola glided past on the Rio di Fontego a few feet away, but the area was as deserted as he'd estimated it would be. It was just ten o'clock.

He wore dark trousers, a dark shirt, his Beretta in its half-holster under his jacket. His bag rested at his feet; he had checked out of the Saviola two hours ago. Supper had killed an hour and a quarter, and he'd spent the rest of the time in a water taxi and on foot from the Rialto Bridge.

173

He looked at his watch again — 10:01 — and when he lowered his arm he heard the muffled throb of a boat engine. Seconds later the launch, small and radio-equipped like the water taxis, came along the *rio* and drifted over to the seawall. The man behind the wheel starboard called softly, *"Signor?"*

Carmody looked back along Via Giordano, saw nothing to worry him, and came out of the shadows. He descended the three steps cut into the seawall, boarded the launch, stowed his bag under the front seat. The driver — bearded, wearing a beret and a black turtleneck — kept his eyes on the canal, waiting for instructions.

Carmody said, "Rio San Spirito. Number fifty-two. Can you find it?"

"San Spirito? Yes, I know it."

"Let's go then."

The darkness was thick in the narrow canals through which they maneuvered; half the time the red-and-green running lights on the launch was the only illumination. Most of the ancient, decaying buildings along the *rio* were dark. Even the occupied ones had shutters drawn across their oblong windows that allowed little light to escape. Carmody watched astern, but the only other crafts were an occasional taxi or a wraithlike gondola gliding into or out of one of the maze of waterways. The silence, broken only by the throb of the launch's inboard, was as heavy as the odor of garbage and salt water.

It was not quite ten-thirty when the driver brought them into the black mouth of another canal and said, "San Spirito, *signor.*"

Carmody looked for familiar landmarks, found one. "Fifty-two is the first building on the near side of that bridge ahead."

The driver cut power, eased the launch in close to the unbroken line of brick-and-cement walls on the right. When they neared the small arched bridge Carmody pointed out the landing platform beyond number fifty-two. The launch drifted up to it. Carmody waited until the driver held steady, then jumped onto the platform.

"Wait here," he said to the driver. "And keep the engine running."

The canal door to Lucarelli's building was at the near end of the seawall, set into the right-angled corner between the *rio* and a high garden wall made of brick. Carmody went there, used a corroded brass knocker.

"Carmody. Open up."

There was the sound of a bolt being shot, then a key turning in the old-fashioned latch. The door edged inward. Carmody went inside, and Lucarelli was standing three feet away with a pistol in his hand. The muzzle dipped when Carmody stopped and stared at him. He said nervously, "All is well, Signor Carmody?"

Carmody took a close look at him. Lucarelli's breath smelled of wine but he was sober enough. Barely.

He said, "Put that gun away," and moved down the hallway into the room where they had talked that afternoon. Three large leather suitcases sat on the floor next to the table. Carmody thought that the biggest of them would contain Lucarelli's run-out money, from which he'd be paid when they reached Sardinia.

The woman, Rita, stood next to the suitcases. She said, "We are leaving now?" in her thickly accented English. She was even twitchier than she had been earlier; she couldn't seem to keep her hands still.

"We're leaving," Carmody told her.

Lucarelli came into the room plucking at his bare upper

lip. The pistol was tucked away in his clothing. He and Rita gathered up the suitcases so Carmody could keep his hands free. He went ahead of them to the door, looked out. The launch sat silently against the platform, the driver waiting at the wheel; as much of San Spirito as he could see was deserted. Carmody stepped out, motioned to Lucarelli and the woman. While the suitcases were being handed into the launch, he stood apart and shifted his gaze back and forth along the canal.

The woman said suddenly in Italian, "My cosmetic case. I left it inside." Her voice seemed high and shrill in the stillness. She moved away, back toward the still-open door to the building.

"Wait, Rita . . ." Lucarelli began, but she had her back to him, almost to the door now.

And in that moment Carmody sensed, rather than saw, the first movement in the shadows beyond the bridge.

The muscles in his neck and shoulders went tight. He swept his jacket back, slid the Beretta out of its holster. The shadows seemed to separate, like an amoeba reproducing, and a formless shape slipped away from the seawall, coming under the bridge. There was the faint pulsation of a boat engine.

Carmody shouted, "Lucarelli! Get down!"

He dropped to one knee, sighted at the moving shape of the boat as it drew nearer, fired twice. One of the bullets broke glass somewhere on the boat; the other missed wide, hit the cement wall across the canal. Then a man-shape reared up at the wheel, and the night erupted in bright chattering flashes. Bullets sprayed the platform, the launch.

None of them hit Carmody because he was already in the canal.

The water was chill, as black and thick as ink; he could

taste the pollution of it, the foulness of oil and garbage. He kicked straight down, at an angle across the narrow width of the *rio*. The Beretta was still in his hand; he shoved it inside the waistband of his trousers before struggling out of his jacket. Swimming blind, groping ahead of him for the wall on the far side, the pressure mounting in his lungs . . . and then his fingers came in contact with the rough surface. He crawled upward along it and poked his head out of the water, dragging air through his mouth, looking back.

The ambush boat had drawn alongside the launch. The dark form of the shooter was hurriedly transferring Lucarelli's suitcases into his own craft, his other hand still clutching a bulky machine pistol. A long way off, somebody was yelling. There was intermittent light along the canal now, but not enough for Carmody to tell if the boat held just the one man or if there was a back-up as well.

The shooter pulled the last suitcase aboard. Turning, he saw Carmody along the far wall. Carmody dove deep as the machine pistol came up and began to chatter again; none of the slugs touched him. Near the bottom he kicked back across the canal to the other side.

Above him, he heard the boat's engine grow loud; the water churned. The shooter wasn't wasting any more time. He didn't want to be seen and he didn't want to risk running into a police boat. By the time Carmody crawled up along the seawall and surfaced again, the ambush boat was a dark blob just swinging out of San Spirito into another canal.

There were more lights showing in nearby buildings, people with their heads stuck out between partially opened shutters. Carmody swam to the launch, caught the port gunwale, hauled himself up and inside.

Lucarelli hadn't reacted quickly enough; he lay dead in

the stern, stitched across the abdomen with enough bullets to nearly cut him in two. The driver had been shot twice in the throat. The launch's deck was slick with blood.

Stop worrying, Lucarelli, I'll get you safely to Sardinia. I've never lost a client yet. Leave everything to me . . .

Impotent rage made Carmody's head ache malignantly. He looked under the front seat, saw that his own suitcase was still there. He pushed it onto the platform, climbed up after it, ran with it to the door of number fifty-two. Inside, he went through the three downstairs rooms and two upstairs, checked inside the bathroom and the closets.

The house was empty.

The woman, Rita, was gone.

Carmody went out a side door into a garden grown wild with wisteria and oleander. The windows of an adjacent building looked down into it, and a fat man in an undershirt stood framed in one, shouting querulously. Three big chestnut trees grew in the garden's center; Carmody stayed in their shadow until he found a gate opening onto one of the narrow interior streets.

As he came running through the gate, a tall youth materialized from the darkness in front of him, lured by the excitement. Carmody didn't want his face seen; he lowered his shoulder, sent the kid sprawling against the garden wall. He ran to the first corner, turned it into another street, ran another block, turned a second corner and came out in a *campiello* with a small stone statue in its center.

He ducked around the statue, went into an alley on the opposite side of the square. With his back against the alley wall, he watched the *campiello* to see if he had pursuit. No one came into it. He stayed where he was for a couple of minutes, catching his breath, shivering inside his wet clothing. Then he moved deeper into the blackness, set his bag down, worked the catches to open it.

Rita, he was thinking, it had to have been Rita.

Besides Piombo and himself — and Piombo could be trusted — the woman and Lucarelli were the only ones who knew about the San Spirito house. And she'd gone back into the house, out of harm's way, just seconds before the shooting started. And the shooter? Lucarelli's rival, Gambresca, or somebody sent by him. She'd found some way to tip Gambresca. For money, or hatred, or revenge, or a combination of all three. Money was part of Gambresca's motive, for sure: the shooter had taken the time to fish the three suitcases out of the launch, so he had to have known what one of them contained.

But why had they done it that way? Why not just put a knife in Lucarelli at the house and walk out with the money? Or tip Gambresca days sooner? They'd been living on San Spirito for more than a week. Maybe she wasn't up to the job of cold-blooded murder herself, or maybe it had taken her all this time to work up the courage for a double-cross, or maybe Lucarelli had had the money hidden in a place only he knew about. Whatever the reason, it was incidental.

Rita and Gambresca — they were what mattered.

While all of this was going through his mind Carmody changed clothes in the darkness. The sodden things went into the suitcase, rolled into a towel. The Beretta went into the pocket of the Madras jacket he now wore.

He left the alley, hunted around until he found a tavern. Inside, locked in the toilet, he broke down the Beretta and cleaned and oiled it with materials from the false bottom of his bag. When he was satisfied that it was in working order he went out into the bar proper and drank two cognacs to get the taste of the canal water out of his mouth.

There was a telephone on the rear wall. Carmody called Della Robbia's number. As soon as he heard the Italian's voice he said, "Carmody. Bad trouble. The whole thing's blown."

Silence for a couple of seconds. Then Della Robbia said, "What happened, s*ignor?*"

"We were ambushed. The man I was taking out is dead. So's your launch driver. One man waiting for us in a boat with a machine pistol — maybe a back-up. It was too dark to see much."

"*Cacchio!*"

"Yeah. A big pile of shit."

"You are all right, Signor Carmody?"

"No physical wounds," Carmody said bitterly. He was holding the phone receiver as if it were the shooter's neck. "Listen, I need you and your connections. The man I was taking out was Renzo Lucarelli. You know him?"

"Lucarelli? Yes . . . yes, of course."

"He had a woman, Rita, who was supposed to go with us. But she ducked off just before we got hit. I think she's a Judas."

"Why would she — ?"

Carmody said, "I don't have all the answers yet — that's what I need you for. You know anything about this Rita?"

"Very little, *signor.* Almost nothing."

"How about a rival of Lucarelli's named Gambresca?"

"A bad one," Della Robbia said. "You believe Gambresca was involved in the shooting?"

"That's how it looks. You know where I can find him?"

"A moment, Signor Carmody, I must think. Yes. He owns a wholesale produce company on Campo Oroglia. It is said he lives above it."

"All right," Carmody said. "Find out what you can about the woman. She may be with Gambresca, she may not be. I want her, Della Robbia, and I want her before she can get out of Venice. Lucarelli is the first client I ever lost and I won't stand still for it."

"I will do what I can," Della Robbia said. "Where are you? Where can I — ?"

"I'll be in touch," Carmody told him and rang off.

He tried to find out from the bartender how to get to the nearest canal that had water taxi service. The bartender didn't speak English. None of the drinkers spoke English. Carmody's Italian was weak; it took him five long, impatient minutes to get directions that made sense.

When he went out again into the night he was running.

There was nobody home at Gambresca's.

Carmody stepped out from under the doorway arch, looked up once more at the sign running across the top of the warehouse. It said *A. Gambresca* in broad black lettering, and below that: *Campo Oroglia 24.* His gaze moved higher, to the dark windows strung along the second floor front. No sign of life. He had been there for several minutes, ringing bells and making noise like a drunk, his fingers restless on the Beretta in his jacket pocket. There hadn't been any response.

Carmody looked at his watch. Almost one-thirty. He crossed the square to enter the same street by which he'd arrived, his steps echoing hollowly in the late-night stillness. The fury inside him boiled like water in a kettle.

What now? Another call to Della Robbia. And if Della Robbia hadn't found out anything? The waiting game, like it or not. He would pick a vantage point somewhere on Campo Oroglia, and he would sit there all night if necessary, until Gambresca showed up.

In the lobby of a small hotel nearby he gave a sleepy night clerk a thousand-lire note for the use of his telephone. Della Robbia answered immediately.

Carmody said, "Well?"

"I have learned something, but perhaps it means little or nothing."

"I'll decide that. What is it?"

"The woman has an uncle, a man named Salviati, who owns a *squero* — a boatyard for the repair and construction of gondolas. The uncle is said to have smuggled contraband and has two boats of high speed at his disposal. It is possible the woman has gone there."

Carmody gave it some thought. Yes, possible. Assuming it was the money that had driven her to sell out Lucarelli, she might have already got her payoff and then headed for her uncle's — a place to hide or a way to leave the city, either one. She'd need someone she could trust, and Gambresca might not be that someone. Another possibility was that she'd gone to the uncle straight from San Spirito, to wait for Gambresca or one of Gambresca's people to bring her blood money.

He asked, "Where is this place, this *squero?*"

"On Rio degli Zecchini."

"So I can get there by water taxi."

"If you can find one at this hour."

"I can find one," Carmody said.

From where he stood in the shadows across the Rio degli Zecchini, Carmody could see the vague shapes of gondolas, some whole and some skeletal, in the *squero*'s low-fenced rear yard. Set back fifty feet from the canal was a two-story, wood-and-brick building that looked as if it had been built in the time of the Doges; it was completely dark. Most of the surrounding buildings were warehouses and the area was deserted. No light showed anywhere except for a pale streetlamp atop a canal bridge nearby.

Carmody put his suitcase into a wall niche, took out the Beretta, held it cupped low against his right leg as he walked to the bridge. On the opposite seawall he stood listening for a time. A ship's horn bayed mournfully on the Lagoon; the canal water, rumpled by the wind, lapped at the seawall. There were no sounds of any kind from the *squero.*

The place's rear entrance was a wooden gate set into a three-sided frame of two-by-fours; the fourth side was the wall of the adjacent building. On the canal side, and on top, the beams sprouted tangles of barbed wire like a fungoid growth. Carmody had had experience with barbed wire before, but he still cut the palm of his left hand in two places when he swung around the frame. The sharp sting of the cuts heaped fuel on his rage.

Moving quickly, he made his way across the yard. The gondolas — long, slender, flat-bottomed, with tapered and upswept prow and stern — were laid out in rows, on davits, in stacks of two and three; they had a ghostly look in the darkness, like giant bones in a graveyard. They also camouflaged his run to the far corner of the building, in case anybody happened to be looking out.

Jalousied shutters were lowered across the double-doored entrance; there were no fronting windows. Carmody edged around the corner, along the side wall. An elongated window halfway down showed him nothing of the interior, just a solid screen of blackness.

Carmody paused, peering toward the back. A high wall marked the rear boundary of the *squero* but it was set several feet beyond the building, forming a narrow passageway. He went there and into the passage; picked his way through a carpeting of refuse, looking for another window. Midway along he found one with louvered shutters closed across it. He squinted upward through one of the canted louvers.

Light.

Movement.

Carmody bent lower so he could see more of the room inside. It was an office of sorts, with a cluttered desk on which a gooseneck lamp burned, two wooden chairs, a table piled with charts and pamphlets, a filing cabinet with a rusted fan on top.

And the woman, Rita.

She stood to one side of the desk, in profile, nervously watching the closed door opposite the window. Her arms were folded across her heavy breasts, as if she were cold; her face was drawn, bloodless. Between her lips was a filter-tipped cigarette that she smoked in short, deep drags.

Carmody glided back the way he'd come, stopped before the unshuttered window at the front part of the building. It was the kind that opened inward on a pair of hinges, with a simple slip catch locking it to the frame. He went to work with the broad flat blade of his Swiss Army knife. After two minutes he put the tips of his fingers against the dirty glass, cautiously pushed the window open.

The interior smelled of paint and linseed oil and dampness. Carmody climbed over the sill, stood motionless on a rough concrete floor. He could see where the door to the office was by a strip of light at its bottom. He could also make out a lathe, a drill press, a table saw, several wood forms, all massed up in the blackness — an obstacle course for him to get through without making any noise.

Slowly, feeling in front of him with his left hand, he

184

moved toward the strip of light. He had to detour twice, the second time abruptly to keep from colliding with a saw-horse. When he reached the door he stopped to listen. She was quiet in there, and since she'd been watching the door minutes earlier, it figured that she was still watching it. He had no way of knowing whether or not she was armed. He hadn't seen a gun, but he'd only had a limited view of the office.

He wrapped his left hand around the knob, twisted it, then threw his left shoulder against the door. The latch was open; the door banged against the table inside, dislodging papers. The woman let out a shriek and stumbled away from the desk, one hand going to her mouth. Her eyes were like buttons about to pop from too much pressure.

Carmody got to her in three long strides, caught her dark hair in his free hand, spun her around and sat her down hard in one of the chairs. Then he knelt in front of her, his angry face less than six inches from hers, and laid the Beretta's muzzle against her cheek.

He could see that she wanted to scream again, but nothing came out when she opened her mouth. Her eyes rolled up in their sockets. Carmody slapped her twice, hard. The blows refocused her vision, brought her out of the faint before she had really gone into it.

She stared at him with a mixture of shock and terror. "Signor Carmody . . ."

"That's right — alive and well."

"But you . . . I believed . . ."

"I know what you believed," he said thinly. "But I was luckier than Lucarelli and the boat driver. Where's the money? And where's Gambresca?"

"Gambresca! That *stronzolo*, he was the one . . ."

"You ought to know, you sold us out to him."

185

She blinked. "I do not understand."

"The hell you don't understand."

"I was so afraid," she whispered. She was trembling now. "I did not wish to die. This is why I run away. Please, I know nothing about Gambresca."

"Are you trying to tell me you didn't set up that ambush?"

"Ambush?"

"The boat, the shooting."

"No! How could I? You cannot think —"

"Why did you run back to the house just before the shooting started?"

"My *cosmeticos,* I forget them."

"Sure you did."

"I tell the truth! Renzo was my man, we go away together, you cannot think I want him to die!"

"Somebody wanted him to die," Carmody said. "Somebody tipped Gambresca. And you and Lucarelli were the only ones besides me and my man in Rome who knew where the hideaway was. You did it for the money, right? For a cut of the run-out money?"

"No, no, no! I did not, I would not . . ."

She was shaking her head, forgetting the gun at her cheek; Carmody pulled the Beretta back a little. It was quiet in the office just then — and in that quiet he heard the faint sound of a footfall in the darkness out front.

The hackles raised on his neck. He came up off his knee, turning, and when he did that he saw the vague shape of a man appear next to the drill press out there, just beyond the outspill of light from the desk lamp. In the man's hand was a familiar, deadly shape.

Carmody threw himself to one side, pushing Rita and the chair over backwards. She screamed again but the sound of it was lost in the stuttering roar of the machine pistol. A slug ripped through the tail of Carmody's jacket, burned across one buttock. Then the gooseneck lamp flew off the desk, shattered, and the office went dark except for bright flashes from the pistol's muzzle.

Carmody managed to get the desk between himself and the doorway. He could hear the rap, rap, rap of the bullets digging into the desk, into the wall above him, as the shooter raked the office with another burst. He twisted his body into the kneehole. He could see out on the other side, but without the muzzle flashes the darkness was too thick for him to locate the shooter. The air stank of burnt gunpowder; the silence had an electric quality. Carmody listened, knowing that the shooter was listening too.

The silence seemed to gain magnitude until it was almost deafening. Either the shooter didn't know where the overhead lights were or he didn't want to take the chance of putting them on. But with the amount of slugs he'd pumped into the office, he had to be thinking that he was the only one left alive. If he'd opened up with that MAC-10 two seconds earlier he'd have been right.

Pretty soon there was a series of scuffling sounds out beyond the doorway. Carmody still didn't move. They were the kinds of sounds somebody makes when he's pretending to leave a place, trying to be clever. The shooter was still out there, waiting. Making up his mind.

Another couple of minutes crawled away. The quiet was so intense it was like a humming in Carmody's ears. Then there was a nearly inaudible sliding sound: the shooter was moving again. Not going away this time. Coming back into the office.

Carmody steadied the Beretta on his left arm.

Nothing happened for a few seconds. Then there was another faint, whispery footfall. And another, not more than ten feet away and almost directly ahead —

Carmody emptied most of the Beretta's clip on a line waist-high and two feet wide.

There was a half-strangled Italian oath; a moment later Carmody heard the metallic clatter of the pistol on concrete, the sound of a body falling heavily. He stayed where he was, listening. A scrabbling movement, a low moan . . . nothing.

It was another couple of minutes before he was satisfied. He crawled out of the kneehole, got to his feet, moved at an angle to the door. He put his pencil flash on, just for an instant, stepping aside as he did so. Then the tension went out of him and he put the light on again, left it on.

The shooter was lying half in and half out of the office doorway, the MAC-10 alongside him. Face down, not moving. Carmody turned him over with the toe of one shoe, shined the light on his face — on the dead, staring eyes.

Gino Della Robbia.

Carmody swore softly. He wasn't surprised; nothing surprised him anymore. But that didn't make Della Robbia's treachery any easier to take.

He swung the light to the rear of the office, located Rita with it. At first he thought she was dead too because she lay crumpled and still. But when he went over there and knelt beside her, he saw that she was breathing. Blood glistened on the side of her head: scalp wound. He didn't see any others. She was lucky. They both were — damned lucky.

He found the switch for the overheads, flipped it on. Then he picked Rita up and sat her in a chair. The movement brought her out of it. For a couple of minutes she was disoriented, hysterical; he slapped her face, got her calmed down. Then she saw Della Robbia and that almost set her off again.

When she could talk she said, "Gino? It was Gino who killed Renzo?"

"And tried to kill me," Carmody said. "Twice."

"But I do not understand . . ."

"It's simple enough. Gambresca had nothing to do with the ambush, just like you had nothing to do with it. Della Robbia, nobody else. For the money. He didn't know how much there was but he did know that it would be plenty — enough to take the risks he took."

She shook her head, winced, sat still.

Carmody said, "You went to him tonight after the ambush, didn't you? Heard me mention his name to Lucarelli, remembered it, looked up his address and went to him."

"Yes. I believed you and Renzo were both dead. I had nowhere else to go."

"And he got you to come here."

"Yes."

"What'd he say to you?"

"That this was the *squero* of a friend. That I should wait here. He gave me a key."

"Wait for what?"

"For him to come. He said he would help me leave Venezia."

Carmody nodded. He was thinking that Della Robbia must have been in a hell of a sweat when he got home from San Spirito and one of the men he thought he'd killed called him on the phone — the one man he should have made sure died first. If he could have found out where Carmody was, he'd have gone there to finish the job. But Carmody hadn't told him and Della Robbia had been afraid to force the issue. So he'd sweated some more and waited for the next call. Then Rita had showed up and he'd thought of this *squero* — the perfect set-up for another ambush. Except that this time he'd been the one who got caught in it.

One question remained: How had Della Robbia found out where Lucarelli's hideout was? Piombo wouldn't have told him. The launch hadn't been followed tonight; Carmody had made sure of that. And he hadn't been followed on any of the previous trips he'd made to Rio San Spirito.

Only one possible answer — one that Carmody should have thought of at the Rio di Fontego tonight. By overlooking the possibility, he had gotten Lucarelli killed and almost lost his own life. Unforgiveable. He would never forget this mistake, and he would never make another like it again.

The answer, the oversight, was that the launch had been equipped with a shortwave radio. Della Robbia must have bribed the driver to open the microphone just before he picked Carmody up, so that when Carmody told him where they were going, Della Robbia had heard the address on a radio on his own boat tuned to the same band. Easy enough then to take a different and quicker route to San Spirito, hide and wait.

Carmody prodded Rita onto her feet, led her through the building and outside. The area was still deserted. It would take a while to find transportation at this hour, but that was a minor inconvenience.

Rita said, "Where are we going, Signor Carmody?"

"Della Robbia's house. Odds are that's where the money is."

"You will keep it all for yourself? The money?"

"No. It's yours — you've earned the right to it. All I want is the fee Lucarelli and I agreed on."

"You . . . you mean this?"

"I mean it," Carmody said. "This too: If you still want to go to Sardinia, I'll take you there. I don't like to leave a job unfinished."

"Yes, I want to go. Oh yes."

"It might take another day or two to rearrange things but I'll find a safe place for you to wait. It won't be too bad."

She looked at him with her large dark eyes. "No," she said, "I do not think it will be bad at all."

Dead Man's Slough

I was halfway through one of the bends in Dead Man's Slough, on my way back to the Whiskey Island marina with three big Delta catfish in the skiff beside me, when the red-haired man rose up out of the water at an islet fifty yards ahead.

It was the last thing I expected to see and I leaned forward, squinting through the boat's Plexiglas windscreen. The weather was full of early-November bluster — high overcast and a raw wind — and the water was too cold and too choppy for pleasure swimming. Besides which, the red-haired guy was fully dressed in khaki trousers and a short-sleeved bush jacket.

He came all the way out of the slough, one hand clapped across the back of his head, and plowed upward through the mud and grass of a tiny natural beach. When he got to its upper edge where the tule grass grew thick and waist-high, he stopped and held a listening pose. Then he whirled around, stood swaying unsteadily as if he were caught in a crosscurrent of the chill wind. He stared out toward me for two or three seconds; the pale oval of his face might have been pulled into a painful grimace, but I couldn't tell for sure at the distance. And then he whirled again in a dazed, frightened way, stumbled in among the rushes and disappeared.

I looked upstream past the islet, where Dead Man's Slough widened into a long reach; the waterway was empty, and so were the willow-lined levees that flanked it. Nor was there any sign of another boat or another human being in the wide channel that bounded the islet on the south. That was not surprising, or at least it wouldn't have been five minutes ago.

The California Delta, fifty miles inland from San Francisco where the Sacramento and San Joaquin rivers merge on a course to San Francisco Bay, has a thousand miles of waterways and a network of islands both large and small, inhabited and uninhabited, linked by seventy bridges and a few hundred miles of levee roads. During the summer months the area is jammed with vacationers, water skiers, fishermen and houseboaters, but in late fall, when the cold winds start to blow, about the only people you'll find are local merchants and farmers and a few late-vacationing anglers like me. I had seen no more than four other people and two other boats in the five hours since I'd left Whiskey Island, and none of those in the half-mile I had just traveled on Dead Man's Slough.

So where had the red-haired man come from?

On impulse I twisted the wheel and took the skiff over toward the islet, cutting back on the throttle as I approached. Wind gusts rustled and bent the carpet of tule grass, but there was no other movement that I could see. Ten yards off the beach, I shut the throttle all the way down to idle; the quick movement of the water carried the skiff the rest of the way in. When the bow scraped up over the soft mud I shut off the engine, pocketed the ignition key and moved aft to tilt the outboard engine out of the water so its propeller blades wouldn't become fouled in the off-shore grass. Then I climbed out and dragged half the boat's length onto the beach as a precaution against it backsliding and drifting off without me.

From the upper rim of the beach I could look all across

the flat width of the islet — maybe fifty yards in all — and for seventy yards or so of its length, to where the terrain humped up in the middle and a pair of willow trees and several wild blackberry bushes blocked off my view. But I couldn't see anything of the red-haired man, or hear anything of him either; there were no sounds except for the low whistling cry of the wind.

An eerie feeling came over me. It was as if I were alone on the islet, alone on all of Dead Man's Slough, and the red-haired guy had been some sort of hallucination. Or some sort of ghostly manifestation. I thought of the old-timer who had rented me the skiff on Whiskey Island — a sort of local historian well versed on Delta lore and legends dating back to the Gold Rush, when steamboats from San Francisco and Sacramento plied these waters with goods and passengers. And I thought of the story he had told me about how the slough got its name.

Back in 1860 an Irish miner named O'Farrell, on his way to San Francisco from the diggings near Sutter's Mill, had disappeared from a sidewheeler at Poker Bend; also missing was a fortune in gold dust and specie he had been carrying with him. Three days later O'Farrell's body was found floating in these waters with his head bashed in and his pockets empty. The murder was never solved. And old-time rivermen swore they had seen the miner's ghost abroad on certain foggy nights, swearing vengeance on the man who had murdered him.

But that wasn't quite all. According to the details of the story, O'Farrell had had red hair — and his ghost was always seen clutching the back of his bloody head with one hand.

Sure, I thought, and nuts to that. Pure coincidence, nothing else. Old-time rivermen were forever seeing ghosts, not only of men but of packets like the *Sagamore* and the *R.K. Page* whose steam boilers had exploded during foolish races in the mid-1800s, killing hundreds of passengers and crewmen. But I did not believe in spooks worth a damn. Nor was I prone to hallucinations or flights of imagination, not at my age and not with my temperament. The red-haired guy was real, all right. Maybe hurt and in trouble, too, judging from his wobbly condition and his actions.

So where had he gone? If he was hiding somewhere in the rushes I couldn't tell the location by looking from here, or even where he had gone into them; tule grass is pretty re-silient and tends to spring back up even after a man plows through it. He could also have gone to the eastern end, beyond the high ground in the middle. The one thing I was sure of was that he was still on the islet: I could see out into the wide channels on the north and south sides, and if he had gone swimming again he would have been visible.

I pulled up the collar on my pea jacket and headed into the rushes on a zigzag course, calling out as I went, offering help if he needed it. Nobody answered me. And there was no sign of any red hair as I worked my way along. After a time I stopped, and when I scanned upward toward the higher ground I saw that I was within thirty yards of the line of blackberry bushes.

I also saw a man come hurrying up onto the hump from the opposite side, between the two willow trees.

He saw me, too, and halted abruptly, and we stood star-ing at each other across the windswept terrain. But he wasn't the red-haired guy. He was dark-looking, heavier, and he wore Levi's, a plaid mackinaw and a gray fisher-man's hat decorated with bright-colored flies. In one hand, held in a vertical position, was a thick-butted fishing rod.

"Hello up there!" I called to him, but he didn't give me

any response. Just stood poised, peering down at me like a wary animal scenting for danger. Which left the first move up to me. I took my hands out of my coat pockets and slow-walked toward him over the marshy earth. He stayed where he was, not moving except to slant the fishing rod across the front of his body, weaponlike. When I got past the blackberry bushes I was ten feet from him, on the firmer ground of the hump; I decided that was far enough and stopped there.

We did some more looking at each other. He was about my age, early fifties, with a craggy outdoorsman's face and eyes the color of butterscotch. There was no anxiety in his expression, nor any hostility either; it was just the set, waiting look of a man on his guard.

Past him I could see the rest of the islet — another sixty yards or so of flattish terrain dominated by shrubs and tules, with a mistletoe-festooned pepper tree off to the left and a narrow rock shelf at the far end. Tied up alongside the shelf was what looked to be a fourteen-foot outboard similar to my rented skiff, except that it sported a gleaming green-and-white paint job. There was nothing else to see along there, or in the choppy expanses of water surrounding us.

Pretty soon the craggy guy said, "Who are you?"

"Just another fisherman," I said, which was more relevant and less provocative than telling him I was a private investigator from San Francisco. "Have you been here long?"

"A little while. Why?"

"Alone?"

"That's right. But I heard *you* shouting to somebody."

"Nobody I know," I said. "A red-haired man I saw drag himself out of the slough a few minutes ago."

He stared at me. "What?"

"Sounds funny, I know, but it's the truth. He was fully dressed and he looked hurt; he disappeared into the tules. I put my boat in and I've been hunting around for him, but no luck so far. You haven't seen him, I take it?"

"No," the craggy guy said. "I haven't seen anybody since I put in after crayfish an hour ago." He paused. "You say this red-haired man was hurt?"

"Seemed that way, yes."

"Bad?"

"Maybe. He looked dazed."

"You think he could have had a boating accident?"

"Could be. But he also seemed scared."

"Scared? Of what?"

"No idea. You heard me shouting, so he must have heard me, too; but he still hasn't shown himself. That might mean he's hiding because he's afraid to be found."

"Might mean something else, too," the craggy guy said. "He could have gone back into the water and swum across to one of the other islands."

"I don't think so. I would have seen him if he'd done that anywhere off this side; and I guess you'd have seen him if he'd done it anywhere off the other side."

"He could also be dead by now if he was hurt as bad as you seem to think."

"That's a possibility," I said. "Or maybe just unconscious. How about helping me look for him so we can find out?"

The craggy guy hesitated. He was still wary, the way a lot of people are of strangers these days — as if he were not quite convinced I was telling him a straight story and thinking that maybe I had designs on his money or his life. But after a time he said, "All right; if there's a man hurt around here, he'll need all the help he can get. Where did you see him come out of the water?"

I turned a little and pointed behind me. "Back there. You can see part of my boat; that's about where it was."

"So if he's still on the island, he's somewhere between here and your boat."

"Seems that way," I said. "Unless he managed to slip over where you were without your seeing him."

"I doubt that. I've got pretty sharp eyes."

"Sure." I thought I might as well introduce myself; maybe that would reassure him. So I gave my name, with a by-the-way after it, and waited while he made up his mind whether or not he wanted to reciprocate.

"Jackson," he said finally. "Herb Jackson."

"Nice to know you, Mr. Jackson. How about if we each take one side and work back toward my skiff?"

He said that was okay with him and we fanned out away from each other, me into the vegetation on the south side. We each used a switchbacking course from the center out to the edges, where the ground was boggy and the footing a little treacherous. Both of us kept silent, but all you could hear were the keening of the wind and the whispery rustle of the tules as I spread through them with my hands and Jackson probed through them with his fishing rod. I caught him looking over at me a couple of times as if he wanted to make sure I intended to stay on my half of the turf.

Neither of us found anything. The only things hidden among the rushes were occasional rocks and chunks of decaying driftwood; and there was no way anybody could have concealed himself in the sparse offshore grasses. You're always hearing about how people submerge in shallow water and breathe through a hollow reed, and maybe that's a possibility in places like Florida and Louisiana, but not in California. Tule grass isn't hollow and you can't breathe

198

through its stalks; you'd swallow water and probably drown if you tried it.

It took us ten minutes to make our way back and down to where my rented boat was. I got there first, and when Jackson came up he halted a good eight feet away and looked down at the empty beach, into the empty skiff, across the empty slough at the empty levee on the far side. Then he put his butterscotch eyes on me.

I said, "He's got to be over where you were somewhere. We've gone over all the ground on this end."

"If he's on the island at all," Jackson said.

"Well, he's got to be." A thought occurred to me. "The outboard on your boat — do you start it with an ignition key or by hand?"

"Key. Why?"

"Did you leave it in the ignition or have you got it with you?"

"In my pocket," he said. "What're you thinking? That he might try to steal my boat?"

"It could happen. But it wouldn't do him much good without power. Unless you keep oars for an emergency."

"No oars." Jackson looked a little worried now, as though he might be imagining his boat adrift and in the hands of a mysterious redheaded stranger. "Damn it, you could be right."

He set off at a soggy run, bulling his way through the rushes and shrubs, slashing at them with whiplike sweeps of the rod. I went after him, off to one side and at a slower pace. He reached the blackberry bushes, cut past them onto the hump and pulled up near the drooping fan of branches on one willow. Then I saw him relax and take a couple of deep breaths; he turned to wait for me.

When I got up there I could see that his boat was still

tied alongside the empty rock shelf. The channels beyond were a couple hundred yards wide at the narrowest point; you could swim that distance easily enough in fifteen minutes — but not on a day like this, with that wind whipping up the water to a froth, and not when you were hurt and so unsteady on your feet you couldn't walk without stumbling.

"So he's still on the island," I said to Jackson. "It shouldn't take us long to find him now."

He had nothing to say to that; he just turned toward the willow, spread the branches, looked in among them and at the ones higher up. I went over and did the same thing at the second tree. The red-haired man was not hiding in either of them — and he wasn't hiding among the blackberry bushes or anywhere else on or near the hump.

We started down toward Jackson's boat, one on each side as before. Rocks, more pieces of driftwood, a rusted coffee can, the carcass of some sort of large bird — nothing else. The pepper tree was on my side, and I paused at the bole and peered up through pungent leaves and thick clusters of mistletoe. Nothing. The shoreline on this end was rockier with shrubs and nettles growing along it instead of tule grass; but there was nobody concealed there, not on my half and not on Jackson's.

Where is he? I thought. He couldn't have just disappeared into thin air. *Where is he?*

The eerie feeling came back over me as I neared the rock shelf; in spite of myself I thought again of O'Farrell, the murdered Gold Rush miner, and his ghost that was supposed to haunt Dead Man's Slough. I shook the thought away, but I didn't feel any better after I had.

I reached the shelf before Jackson and stopped abaft the boat. She was a sleek little lady, not more than a year old, with bright chrome fittings to go with the green-and-white paint job; the outboard was a thirty-five-horsepower Evinrude. In the stern, I saw then, was a tackle box, a wicker creel, an Olympic spincast outfit and a nifty Shakespeare graphite-and-fiberglass rod. A heavy sheepskin jacket was draped over the back of the naugahyde seat.

When I heard Jackson come up near me a few seconds later I pivoted around to face him. He said, "I don't like this at all."

Neither did I, not one bit. "Yeah," I said.

He gave me a narrow look. He had that rod slanted across the front of his body again. "You sure you're not just playing games with me, mister?"

"Why would I want to play games with you?"

"I don't know. All I know is we've been over the entire island without finding this redhead of yours. There's nothing here except tule grass and shrubs and three trees; we couldn't have overlooked anything as big as a man."

"I guess not," I said.

"Then where is he — if he exists at all?"

"Dead, maybe."

"Dead?"

"He's not on the island; that means he had to have tried swimming across one of the channels. But you or I would've seen him at some point if he'd got halfway across any of them."

"You think he drowned?"

"I'm afraid so," I said. "He was hurt and probably weak — and that water is turbulent and ice-cold. Unless he was an exceptionally strong swimmer and in the best possible shape, he couldn't have lasted long."

Jackson thought that over, rubbing fingertips along his craggy jaw. "You might be right, at that," he said. "So what do we do now?"

"There's not much we can do. One of us should notify the county sheriff, but that's about all. The body'll turn up sooner or later."

"Sure," Jackson said. "Tell you what: I'll call the sheriff from the camp in Hogback Slough; I'm heading in there right away."

"Would you do that?"

"Be glad to. No problem."

"Well, thanks. He can reach me on Whiskey Island if he wants to talk to me about it."

"I'll tell him that."

He nodded to me, lowered the rod a little, then moved past me to the boat. I retreated a dozen yards over the rocky ground, watching him as he untied the bowline from a shrub and climbed in under the wheel. Thirty seconds later, when I was halfway up to the willow trees, the outboard made a guttural rumbling noise and its propeller blades began churning the water. Jackson maneuvered backward away from the shelf, waved as he shifted into a forward gear and opened the throttle wide; the boat got away in a hurry, bow lifting under the surge of power. From up on the hump I watched it dwindle as he cut down the center of the southern channel toward the entrance to Hogback Slough.

So much for Herb Jackson, I thought then. Now I could start worrying about the red-haired man again.

What I had said about being afraid he'd drowned was a lie. But he was not a ghost and he had not pulled any magical vanishing act; he was still here, and I was pretty sure he was still alive. It was just that Jackson and I had overlooked something — and it had not occurred to me what it was until Jackson said there was nothing here except tule grass and shrubs and three trees. That was not quite true. There *was* something else on the islet, and it made one place we had failed to search; that was where the man had to be.

I went straight to it, hurrying, and when I got there I said my name again in a loud voice and added that I was a detective from San Francisco.

Then I said, "He's gone now; there's nobody around but me. You're safe."

Nothing happened for fifteen seconds. Then there were sounds and struggling movement, and I waded in quickly to help him with some careful lifting and pushing.

And there he was, burrowing free of a depression in the soft mud, out from under my rented skiff just above the waterline where I had beached the forward half of it.

When he was clear of the boat I released my grip on the gunwale and eased him up on his feet. He kept trying to talk, but he was in no shape for that yet; most of what he said was gibberish. I got him into the skiff, wrapped him in a square of canvas from the stern — he was shivering so badly you could almost hear his bones clicking together — and cleaned some of the mud off him. The area behind his right ear was pulpy and badly lacerated, but if he was lucky he didn't have anything worse than a concussion.

While I was doing that he calmed down enough to be coherent, and the first thing he said was, "He tried to kill me. He tried to murder me."

"I figured as much. What happened?"

"We were in his boat; we'd just put in to the island because he said there was something wrong with the ignition. He asked me to take a look, so I pulled off my coat and leaned down under the wheel. Then my head seemed to explode. The next thing I knew, I was floundering in the south-side channel."

"He hit you with that fishing rod of his, probably," I said. "The current carried you along after he dumped you overboard and the cold water brought you around. Why does he want you dead?"

"It must be the insurance. We own a company in Sacramento and we have a partnership policy — double indemnity for accidental death. I knew Frank was in debt, but I never thought he'd go this far."

"Frank? Then his name isn't Herb Jackson?"

"No. It's Saunders, Frank Saunders. Mine's Rusty McGuinn."

Irish, I thought. Like O'Farrell. That figures.

I got out again to slide the skiff off the beach and into the slough. When I clambered back in, McGuinn said, "You knew he was after me, didn't you? That's why you didn't give me away when the two of you were together."

"Not exactly." I started the engine and got us under way at a good clip upstream. "I didn't have any idea who you were or where you'd come from until I looked inside Jackson's — or Saunders' — boat. He told me he was alone and he'd put in after crayfish. But he was carrying one rod and there were two more casting outfits in the boat; you don't need all that stuff for crayfish, and no fisherman alone is likely to carry *three* outfits for any reason. There was a heavy sheepskin jacket there, too, draped over the seat; but he was already wearing a heavy mackinaw, and I remembered you only had on a short-sleeved jacket when you came out of the water. It all began to add up then. I talked him into leaving as soon as I could."

"How did you do that?"

"By telling him what he wanted to hear — that you must be dead."

"But how did you know where I was hiding?"

I explained how Saunders had triggered the answer for me. "I also tried to put myself in your place. You were hurt and scared; your first thought would be to get away as fast as possible. Which meant by boat, not by swimming. So it figured you hid nearby until I was far enough away and then slipped back to the skiff.

"But this boat — like Saunders' — starts with a key, and I had it with me. You could have set yourself adrift, but then Saunders might have seen you and come chasing in his boat. In your condition it made sense you might burrow under the skiff, with a little space clear at one side so you could breathe."

"Well, I owe you a debt," McGuinn said. "You saved my life."

"Forget it," I said, a little ruefully. Because the truth was I had almost got him killed. I had told Saunders he was on the island and insisted on a two-man search party; and I had failed to tumble to who and what Saunders was until it was almost too late. If McGuinn hadn't been so well hidden, if we'd found him, Saunders would probably have jumped me and I might not have been able to handle him; McGuinn and I could both be dead now. I'm not a bad detective, usually; other times, though, I'm a near bust.

The channel that led to Whiskey Island loomed ahead. Cheer up, I told myself — the important thing is that this time, 120 years after the first one, the red-haired Irish bludgeon victim is being brought out alive and the man who assaulted him is sure to wind up in prison. The ghost of O'Farrell, the Gold Rush miner, won't have any company when it goes prowling and swearing vengeance on those foggy nights in Dead Man's Slough.

A Killing in Xanadu

The name of the place, like that of the principality in Coleridge's *Kubla Khan* and of the newspaper tycoon's estate in *Citizen Kane*, was Xanadu. "In Xanadu did Kubla Khan a stately pleasure-dome decree . . ." This one was neither a principality nor an estate, but you could call it a pleasure-dome — or rather, a whole series of pleasure-domes overlooking a rugged portion of California's Big Sur seacoast, not all that far from the Hearst Castle. Which tied off one of the historical references because William Randolph Hearst was supposedly the model for the tycoon in Orson Welles' classic film.

What it was, this particular Xanadu, was a resort playground for the wealthy Establishment. Eighteen-hole golf course, tennis and racketball courts, Olympic-sized swimming pool, sauna and steam rooms, two restaurants, three bars, a disco nightclub, and forty or fifty rustic cottages nestled on craggy terrain among tall redwoods. And the tariff was a mere $1500 per week per person, not including meals, drinks, or gratuities.

Nice play if you can get it.

I couldn't get it myself, but that was all right; it was not my idea of a vacation wonderland anyway. The reason I went down there on a windy Thursday in August was to pay a call on one of those who could get it — a San Francisco socialite named Lauren Speers. She was worth a few hundred thousand, all inherited money, and numbered politicians, actors, capitalists, and other influential types among her friends; she also had striking red hair and green eyes

and was beautiful enough if you liked them forty and dissi-
pated. I know all of that not because she was my client, but
because the man who *was* my client, an attorney named
Adam Brister, had told me so and shown me a color photograph. Ms. Speers and I had never laid eyes on each other.
Ms. Speers' money and I had never laid eyes on each other
either, nor were we ever likely to.

Brister was no better acquainted with her than I was. He
had been retained by one Vernon Inge of Oakland, who
owned a car which he claimed La Speers had sideswiped
with her Porsche in a hit-and-run accident a couple of
weeks ago. The accident had rendered Inge a nasty whip-
lash that kept him from performing his job as a baker. Or so
he and Brister alleged in a damage suit against Speers.

The lawsuit was where I came in: I went to Xanadu to
serve the lady with a court summons.

So much for the glamorous role of the private eye in
modern society. No rich client, no smoky-hot liaison with a
beautiful woman, no fat fee. Just two hundred bucks plus
expenses to track down a woman who moved around more
than the governor, hand her some papers, listen to abusive
language — they always throw abusive language at you —
and then steal away again into the real world.

But first I had to pass out of the real world, through the
portals into Xanadu, and I did that at two-fifteen. A short
entrance drive wound upward past part of the golf course,
then among lush redwoods and giant ferns, and emerged
into a parking area shaped like a bowl. Three-quarters of it
was reserved for guest parking; the other quarter was taken
up with rows of three-wheeled machines that looked like
golf carts, with awnings over them done in pastel ice-cream
colors. From what I had been able to find out about
Xanadu, the carts were used by guests to get from one

pleasure-dome to another, along a network of narrow and sometimes steep paths. Exercise was all well and good in its proper place — tennis court, swimming pool, disco — but the rich folk no doubt considered walking uphill a vulgarity.

Beyond where the carts were was a long slope, with a wide path cut into it and a set of stairs alongside that seemed more ornamental than functional. At the top of the slope, partially visible from below, were some of the resort buildings, all painted in pastel colors like the cart awnings. The muted sounds of people at play drifted down on the cool wind from the ocean.

I put my car into a slot marked *Visitors Parking*. A black guy in a starched white uniform came over to me as I got out. He was about my age, early fifties, with a lot of gray in his hair, and his name was Horace. Or so it said on the pocket of his uniform, in pink script like the sugar-writing on a birthday cake.

He looked at me and I looked at him. I was wearing my best suit, but my best suit was the kind the inhabitants of Xanadu wore to costume parties or gave away to the Salvation Army. But that was okay by Horace. Some people who work at fancy places like this get to be snobs in their own right; not him. His eyes said that I would never make it up that hill over yonder, not for more than a few minutes at a time, but then neither would he and the hell with it.

I let him see that I felt the same way and a faint smile turned one corner of his mouth. "Here on business?" he asked.

"Yes. I'm looking for Lauren Speers."

"She's out right now. Took her car a little past one."

"Do you have any idea when she'll be back?"

"Depends on how thirsty she gets, I suppose."

"Pardon?"

"The lady drinks," Horace said, and shrugged.

"You mean she'd been drinking before she left?"

"Martinis. Starts in at eleven every morning, quits at one, sleeps until four. Then it's Happy Hour. But not today. Today she decided to go out. If I'd seen her in time I'd have tried to talk her out of driving, but she was in that sports job of hers and gone before I even noticed her."

"Must be nice to be rich," I said.

"Yeah," he said.

"Can you tell me which cottage is hers?"

"Number forty-one. Straight ahead past the swimming pool. Paths are all marked. Miss Dolan'll likely be there if you want to wait at the cottage."

"Who's Miss Dolan?"

"Miss Speers' secretary — Bernice Dolan. She's writing a book, you know. Miss Speers, I mean."

"No, I didn't know. What kind of book?"

"All about her life. Ought to be pretty spicy."

"From what I know about her, I guess it will be."

"But I'll never read it," Horace said. "Bible, now, that's much more interesting. If you know what I mean."

I said I knew what he meant. And thanked him for his help. I did not offer him any money; if I had he would have been offended. He would take gratuities from the guests because that was part of his job, but it had already been established that he and I were social equals. And that made an exchange of money unseemly.

I climbed the stairs — I wouldn't have driven one of those cute little carts even if it was allowed, which it wasn't or Horace would have offered me one — and found my way to the swimming pool. You couldn't have missed it; it was laid out between the two largest buildings, surrounded by a lot of bright green lawn and flagstone terracing, with a

209

stone-faced outdoor bar at the near end. Twenty or thirty people in various stages of undress occupied the area. A few of them were in the pool, but most were sitting at wrought-iron tables, being served tall drinks by three white-jacketed waiters. None of the waiters, I noticed, was black.

Nobody paid any attention to me as I passed by, except for a hard-looking thirtyish blonde who undressed me with her eyes — women do it too, sometimes — and then put my clothes back on again and threw me out of her mental bedroom. Fiftyish gentlemen with shaggy looks and a beer belly were evidently not her type.

Past the pool area, where the trees began, were a pair of paths marked with redwood-burl signs. The one on the left, according to the sign, would take me to number 41, so I wandered off in that direction. And ten minutes later I was still wandering, uphill now, with 41 still nowhere in sight. I was beginning to realize that the fancy little carts were not such an affectation as I had first taken them to be.

I had passed three cottages so far — or the walks that led to three cottages. The buildings themselves were set back some distance from the main path, half-hidden by trees, and were all lavish chalet types with wide porches and pastel-colored wrought-iron trim. Unlike the stairs from the parking area, the wrought iron was just as functional as it was ornamental: the curved bars and scrollwork served as a kind of burglar proofing over the windows. Xanadu may have been a whimsical pleasure resort, but its rulers nonetheless had their defenses up.

Here in the woods it was much cooler, almost cold, because of the ocean breeze and because the afternoon sunlight penetrated only in dappled patches. I was wishing that I'd worn a coat over my suit when I came around a bend and glimpsed a fourth cottage through the redwoods. Another burl sign stood adjacent to the access path, and I could just make out the numerals 41 emblazoned on it.

I took a few more steps toward the sign. And from behind me, then, I heard a sound like that of a lawnmower magnified: one of the carts approaching. I moved off the path as the sound grew louder. A couple of seconds later the thing came around the curve at my back, going at an erratic clip, and shot past me. Inside was a red-haired woman wearing white. The cart veered over to number 41's walk, skidded to a stop, and the redhead got out and hurried toward the cottage. The white garment she wore was a thin coat, buttoned up against the wind, and she had a big straw bag in her right hand; the long red hair streamed out behind her like a sheet of flame. The way she'd handled the cart indicated Ms. Lauren Speers was every bit as sloshed as Horace had led me to believe, but she carried herself on her feet pretty well. The serious drinker, male or female, learns how to walk if not drive in a straight line.

I called out to her but she either didn't hear me or chose to ignore me: she kept on going without breaking stride or glancing in my direction. I ran the rest of the way to the cottage path, turned in along it. She was already on the porch by then, digging in her bag with her free hand; I could see her through a gap in the fronting screen of trees. She found a key and had it in the lock before I could open my mouth to call to her again. In the next second she was inside, with the door shut behind her.

Well, hell, I thought.

I stopped and spent thirty seconds or so catching my breath. Running uphill had never been one of my favorite activities, even when I was in good physical shape. Then I checked the papers Adam Brister had given me to serve. And then I started along the path again.

I was twenty yards from the porch, with most of the cottage visible ahead of me, when the gun went off.

It made a flat cracking sound in the stillness, muffled by the cottage walls but distinct enough to be unmistakable. I pulled up, stiffening, the hair turning bristly on my neck. There was no second shot, not in the three or four seconds I stood motionless and not when I finally went charging ahead onto the porch.

I swatted on the door a couple of times with the edge of my hand. Nothing happened inside. But after a space there was a low cry and a woman's voice said querulously, "Bernice? Oh my God — Bernice!" I caught hold of the knob, turned it; it was locked. The hell with propriety, I thought, and stepped back a pace and slammed the bottom of my shoe against the latch just below the knob.

Metal screeched and wood splinters flew; the door burst open. And I was in a dark room with redwood walls, a beamed ceiling, a fireplace along one wall, rustic furniture scattered here and there. Off to the left was a dining area and a kitchen; off to the right was a short hallway that would lead to the bedrooms and the bath. There were two women in the room, one of them lying crumpled on a circular hooked rug near the fireplace, the other one standing near the entrance to the hallway. Equidistant between them, on the polished-wood floor at the rug's perimeter, was a .25 caliber automatic.

The standing woman was Lauren Speers. She had shed the white coat — it was on a long couch with her straw bag — and she was wearing shorts and a halter, both of them white and brief, showing off a good deal of buttery tan skin. She stood without moving, staring down at the woman on the rug, the knuckles of one hand pressing her lips flat against her teeth. Her expression was one of bleary shock, as if she had too much liquor inside her to grasp the full meaning of what had happened here. Or to have registered my violent entrance. Even when I moved deeper into the room, over in front of her, she did not seem to know I was there.

I went for the gun first. You don't leave a weapon lying around on the floor after somebody has just used it. I picked it up by the tip of the barrel — still warm — and dropped it into my coat pocket. Lauren Speers still didn't move, still didn't acknowledge my presence; her eyes were half-rolled up in their sockets. And I realized that she had fainted standing up, that it was only a matter of seconds before her legs gave out and she fell.

Before that could happen I put an arm around her waist and half-carried her to the nearest chair, put her into it. She was out, all right; her head lolled to one side. I could smell the sour odor of gin on her breath. The whole room smelled of gin, in fact, as if somebody had been using the stuff for disinfectant.

The woman on the rug was dead. I knew that even without checking for a pulse; had known it the instant I saw her wide-open eyes and the blood on her blouse beneath one twisted arm. She was in her late thirties, attractive in a regular-featured way, with short brown hair and a thin mouth. Wearing blouse, skirt, open-toed sandals.

Looking at her made my stomach feel queasy, filled me with a sense of revulsion and awe. It was the same reaction I always had to violent death, because it was such an ugliness, such a waste. I swallowed against the taste of bile and turned away.

Lauren Speers was still sprawled where I'd put her in the chair, unmoving. I went past her, down the short hall, and looked into the two bedrooms and the bath. All three were empty. And the windows in all three were closed and locked; I could see that at a glance.

I came back out and looked into the kitchen. That was empty too. I started across to a set of sliding glass doors that led onto a rear balcony, but before I got there I noticed something on the floor between the couch and a burl coffee table — a piece of white paper folded lengthwise, lying there tent-fashion. I detoured over and used my handkerchief to pick it up.

It was a sheet of notepaper with six lines of writing in a neat, backslanted feminine hand: three names followed by three series of numbers. All of the names and numbers had heavy lines drawn through them, like items crossed off on a grocery list.

Rykman 56 57 59 62 63 116–125 171–175—25,000
Boyer 214–231 235 239–247 255—25,000
Huddleston 178 170 205–211 360–401 415–420—50,000

None of that meant anything to me. I put the paper into the same pocket with the gun, moved on to the sliding doors. They were securely locked, with one of those twist latches that are supposed to be impossible to force from outside. Adjacent was a wide dormer-style window split into vertical halves that fastened in the center, so you could open them inward on a hot day to let in the sea breeze. The halves were also locked — a simple bar-type catch on one that flipped over and fit inside a bracket on the other — and there was more of the wrought-iron burglar-proofing bolted over them on the outside.

I stood at the glass doors, looking out. From there you had an impressive view down a long rocky slope to where the Pacific roiled up foam in a secluded cove, framed on both sides by skyscraping redwoods. But it wasn't the view that had my attention; it was what looked to be a strip of film about three inches in length, that was caught on a railing splinter off to one side and fluttering in the wind. I debated whether or not to unlatch the doors and go out there for a closer look. I was still debating when somebody came clumping up onto the front porch.

The noise brought me around. The front door was still open, and I watched it fill up with six feet of a youngish flaxen-haired guy dressed in tennis whites and carrying a covered racket. He said, "What's going on here? Who are you?" Then he got to where he could see the body on the rug, and Lauren Speers unconscious in the chair, and he said, "Christ!" in an awed voice.

Right away, to avoid trouble, I told him my name, my profession, and the fact that I had come here to see Lauren Speers on a business matter, only to stumble on a homicide instead. He was Joe Craig, he said, one of Xanadu's tennis professionals, and he had come over from his own staff cottage nearby to pick up Speers for a three o'clock tennis appointment. He seemed stunned, confused; his eyes kept shifting away from me to the body.

There was a telephone on another burl table beside the couch. I went to it and rang up the resort office. And spent five minutes and a lot of breath explaining three times to three different people that there had been a shooting in Number 41 and somebody was dead. None of the three wanted to believe it. A killing in Xanadu? Things like that just didn't happen. The first one referred me to the second and the second to the third; the third, who said he was Resident Director Mitchell, maintained his disbelief for a good two minutes before a kind of horrified indignation took over and he promised to notify the county police right away.

Craig had gone over to Lauren Speers and was down on one knee beside her, chafing one of her hands without result. "Maybe we should take her outside," he said. "Let her have some air."

That was a good idea. I helped him get her up out of the chair, and as we hauled her across to the door I asked him, "Do you know the dead woman?"

"God, yes. Bernice Dolan, Ms. Speers' secretary. Did Ms. Speers do that to her? Shoot her like that?"

"So it would seem." On the porch we put her onto a wrought-iron chaise longue and Craig went after her hand again. "There's nobody else here, the balcony doors and all the windows are locked from the inside, and I was down on the path with a clear look at the front door when it happened."

He shook his head. "I knew they weren't getting along," he said, "but I never thought it would lead to anything like this."

"How did you know they weren't getting along?"

"Bernice told me. We dated a couple of times — nothing serious." Another headshake. "I can't believe she's . . . dead."

"What was the trouble between them?"

"Well, Ms. Speers is writing a book — or rather, dictating one. All about some of the important people she's known and some of the things she's been mixed up in in the past. And full of scandalous material, apparently. She'd got her hands on all sorts of letters and documents and she quoted some of them at length. Bernice'd had editorial experience in New York and kept telling her she couldn't do that because some of the material was criminal and most of it was libelous. But that didn't matter to Ms. Speers; she said she was going to publish it anyway. They were always arguing about it."

"Why didn't she just fire Bernice?"

"I guess she was afraid Bernice would go to some of the people mentioned in the book, out of spite or something, and stir up trouble that'd affect publication."

"Were their arguments ever violent?"

"I think so. Bernice was afraid of her. She'd have quit herself if she hadn't needed the money."

But even if Lauren Speers was prone to violence, I thought, why would she shoot her secretary no more than two minutes after returning from an after-lunch drive? That was how long it had been between the time I saw her go inside and the time the gun went off: two minutes maximum.

Craig's hand-chafing was finally beginning to have an effect. La Speers made a low moaning sound, her eyelids fluttered and slid up, and she winced. Her stare was glassy and blank for three or four seconds; the pupils looked as if they were afloat in bloody milk. Then memory seemed to come back to her and her eyes focused, her body jerked as if an electrical current had passed through it.

"Oh my God!" she said. "Bernice!"

"Easy," Craig said. "It's all over now, Mrs. Speers."

"Joe? What are you doing here?"

"Our tennis date, remember?"

"I don't remember anything. Oh God, my head . . ."
Then she saw me standing there. "Who're you?"

We got it established who I was and more or less why I was present. She did not seem to care; she pushed herself off the chaise longue before I was done talking and went inside. She was none too steady on her feet, but when Craig tried to take her arm she smacked his hand away. One long look at the body produced a shudder and sent her rushing into the kitchen. I heard the banging of cupboard doors and the clink of glassware, and a few seconds later she came back with a cut-glass decanter in her right hand and an empty tumbler in her left. The decanter was full of something colorless that was probably gin.

I went over as she started to pour and took both decanter and tumbler away from her. "No more liquor. You've had plenty."

Her eyes snapped at me, full of savagery. "You fat son of a bitch — how dare you! Give it back to me!"

"No," I said, thinking: fat son of a bitch. Yeah. I put my back to her and went down the hall into the bathroom. She came after me, calling me more names; clawed at my arm and hand while I emptied the gin into the washbasin. I yelled to Craig to get her off me and he came and did that.

There was blood on the back of my right hand where she'd scratched me. I washed it off, dabbed the scratch with iodine from the medicine cabinet. Speers was back on the chaise longue when I returned to the porch, Craig beside her looking nonplussed. She was shaking and she looked sick, shrunken, as if all her flesh had contracted inside her skin. But the fury was still alive in those green eyes: They kept right on ripping away at me.

I asked her, "What happened here today, Ms. Speers?"

"Go to hell," she said.

"Why did you kill your secretary?"

"Go to — What? My God, you don't think *I* did that?"

"It looks that way."

"But I didn't, I couldn't have . . ."

"You were drunk," I said. "Maybe that explains it."

"Of course I was drunk. But I don't kill people when I'm drunk. I go straight to bed and sleep it off."

"Except today, maybe."

"I told you, you bastard, I didn't kill her!"

"Look, lady," I said, "I'm tired of you calling me names. I don't like it and I don't want to listen to it anymore. Maybe you killed Bernice Dolan and maybe you didn't. If you didn't, then you'd better start acting like a human being. The way you've been carrying on, you look guilty as sin."

She opened her mouth, shut it again. Some of the heat faded out of her eyes. "I didn't do it," she said, much calmer, much more convincing.

"All right. What did happen?"

"I don't know. I heard the shot, I came out of the bedroom, and there she was all twisted and bloody, with the gun on the floor . . ."

"A twenty-five caliber automatic. Your gun?"

"Yes. My gun."

"Where do you usually keep it?"

"In the nightstand drawer in my bedroom."

"Did you take it out today for any reason?"

"No."

"Did Bernice have it when you got back?"

A blank look. "Got back?"

"From wherever it was you went this afternoon."

"Away from Xanadu? In my car?"

"Are you saying you don't remember?"

"Okay, I have memory lapses sometimes when I've been drinking. Blackouts — an hour or two. But I don't usually go out driving . . ." The misery in her voice made her sound vulnerable, almost pathetic. I still didn't like her much, but she was in a bad way — physically, emotionally, and circumstantially — and she needed all the help she could get. Beginning with me. Maybe. "I thought I came straight here after lunch. I remember starting back in the cars . . . but

219

that's all. Nothing else until I heard the shot and found Bernice."

Out on the main path I heard the whirring of an oncoming cart. A short time later two middle-aged guys, both dressed in expensive summer suits, came running through the trees and up onto the porch. The taller of them, it developed, was Resident Director Mitchell; the other one was Xanadu's chief of security. The first thing they did was to go inside and gape at the body. When they came out again I explained what had happened as far as I knew it, and what I was doing in Xanadu in the first place. Speers did not react to the fact that I was here to serve her with a court summons. Death makes every other problem inconsequential.

She had begun to look even sicker; her skin had an unhealthy grayish tinge. When Mitchell and the security chief moved off the porch for a conference she got up and hurried into the cottage. I went in after her, to make sure she didn't touch anything or go for another stash of gin. But it was the bathroom she wanted this time; five seconds after she shut the door, retching sounds filtered out through it.

I stepped into her bedroom and took a turn around it without putting my hands on any of its surfaces. The bed was rumpled and the rest of the room looked the same — scattered clothing, jars of cosmetics, bunches of dog-eared paperback books. There were also half a dozen framed photographs of well-groomed men, all of them signed with the word "love."

The retching noises had stopped when I came out and I could hear water running in the bathroom. I moved down to the other, smaller bedroom. Desk with an electric portable typewriter and a dictating machine on its top. No photographs and nothing else much on the furniture. No sign of a manuscript, either; that would be locked away somewhere, I thought.

The sliding closet door was ajar, so I put my head through the opening. The closet was empty except for two bulky suitcases. I nudged both with my foot and both seemed to be packed full.

Half a minute after I returned to the living room, Lauren Speers reappeared. When she saw me she ducked her head and said, "Don't look at me. I look like hell." But I looked at her anyway. I also blocked her way to the door.

With my handkerchief I took out the piece of notepaper I had found earlier and held it up where she could see what was written on it. "Do you have any idea what this is, Ms. Speers?" She started to reach for it but I said, "No, don't touch it. Just look."

She looked. "I never saw it before," she said.

"Is the handwriting familiar?"

"Yes. It's Bernice's."

"From the looks of it, she was left-handed."

"Yes, she was. If that matters."

"The three names here — are they familiar?"

"I think so. James Huddleston is the former state attorney general. Edward Boyer and Samuel Rykman are both prominent business people."

"Close friends of yours?"

Her mouth turned crooked. "Not anymore."

"Why is that?"

"Because they're bastards. And one is an out-and-out thief."

"Which one?"

She shook her head — there was a feral gleam in her eyes now — and started past me. I let her go. Then I put the paper away again and followed her onto the porch.

221

The security chief had planted himself on the cottage path to wait for the county police; Craig was down there with him. The Resident Director had disappeared somewhere, probably to go do something about protecting Xanadu's reputation. Nobody was paying any attention to me, so I went down and along a packed-earth path that skirted the far side of the cottage.

At the rear there were steps leading up onto the balcony. I climbed them and took a look at the strip of film I had noticed earlier, caught on a wood splinter through one of several small holes along its edge. It was the stiff and sturdy kind they use to make slides — the kind that wouldn't bend easily under a weight laid on it edgewise.

I paced around for a time, looking at this and that. Then I stood still and stared down at the ocean spray boiling over the rocks below, not really seeing it, looking at some things inside my head instead. I was still doing that when more cart noises sounded out front, two or three carts this time judging from the magnified whirring and whining. County cops, I thought. Nice timing, too.

When I came back around to the front two uniformed patrolmen, a uniformed officer in captain's braid, a civilian carrying a doctor's satchel, and another civilian with photographic equipment and a field lab kit were being met by the security chief. I went over and joined them.

The captain, whose name was Orloff, asked me, "You're the private detective, is that right? The man who found the body?"

"That's right." I relinquished the .25 automatic, saying that I had only handled it by the barrel. Not that it would have mattered if I *had* taken it by the grip. If there were any fingerprints on it, they would belong to Lauren Speers.

"It was just after the shooting that you arrived?"

"Not exactly," I said, "I was in the vicinity before the shooting. I went inside after I heard the shot — not much more than a minute afterward."

"So you didn't actually see the woman shoot her secretary."

"No," I said. "But I wouldn't have seen that if I'd been inside when it happened. Ms. Speers didn't kill Bernice Dolan. The man right over there, Joe Craig, did that."

There was one of those sudden electric silences. Both Craig and Lauren Speers were near enough to hear what I had said; he stiffened and gaped at me and she came up out of her chair on the porch. Craig's face tried to arrange itself into an expression of disbelief, but he was not much of an actor; if this had been a Hollywood screen test, he would have flunked it hands down.

He said, "What the hell kind of crazy accusation is that?" Which was better — more conviction — but it still sounded false.

His guilt was not so obvious to Orloff or any of the others. They kept looking from Craig to me as if trying to decide who to believe. The security guy said, "How could Joe be guilty? The balcony door and all the windows are locked from the inside; you said so yourself. You also said there was no one else in the cottage except Ms. Speers and the dead woman when you entered."

"That's right," I said. "But Craig wasn't in the cottage when he shot the secretary. And everything wasn't locked up tight, either."

Craig said, "Don't listen to him, he doesn't know what he's saying —"

"The living room smells of gin," I said to the security guy. "You must have noticed that when you were in there. It smelled just the same when I first entered. But if you fire a handgun in a closed room you get the smell of cordite. No cordite odor means the gun was fired outside the room."

"That's true enough," Orloff said. "Go on."

"I'd been here less than ten minutes when Craig showed up," I said. "He claimed he'd come to keep a tennis date with Ms. Speers. But the parking lot attendant told me earlier that she drinks her lunch every day and then comes here to sleep it off until Happy Hour at four o'clock. People on that kind of heavy drinking schedule don't make dates to go play tennis at three o'clock.

"Craig said something else, too — much more damning. When I asked him if he knew the dead woman he identified her as Bernice Dolan. Then he said, 'Did Ms. Speers do that to her? Shoot her like that?' But I didn't say anything about hearing a gunshot until later; and the way the body is crumpled on the rug, with one arm flung over the chest, all you can see is blood, not the type of wound. So how did he know she was shot? She could just as easily have been stabbed to death."

There was not much bravado left in Craig; you could almost see him wilting, like an uprooted weed drying in the sun. "I assumed she was shot," he said weakly, "I just . . . assumed it."

Lauren Speers had come down off the porch and was staring at him. "Why?" she said. "For god's sake, *why?*"

He shook his head at her. But I said, "For money, that's why. A hundred thousand dollars in extortion payoffs, at least some of which figures to be in his own cottage right now."

That pushed Craig to the breaking point. He back-pedaled a couple of steps and might have kept right on backing if one of the patrolmen hadn't grabbed his arm.

Lauren Speers said, "I don't understand. What extortion?"

224

"From those three men I asked you about a few minutes ago — Huddleston, Boyer, and Rykman. They figure prominently in the book you're writing, don't they? Large sections of it are devoted to them and contain material either scandalous or criminal?"

"How do you know about that?"

"Craig told me; he was trying to make it seem like you had a motive for killing Bernice. And you told me when you said those three men were bastards and one of them was an out-and-out thief. This little piece of paper took care of the rest." I fished it out of my coat pocket again and handed it to Orloff. "The first series of numbers after each name are page numbers — pages in the book manuscript on which the most damaging material about that person appears. The numbers after the dash are the amounts extorted from each man."

"Where did you get this?"

"It was on the floor between the couch and the coffee table. Right near where Ms. Speers' bag was. I think that's where it came from — out of the handbag."

She said, "How could it have been in my bag?"

"Bernice put it there. While she was out impersonating you this afternoon."

Now everybody looked bewildered. Except Craig, of course: he only looked sick — much sicker than Lauren Speers had earlier.

"Impersonating me?" she said.

"That's right. Wearing a red wig and your white coat, and carrying your bag. You didn't go anywhere after lunch except back here to bed; it was Bernice who took your car and left Xanadu. And it was Bernice who passed me in the car, Bernice I saw enter the cottage a couple of minutes before she was shot."

The security guy asked, "How can you be sure about that?"

"Because Bernice was left-handed," I said. "And Ms. Speers is right-handed; I could tell that a while ago when she started to pour from a decanter into a glass — decanter in her right hand, glass in her left. But the woman who got out of the car carried the straw bag in her right hand; and when she got to the cottage door she used her left hand to take out the key and to open the door."

Lauren Speers looked at a lock of her red hair, as if to make sure it was real. "Why would Bernice impersonate me?"

"She and Craig were in on the extortion scheme together and it was part of the plan. They must have worked it something like this: as your secretary she had access to your book manuscript, your personal stationery, your signature, and no doubt your file of incriminating letters and documents. She also had access to your personal belongings and your car keys, particularly from one to four in the afternoons while you were sleeping. And she'd have known from your records how to contact Huddleston and the other two.

"So she and Craig wrote letters to each of them, on your stationery over your forged signature, demanding large sums of money to delete the material about them from your book and to return whatever documents concerned them; they probably also enclosed photocopies of the manuscript pages and the documents as proof. The idea was to keep themselves completely in the clear if the whole thing backfired. You'd get the blame in that case, not them.

"To maintain the illusion, Bernice had to pretend to be you when she collected the payoff. I don't know what sort of arrangements she and Craig made, but they wouldn't have allowed any of the three men to deliver the money personally. An intermediary, maybe, someone who didn't know you. Or maybe a prearranged drop site. In any event, Bernice always dressed as you at collection time."

Orloff asked, "Why do you think Craig killed her?"

"The old doublecross," said. "They'd collected all the extortion money; that's evident from the way each of the three names is crossed out on that paper. Today was the last pickup and I think they had it worked out that she would resign from Ms. Speers' employ and Craig would resign from Xanadu and they'd go off somewhere together: her closet is all cleaned out and her bags are packed. But Craig had other ideas. He knew when she was due back here and he was waiting for her — outside on the rear balcony. When she let herself in he knocked on the window and gestured for her to open the two halves. After she complied he must have said something like, 'Quick, lock the front door, take off the coat, and give me the wig and the money.' She must have thought there was some reason for the urgency, and she trusted him; so she did what he asked. And when she pulled the money out of the bag she also pulled out the slip of paper. In her haste it fell unnoticed to the floor.

"As soon as Craig had the wig and the money he took out the gun, which he'd swiped from Ms. Speers' nightstand, and shot her. And then he threw the gun inside and pulled the halves of the window closed."

"And locked them somehow from the outside," the security guy said, "in the minute or two before you broke in? How could he do that?"

"Simply, considering the catch on those window halves is a bar type that flops over into a bracket. The gimmick he used was a thin but stiff strip of film. He lost it afterward without realizing it: you'll still find it caught on a splinter on the balcony railing. The way he did it was to insert the film strip between the two halves and flip the catch over until it rested on the strip's edge. Next he pulled the halves all the way closed, using his thumb and forefinger on the inner frames of each, and with his other hand he eased the strip downward until the catch dropped into the bracket. Then he withdrew the strip from the crack. With a little practice, you could do the whole thing in thirty seconds.

"So far he had himself a perfect crime. All he'd have had to do was return to his cottage, get rid of the wig, stash the money, pick himself up a witness or two, and come back here and 'find' Ms. Speers locked up with the body. Under the circumstances he'd arranged, she would be the only one who could have committed the murder.

"What screwed him up was me showing up when I did. He heard me pounding on the door as he was working his trick with the film strip; he had just enough time to slip away into the woods before I broke in. But who was I? What had I seen and heard? The only way he could find out was to come back as soon as he'd dumped the wig and money. The fact that he showed up again in less than ten minutes means he didn't dump them far away; they won't be hard to find. And there might even be a fingerprint on that film strip to nail your case down tight —"

Lauren Speers moved. Before anybody could stop her she charged over to where Craig was and slugged him in the face. Not a slap — a roundhouse shot with her closed fist. He staggered but didn't go down. She went after him, using some of the words she had used on me earlier, and hit him again and tried to kick him here and there. It took Orloff, the security guy, and one of the patrolmen to pull her off.

It was another couple of hours before they let me leave Xanadu. During that time Orloff and his men found all of the extortion money — $100,000 in cash — hidden in one of Craig's bureau drawers; they also found the red wig in the garbage can behind his cottage. That was enough, along with my testimony, for them to arrest him on suspicion of homicide. From the looks of him, they'd have a full confession an hour after he was booked.

Just before I left I served Lauren Speers with the court summons. She took it all right; she said it was the least she could do after I had practically saved her life. She also took one of my business cards and promised she would send me a check "as an appreciation," but I doubted that she would. She was a lady too lost in alcohol and bitter memories, too involved in a quest for notoriety and revenge, to remember that sort of promise — running fast and going nowhere, as the comedian Fred Allen had once said, on a treadmill to oblivion.

So I went back to San Francisco and the following day I collected my two hundred plus expenses from Adam Brister. And that night, instead of reading one of the pulp magazines I collect and admire, I read Coleridge's *Kubla Khan* in a book from the public library. It was a pretty fine piece of work, all right, and so was his Xanadu. A place of idyllic beauty. The stuff of dreams.

The one at Big Sur was the stuff of dreams too — dreams of tinsel and plastic and pastel colors; of beauty measured by wealth, happiness by material possessions. Some people could find fulfillment with those dreams and in that place. Others, like Lauren Speers, were not so fortunate.

For them, the pleasure-domes of Xanadu could be the stuff of nightmares.

Stakeout

Four o'clock in the morning. And I was sitting huddled and ass-numb in my car in a freezing rainstorm, waiting for a guy I had never seen in person to get out of a nice warm bed and drive off in his Mercedes, thus enabling me to follow him so I could find out where he lived.

Thrilling work if you can get it. The kind that makes any self-respecting detective wonder why he didn't become a plumber instead.

Rain hammered against the car's metal surfaces, sluiced so thickly down the windshield that it transformed the glass into an opaque screen; all I could see were smeary blobs of light that marked the street lamps along this block of 47th Avenue. Wind buffeted the car in forty-mile-an-hour gusts off the ocean nearby. Condensation had formed again on the driver's door window, even though I had rolled it down half an inch; I rubbed some of the mist away and took another bleary-eyed look across the street.

This was one of San Francisco's older middle-class residential neighborhoods, desirable — as long as you didn't mind fog-belt living — because Sutro Heights Park was just a block away and you were also within walking distance of Ocean Beach, the Cliff House, and Land's End. Most of the houses had been built in the thirties and stood shoulder-to-shoulder with their neighbors, but they seemed to have more individuality than the bland row houses dominating the avenues farther inland; out here, California Spanish was the dominant style. Asians had bought up much of the city's west side housing in recent years, but fewer of those close to the ocean than anywhere else. A lot of homes in pockets such as this were still owned by older-generation, blue-collar San Franciscans.

The house I had under surveillance, number 9279, was one of the Spanish stucco jobs, painted white with a red tile roof. Yucca palms, one large and three small, dominated its tiny front yard. The three-year-old Mercedes with the Washington state license plates was still parked, illegally, across the driveway. Above it, the house's front windows remained dark. If anybody was up yet I couldn't tell it from where I was sitting.

I shifted position for the hundredth time, wincing as my stiffened joints protested with creaks and twinges. I had been here four and a half hours now, with nothing to do except to sit and wait and try not to fall asleep; to listen to the rain and the rattle and stutter of my thoughts. I was weary and irritable and I wanted some hot coffee and my own warm bed. It would be well past dawn, I thought bleakly, before I got either one.

Stakeouts . . . God, how I hated them. The passive waiting, the boredom, the slow, slow passage of dead time. How many did this make over the past thirty-odd years? How many empty, wasted, lost hours? Too damn many, whatever the actual figure. The physical discomfort was also becoming less tolerable, especially on nights like this, when not even a heavy overcoat and gloves kept the chill from penetrating bone-deep. I had lived fifty-eight years; fifty-eight is too old to sit all-night stakeouts on the best of cases, much less on a lousy split-fee skip-trace.

I was starting to hate Randolph Hixley, too, sight unseen. He was the owner of the Mercedes across the street and my reason for being here. To his various and sundry employers, past and no doubt present, he was a highly paid freelance computer consultant. To his ex-wife and two kids, he was a probable deadbeat who currently owed some $24,000 in back alimony and child support. To me and Puget Sound Investigations of Seattle, he was what should have been a small but adequate fee for routine work. Instead, he had developed into a minor pain in the ass. Mine.

Hixley had quit Seattle for parts unknown some four months ago, shortly after his wife divorced him for what she referred to as "sexual misconduct," and had yet to make a single alimony or child support payment. For reasons of her own, the wife had let the first two barren months go by without doing anything about it. On the occasion of the third due date, she had received a brief letter from Hixley informing her in tear-jerk language that he was so despondent over the breakup of their marriage he hadn't worked since leaving Seattle and was on the verge of becoming one of the homeless. He had every intention of fulfilling his obligations, though, the letter said; he would send money as soon as he got back on his feet. So would she bear with him for a while and please not sic the law on him? The letter was postmarked San Francisco, but with no return address.

The ex-wife, who was no dummy, smelled a rat. But because she still harbored some feelings for him, she had gone to Puget Sound Investigations rather than to the authorities, the object being to locate Hixley and determine if he really was broke and despondent. If so, then she would show the poor dear compassion and understanding. If not, then she would obtain a judgment against the son-of-a-bitch and force him to pay up or get thrown in the slammer.

Puget Sound had taken the job, done some preliminary work, and then called a San Francisco detective — me — and farmed out the tough part for half the fee. That kind of cooperative thing is done all the time when the client isn't wealthy enough and the fee isn't large enough for the primary agency to send one of its own operatives to another state. No private detective likes to split fees, particularly when he's the one doing most of the work, but ours is sometimes a back-scratching business. Puget Sound had done a favor for me once; now it was my turn.

Skip-tracing can be easy or it can be difficult, depending on the individual you're trying to find. At first I figured Randolph Hixley, broke or not, might be one of the difficult ones. He had no known relatives or friends in the Bay Area. He had stopped using his credit cards after the divorce, and had not applied for new ones, which meant that if he was working and had money, he was paying his bills in cash. In Seattle, he'd provided consultancy services to a variety of different companies, large and small, doing most of the work at home by computer link. If he'd hired out to one or more outfits in the Bay Area, Puget Sound had not been able to turn up a lead as to which they might be, so I probably wouldn't be able to either. There is no easy way to track down that information, not without some kind of insider pull with the IRS.

And yet despite all of that, I got lucky right away — so lucky I revised my thinking and decided, prematurely and falsely, that Hixley was going to be one of the easy traces after all. The third call I made was to a contact in the San Francisco City Clerk's office, and it netted me the information that the 1987 Mercedes 560 SL registered in Hixley's name had received two parking tickets on successive Thursday mornings, the most recent of which was the previous week. The tickets were for identical violations: illegal parking across a private driveway and illegal parking during posted street-cleaning hours. Both citations had been issued between seven and seven-thirty A.M. And in both instances, the address was the same: 9279 47th Avenue.

I looked up the address in my copy of the reverse city directory. 9279 47th Avenue was a private house occupied by one Anne Carswell, a commercial artist, and two other Carswells, Bonnie and Margo, whose ages were given as eighteen and nineteen, respectively, and who I presumed were her daughters. The Carswells didn't own the house; they had been renting it for a little over two years.

Since there had been no change of registration on the Mercedes — I checked on that with the DMV — I assumed that the car still belonged to Randolph Hixley. And I figured things this way: Hixley, who was no more broke and despondent than I was, had met and established a relationship with Anne Carswell, and taken to spending Wednesday nights at her house. Why only Wednesdays? For all I knew, once a week was as much passion as Randy and Anne could muster up. Or it could be the two daughters slept elsewhere that night. In any case, Wednesday was Hixley's night to howl.

So the next Wednesday evening I drove out there, looking for his Mercedes. No Mercedes. I made my last check at midnight, went home to bed, got up at six A.M., and drove back to 47th Avenue for another look. Still no Mercedes.

Well, I thought, they skipped a week. Or for some reason they'd altered their routine. I went back on Thursday night. And Friday night and Saturday night. I made spot checks during the day. On one occasion I saw a tall, willowy redhead in her late thirties — Anne Carswell, no doubt — driving out of the garage. On another occasion I saw the two daughters, one blond, one brunette, both attractive, having a conversation with a couple of sly college types. But that was all I saw. Still no Mercedes, still no Randolph Hixley.

234

I considered bracing one of the Carswell women on a ruse, trying to find out that way where Hixley was living. But I didn't do it. He might have put them wise to his background and the money he owed, and asked them to keep mum if anyone ever approached them. Or I might slip somehow in my questioning and make her suspicious enough to call Hixley. I did not want to take the chance of warning him off.

Last Wednesday had been another bust. So had early Thursday — I drove out there at five A.M. that time. And so had the rest of the week. I was wasting time and gas and sleep, but it was the only lead I had. All the other skip-trace avenues I'd explored had led me nowhere near my elusive quarry.

Patience and perseverance are a detective's best assets; hang in there long enough and as often as not you find what you're looking for. Tonight I'd finally found Hixley and his Mercedes, back at the Carswell house after a two-week absence.

The car hadn't been there the first two times I drove by, but when I made what would have been my last pass, at twenty of twelve, there it was, once again illegally parked across the driveway. Maybe he didn't give a damn about parking tickets because he had no intention of paying them. Or maybe he disliked walking fifty feet or so, which was how far away the nearest legal curb space was. Or, hell, maybe he was just an arrogant bastard who thumbed his nose at the law any time it inconvenienced him. Whatever his reason for blocking Anne Carswell's driveway, it was his big mistake.

The only choice I had, spotting his car so late, was to stake it out and wait for him to show. I would have liked to go home and catch a couple of hours sleep, but for all I knew he wouldn't spend the entire night this time. If I left

235

and came back and he was gone, I'd have to go through this whole rigmarole yet again.

So I parked and settled in. The lights in the Carswell house had gone off at twelve-fifteen and hadn't come back on since. It had rained off and on all evening, but the first hard rain started a little past one. The storm had steadily worsened until, now, it was a full-fledged howling, ripping blow. And still I sat and still I waited. . . .

A blurred set of headlights came boring up 47th toward Geary, the first car to pass in close to an hour. When it went swishing by I held my watch up close to my eyes: 4:07. Suppose he stays in there until eight or nine? I thought. Four or five more hours of this and I'd be too stiff to move. It was meatlocker cold in the car. I couldn't start the engine and put the heater on because the exhaust, if not the idle, would call attention to my presence. I'd wrapped my legs and feet in the car blanket, which provided some relief; even so, I could no longer feel my toes when I tried to wiggle them.

The hard drumming beat of the rain seemed to be easing a little. Not the wind, though; a pair of back-to-back gusts shook the car, as if it were a toy in the hands of a destructive child. I shifted position again, pulled the blanket more tightly around my ankles.

A light went on in the Carswell house.

I scrubbed mist off the driver's door window, peered through the wet glass. The big front window was alight over there, behind drawn curtains. That was a good sign: People don't usually put their living room lights on at four A.M. unless somebody plans to be leaving soon.

Five minutes passed while I sat chafing my gloved hands together and moving my feet up and down to improve circulation. Then another light went on — the front porch light this time. And a few seconds after that, the door opened

236

and somebody came out onto the stoop.

It wasn't Randolph Hixley; it was a young blond woman wearing a trenchcoat over what looked to be a lacy nightgown. One of the Carswell daughters. She stood still for a moment, looking out over the empty street. Then she drew the trenchcoat collar up around her throat and ran down the stairs and over to Hixley's Mercedes.

For a few seconds she stood hunched on the sidewalk on the passenger side, apparently unlocking the front door with a set of keys. She pulled the door open, as if making sure it was unlocked, then slammed it shut again. She turned and ran back up the stairs and vanished into the house.

I thought: Now what was that all about?

The porch light stayed on. So did the light in the front room. Another three minutes dribbled away. The rain slackened a little more, so that it was no longer sheeting; the wind continued to wail and moan. And then things got even stranger over there.

First the porch light went off. Then the door opened and somebody exited onto the stoop, followed a few seconds later by a cluster of shadow-shapes moving in an awkward, confused fashion. I couldn't identify them or tell what they were doing while they were all grouped on the porch; the tallest yucca palm cast too much shadow and I was too far away. But when they started down the stairs, there was just enough extension of light from the front window to individuate the shapes for me.

There were four of them, by God — three in an uneven line on the same step, the fourth backing down in front of them as though guiding the way. Three women, one man. The man — several inches taller, wearing an overcoat and hat, head lolling forward as if he were drunk or unconscious — was being supported by two of the women.

237

They all managed to make it down the slippery stairs without any of them suffering a misstep. When they reached the sidewalk, the one who had been guiding ran ahead to the Mercedes and dragged the front passenger door open. In the faint outspill from the dome light, I watched the other two women, with the third one's help, push and prod the man inside. Once they had the door shut again, they didn't waste any time catching their breaths. Two of them went running back to the house; the third hurried around to the driver's door, bent to unlock it. She was the only one of the three, I realized then, who was fully dressed: raincoat, rainhat, slacks, boots. When she slid in under the wheel I had a dome-lit glimpse of reddish hair and a white, late-thirties face under the rainhat. Anne Carswell.

She fired up the Mercedes, let the engine warm for all of five seconds, switched on the headlights, and eased away from the curb at a crawl, the way you'd drive over a surface of broken glass. The two daughters were already back inside the house, with the door shut behind them. I had long since unwrapped the blanket from around my legs; I didn't hesitate in starting my car. Or in trying to start it: The engine was cold and it took three whiffing tries before it caught and held. If Anne Carswell had been driving fast, I might have lost her. As it was, with her creeping along, she was only halfway along the next block behind me when I swung out into a tight U-turn.

I ran dark through the rain until she completed a slow turn west on Point Lobos and passed out of sight. Then I put on my lights and accelerated across Geary to the Point Lobos intersection. I got there in time to pick up the Mercedes' taillights as it went through the flashing yellow traffic signal at 48th Avenue. I let it travel another fifty yards downhill before I turned onto Point Lobos in pursuit.

Five seconds later, Anne Carswell had another surprise for me.

I expected her to continue down past the Cliff House and around onto the Great Highway; there is no other through direction once you pass 48th. But she seemed not to be leaving the general area after all. The Mercedes' brake lights came on and she slow-turned into the Merrie Way parking area above the ruins of the old Sutro Baths. The combination lot and overlook had only the one entrance/exit; it was surrounded on its other three sides by cliffs and clusters of wind-shaped cypress trees and a rocky nature trail that led out beyond the ruins to Land's End.

Without slowing, I drove on past. She was crawling straight down the center of the unpaved, potholed lot, toward the trees at the far end. Except for the Mercedes, the rain-drenched expanse appeared deserted.

Below Merrie Way, on the other side of Point Lobos, there is a newer, paved parking area carved out of Sutro Heights park for sightseers and patrons of Louis' Restaurant opposite and the Cliff House bars and eateries farther down. It, too, was deserted at this hour. From the overlook above, you can't see this curving downhill section of Point Lobos; I swung across into the paved lot, cut my lights, looped around to where I had a clear view of the Merrie Way entrance. Then I parked, shut off the engine, and waited.

For a few seconds I could see a haze of slowly moving light up there, but not the Mercedes itself. Then the light winked out and there was nothing to see except wind-whipped rain and dark. Five minutes went by. Still nothing to see. She must have parked, I thought — but to do what?

Six minutes, seven. At seven and a half, a shape materialized out of the gloom above the entrance — somebody on

239

foot, walking fast, bent against the lashing wind. Anne Carswell. She was moving at an uphill angle out of the overlook, climbing to 48th Avenue.

When she reached the sidewalk, a car came through the flashing yellow at the intersection and its headlight beams swept over her; she turned away from them, as if to make sure her face wasn't seen. The car swished down past where I was, disappeared beyond the Cliff House. I watched Anne Carswell cross Point Lobos and hurry into 48th at the upper edge of the park.

Going home, I thought. Abandoned Hixley and his Mercedes on the overlook and now she's hoofing it back to her daughters.

What the hell?

I started the car and drove up to 48th and turned there. Anne Carswell was now on the opposite side of the street, near where Geary dead-ends at the park; when my lights caught her she turned her head away as she had a couple of minutes ago. I drove two blocks, circled around onto 47th, came back a block and then parked and shut down again within fifty yards of the Carswell house. Its porch light was back on, which indicated that the daughters were anticipating her imminent return. Two minutes later she came fast-walking out of Geary onto 47th. One minute after that, she climbed the stairs to her house and let herself in. The porch light went out immediately, followed fifteen seconds later by the light in the front room.

I got the car moving again and made my way back down to the Merrie Way overlook.

The Mercedes was still the only vehicle on the lot, parked at an angle just beyond the long terraced staircase that leads down the cliffside to the pitlike bottom of the ruins. I pulled in alongside, snuffed my lights. Before I got out, I armed myself with the flashlight I keep clipped under the dash.

Icy wind and rain slashed at me as I crossed to the Mercedes. Even above the racket made by the storm, I could hear the barking of sea lions on the offshore rocks beyond the Cliff House. Surf boiled frothing over those rocks, up along the cliffs and among the concrete foundations that are all that's left of the old bathhouse. Nasty night, and a nasty business here to go with it. I was sure of that now.

I put the flashlight up against the Mercedes' passenger window, flicked it on briefly. He was in there, all right; she'd shoved him over so that he lay half sprawled under the wheel, his head tipped back against the driver's door. The passenger door was unlocked. I opened it and got in and shut the door again to extinguish the dome light. I put the flash beam on his face, shielding it with my hand.

Randolph Hixley, no doubt of that; the photograph Puget Sound Investigations had sent me was a good one. No doubt, either, that he was dead. I checked for a pulse, just to make sure. Then I moved the light over him, slowly, to see if I could find out what had killed him.

There weren't any discernible wounds or bruises or other marks on his body; no holes or tears or bloodstains on his damp clothing. Poison? Not that, either. Most any deadly poison produces convulsions, vomiting, rictus; his facial muscles were smooth and when I sniffed at his mouth I smelled nothing except Listerine.

Natural causes, then? Heart attack, stroke, aneurysm? Sure, maybe. But if he'd died of natural causes, why would Anne Carswell and her daughters have gone to all the trouble of moving his body and car down here? Why not just call Emergency Services?

On impulse I probed Hixley's clothing and found his

wallet. It was empty — no cash, no credit cards, nothing except some old photos. Odd. He'd quit using credit cards after his divorce; he should have been carrying at least a few dollars. I took a close look at his hands and wrists. He was wearing a watch, a fairly new and fairly expensive one. No rings or other jewelry but there was a white mark on his otherwise tanned left pinkie, as if a ring had been recently removed.

They rolled him, I thought. All the cash in his wallet and a ring off his finger. Not the watch because it isn't made of gold or platinum and you can't get much for a watch, anyway, these days.

But why? Why would they kill a man for a few hundred bucks? Or rob a dead man and then try to dump the body? In either case, the actions of those three women made no damn sense. . . .

Or did they?

I was beginning to get a notion.

I backed out of the Mercedes and went to sit and think in my own car. I remembered some things, and added them together with some other things, and did a little speculating, and the notion wasn't a notion anymore — it was the answer.

Hell, I thought then, I'm getting old. Old and slow on the uptake. I should have seen this part of it as soon as they brought the body out. And I should have tumbled to the other part a week ago, if not sooner.

I sat there for another minute, feeling my age and a little sorry for myself because it was going to be quite a while yet before I got any sleep. Then, dutifully, I hauled up my mobile phone and called in the law.

They arrested the three women a few minutes past seven

A.M. at the house on 47th Avenue. I was present for identification purposes. Anne Carswell put up a blustery protest of innocence until the inspector in charge, a veteran named Ginzberg, tossed the words "foul play" into the conversation; then the two girls broke down simultaneously and soon there were loud squawks of denial from all three: "We didn't hurt him! He had a heart attack, he died of a heart attack!" The girls, it turned out, were not named Carswell and were not Anne Carswell's daughters. The blonde was Bonnie Harper; the brunette was Margo LaFond. They were both former runaways from southern California.

The charges against the trio included failure to report a death, unlawful removal of a corpse, and felony theft. But the main charge was something else entirely.

The main charge was operating a house of prostitution.

Later that day, after I had gone home for a few hours' sleep, I laid the whole thing out for my partner, Eberhardt.

"I should have known they were hookers and Hixley was a customer," I said. "There were enough signs. His wife divorced him for 'sexual misconduct'; that was one. Another was how unalike those three women were — different hair colors, which isn't typical in a mother and her daughters. Then there were those sly young guys I saw with the two girls. They weren't boyfriends, they were customers too."

"Hixley really did die of a heart attack?" Eberhardt asked.

"Yeah. Carswell couldn't risk notifying Emergency Services; she didn't know much about Hixley and she was afraid somebody would come around asking questions. She had a nice discreet operation going there, with a small but high-paying clientele, and she didn't want a dead man to rock the boat. So she and the girls dressed the corpse and

243

hustled it out of there. First, though, they emptied Hixley's wallet and she stripped a valuable garnet ring off his pinkie. She figured it was safe to do that; if anybody questioned the empty wallet and missing ring, it would look like the body had been rolled on the Merrie Way overlook, after he'd driven in there himself and had his fatal heart attack. As far as she knew, there was nothing to tie Hixley to her and her girls — no direct link, anyhow. He hadn't told her about the two parking tickets."

"Uh-huh. And he was in bed with all three of them when he croaked?"

"So they said. Right in the middle of a round of fun and games. That was what he paid them for each of the times he went there — seven hundred and fifty bucks for all three, all night."

"Jeez, three women at one time," Eberhardt paused, thinking about it. Then he shook his head. *"How?"* he said.

I shrugged. "Where there's a will, there's a way."

"Kinky sex — I never did understand it. I guess I'm old-fashioned."

"Me too. But Hixley's brand is pretty tame, really, compared to some of the things that go on nowadays."

"Seems like the whole damn world gets a little kinkier every day," Eberhardt said. "A little crazier every day, too. You know what I mean?"

"Yeah," I said, "I know what you mean."

La Bellezza Delle Bellezze

1.

That Sunday, the day before she died, I went down to Aquatic Park to watch the old men play bocce. I do that sometimes on weekends when I'm not working, when Kerry and I have nothing planned. More often than I used to, out of nostalgia and compassion and maybe just a touch of guilt, because in San Francisco bocce is a dying sport.

Only one of the courts was in use. Time was, all six were packed throughout the day and there were spectators and waiting players lined two and three deep at courtside and up along the fence on Van Ness. No more. Most of the city's older Italians, to whom bocce was more a religion than a sport, have died off. The once large and close-knit North Beach Italian community has been steadily losing its identity since the fifties — families moving to the suburbs, the expansion of Chinatown and the gobbling up of North Beach real estate by wealthy Chinese — and even though there has been a small new wave of immigrants from Italy in recent years, they're mostly young and upscale. Young, upscale Italians don't play bocce much, if at all; their interests lie in soccer, in the American sports where money and fame and power have replaced a love of the game itself. The Di Massimo bocce courts at the North Beach Playground are mostly closed now; the only place you can find a game every Saturday and Sunday is on the one Aquatic Park court. And the players get older, and sadder, and fewer each year.

There were maybe fifteen players and watchers on this Sunday, almost all of them older than my fifty-eight. The two courts nearest the street are covered by a high, pillar-supported roof, so that contests can be held even in wet weather; and there are wooden benches set between the pillars. I parked myself on one of the benches midway along. The only other seated spectator was Pietro Lombardi, in a patch of warm May sunlight at the far end, and this surprised me. Even though Pietro was in his seventies, he was one of the best and spryest of the regulars, and also one of the most social. To see him sitting alone, shoulders slumped and head bowed, was puzzling.

Pining away for the old days, maybe, I thought — as I had just been doing. And a phrase popped into my head, a line from Dante that one of my uncles was fond of quoting when I was growing up in the Outer Mission: *Nessun maggior dolore che ricordarsi del tempo felice nella miseria.* The bitterest of woes is to remember old happy days.

Pietro and his woes didn't occupy my attention for long. The game in progress was spirited and voluble, as only a game of bocce played by elderly *'paesanos* can be, and I was soon caught up in it.

Bocce is simple — deceptively simple. You play it on a long narrow packed-earth pit with low wooden sides. A wooden marker ball the size of a walnut is rolled to one end; the players stand at the opposite end and in turn roll eight larger, heavier balls, grapefruit-sized, in the direction of the marker, the object being to see who can put his bocce ball closest to it. One of the required skills is slow-rolling the ball, usually in a curving trajectory, so that it kisses the marker and then lies up against it — the perfect shot — or else stops an inch or two away. The other required skill is knocking an opponent's ball away from any such close lie without disturbing the marker. The best players, like Pietro Lombardi, can do this two out of three times on the fly — no mean feat from a distance of fifty feet. They can also do it by caroming the ball off the pit walls, with topspin or reverse spin after the fashion of pool-shooters.

Nobody paid much attention to me until after the game in progress had been decided. Then I was acknowledged with hand gestures and a few words — the tolerant acceptance accorded to known spectators and occasional players. Unknowns got no greeting at all; these men still clung to the old ways, and one of the old ways was clannishness.

Only one of the group, Dominick Marra, came over to where I was sitting. And that was because he had something on his mind. He was in his mid-seventies, white-haired, white-mustached; a bantamweight in baggy trousers held up by galluses. He and Pietro Lombardi had been close friends for most of their lives. Born in the same town — Agropoli, a village on the Gulf of Salerno not far from Naples; moved to San Francisco with their families a year apart, in the late twenties; married cousins, raised large families, were widowed at almost the same time a few years ago. The kind of friendship that is almost a blood tie. Dominick had been a baker; Pietro had owned a North Beach trattoria that now belonged to one of his daughters.

What Dominick had on his mind was Pietro. "You see how he sits over there, hah? He's got trouble — *la miseria*."

"What kind of trouble?"

"His granddaughter. Gianna Fornessi."

"Something happen to her?"

"She's maybe go to jail," Dominick said.

"What for?"

"Stealing money."

"I'm sorry to hear it. How much money?"

"Two thousand dollars."

"Who did she steal it from?"

"Che?"

"Who did she steal the money from?"

Dominick gave me a disgusted look. "She don't steal it. Why you think Pietro he's got *la miseria,* hah?"

I knew what was coming now; I should have known it the instant Dominick starting confiding to me about Pietro's problem. I said, "You want me to help him and his granddaughter."

"Sure. You a detective."

"A busy detective."

"You got no time for old man and young girl? *Compaesani?"*

I sighed, but not so he could hear me do it. "All right, I'll talk to Pietro. See if he wants my help, if there's anything I can do."

"Sure he wants your help. He just don't know it yet."

We went to where Pietro was sitting alone in the sun. He was taller than Dominick, heavier, balder. And he had a fondness for Toscanas, those little twisted black Italian cigars; one protruded now from a corner of his mouth. He didn't want to talk at first but Dominick launched into a monologue in Italian that changed his mind and put a glimmer of hope in his sad eyes. Even though I've lost a lot of the language over the years, I can understand enough to follow most conversations. The gist of Dominick's monologue was that I was not just a detective but a miracle worker, a cross between Sherlock Holmes and the messiah. Italians are given to hyperbole in times of excitement or stress, and there isn't much you can do to counteract it — especially when you're one of the *compaesani* yourself.

"My Gianna, she's good girl," Pietro said. "Never give trouble, even when she's little one. *La bellezza delle bellezze,* you understand?"

The beauty of beauties. His favorite grandchild, probably. I said, "I understand. Tell me about the money, Peitro."

"She don't steal it," he said. "*Una ladra,* my Gianna? No, no, it's all big lie."

"Did the police arrest her?"

"They got no evidence to arrest her."

"But somebody filed charges, is that it?"

"Charges," Pietro said. "Bah," he said and spat.

"Who made the complaint?"

Dominick said, "Ferry," as if the name were an obscenity.

"Who's Ferry?"

He tapped his skull. "*Caga di testa,* this man."

"That doesn't answer my question."

"He live where she live. Same apartment building."

"And he says Gianna stole two thousand dollars from him."

"Liar," Pietro said. "He lies."

"Stole it how? Broke in or what?"

"She don't break in nowhere, not my Gianna. This Ferry, this *bastardo,* he says she take the money when she's come to pay rent and he's talk on telephone. But how she knows where he keep his money? Hah? How she knows he have two thousand dollars in his desk?"

"Maybe he told her."

"Sure, that's what he says to police," Dominick said. "Maybe he told her," he says. "He don't tell her nothing."

"Is that what Gianna claims?"

Pietro nodded. Threw down what was left of his Toscana and ground in into the dirt with his shoe — a gesture of

249

anger and frustration. "She don't steal that money," he said. "What she need to steal money for? She got good job, she live good, she don't have to steal."

"What kind of job does she have?"

"She sell drapes, curtains. In . . . what you call that business, Dominick?"

"Interior decorating business," Dominick said.

"*Si*. In interior decorating business."

"Where does she live?" I asked.

"Chestnut Street."

"Where on Chestnut Street? What number?"

"Seventy-two fifty."

"You make that Ferry tell the truth, hah?" Dominick said to me. "You fix it up for Gianna and her goombah?"

"I'll do what I can."

"*Va bene*. Then you come tell Pietro right away."

"If Pietro will tell me where he lives —"

There was a sharp whacking sound as one of the bocce balls caromed off the side wall near us, then a softer clicking of ball meeting ball, and a shout went up from the players at the far end: another game won and lost. When I looked back at Dominick and Pietro they were both on their feet. Dominick said, "You find Pietro okay, good detective like you," and Pietro said, "*Grazie, mi amico,*" and before I could say anything else the two of them were off arm in arm to join the others.

Now I was the one sitting alone in the sun, holding up a burden. Primed and ready to do a job I didn't want to do, probably couldn't do, and would not be paid well for if at all. Maybe this man Ferry wasn't the only one involved who had *caga di testa* — shit for brains. Maybe I did too.

2.

The building at 7250 Chestnut Street was an old three-storied, brown-shingled job, set high in the shadow of Coit Tower and across from the retaining wall where Telegraph Hill falls off steeply toward the Embarcadero. From each of the apartments, especially the ones on the third floor, you'd have quite a view of the bay, the East Bay, and both bridges. Prime North Beach address, this. The rent would be well in excess of two thousand a month.

A man in a tan trenchcoat was coming out of the building as I started up the steps to the vestibule. I called out to him to hold the door for me — it's easier to get apartment dwellers to talk to you once you're inside the building — but either he didn't hear me or he chose to ignore me. He came hurrying down without a glance my way as he passed. City-bred paranoia, I thought. It was everywhere these days, rich and poor neighborhoods both, like a nasty strain of social disease. Bumpersticker for the nineties: *Fear Lives.*

There were six mailboxes in the foyer, each with Dymo-Label stickers identifying the tenants. Gianna Fornessi's name was under box #4, along with a second name: Ashley Hansen. It figured that she'd have a roommate; salespersons working in the interior design trade are well but not extravagantly paid. Box #1 bore the name George Ferry and that was the bell I pushed. He was the one I wanted to talk to first.

A minute died away, while I listened to the wind that was savaging the trees on the hillside below. Out on the bay hundreds of sailboats formed a mosaic of white on blue. Somewhere among them a ship's horn sounded — to me, a sad false note. Shipping was all but dead on this side of the bay, thanks to wholesale mismanagement of the port over the past few decades.

The intercom crackled finally and a male voice said, "Who is it?" in wary tones.

I asked if he was George Ferry, and he admitted it, even more guardedly. I gave him my name, said that I was there to ask him a few questions about his complaint against Gianna Fornessi. He said, "Oh Christ." There was a pause, and then, "I called you people yesterday, I told Inspector Cullen I was dropping the charges. Isn't that enough?"

He thought I was a cop. I could have told him I wasn't; I could have let the whole thing drop right there, since what he'd just said was a perfect escape clause from my commitment to Pietro Lombardi. But I have too much curiosity to let go of something, once I've got a piece of it, without knowing the particulars. So I said, "I won't keep you long, Mr. Ferry. Just a few questions."

Another pause. "Is it really necessary?"

"I think it is, yes,"

An even longer pause. But then he didn't argue, didn't say anything else — just buzzed me in.

His apartment was on the left, beyond a carpeted, dark-wood staircase. He opened the door as I approached it. Mid-forties, short, rotund, with a nose like a blob of putty and a Friar Tuck fringe of reddish hair. And a bruise on his left cheekbone, a cut along the right corner of his mouth. The marks weren't fresh, but then they weren't very old either. Twenty-four hours, maybe less.

He didn't ask to see a police ID; if he had I would have told him immediately that I was a private detective, because nothing can lose you a California investigator's license faster than impersonating a police officer. On the other hand, you can't be held accountable for somebody's false assumption. Ferry gave me a nervous once-over, holding his head tilted downward as if that would keep me from seeing his bruise and cut, then stood aside to let me come in.

The front room was neat, furnished in a self-consciously masculine fashion: dark woods, leather, expensive sporting prints. It reeked of leather, dust, and his lime-scented cologne.

As soon as he shut the door Ferry went straight to a liquor cabinet and poured himself three fingers of Jack Daniels, no water or mix, no ice. Just holding the drink seemed to give him courage. He said, "So. What is it you want to know?"

"Why you dropped your complaint against Gianna Fornessi."

"I explained to Inspector Cullen . . ."

"Explain to me, if you don't mind."

He had some of the sour mash. "Well, it was all a mistake . . . just a silly mistake. She didn't take the money after all."

"You know who did take it, then?"

"Nobody took it. I . . . misplaced it."

"Misplaced it. Uh-huh."

"I thought it was in my desk," Ferry said. "That's where I usually keep the cash I bring home. But I'd put it in my safe deposit box along with some other papers, without realizing it. It was in an envelope, you see, and the envelope got mixed up with the other papers."

"Two thousand dollars is a lot of cash to keep at home. You make a habit of that sort of thing?"

"In my business . . ." The rest of the sentence seemed to hang up in his throat; he oiled the route with the rest of his drink. "In my business I need to keep a certain amount of cash on hand, both here and at the office. The amount I keep here isn't usually as large as two thousand dollars, but I —"

"What business are you in, Mr. Ferry?"

"I run a temp employment agency for domestics."

"Temp?"

"Short for temporary," he said. "I supply domestics for part-time work in offices and private homes. A lot of them are poor, don't have checking accounts, so they prefer to be paid in cash. Most come to the office, but a few —"

"Why did you think Gianna Fornessi had stolen the two thousand dollars?"

". . . What?"

"Why Gianna Fornessi? Why not somebody else?"

"She's the only one who was here. Before I thought the money was missing, I mean. I had no other visitors for two days and there wasn't any evidence of a break-in."

"You and she are good friends, then?"

"Well . . . no, not really. She's a lot younger . . ."

"Then why was she here?"

"The rent," Ferry said. "She was paying her rent for the month. I'm the building manager, I collect for the owner. Before I could write out a receipt I had a call, I was on the phone for quite a while and she . . . I didn't pay any attention to her and I thought she must have . . . you see why I thought she'd taken the money?"

I was silent.

He looked at me, looked at his empty glass, licked his lips, and went to commune with Jack Daniels again. While he was pouring I asked him, "What happened to your face, Mr. Ferry?"

His hand twitched enough to clink bottle against glass. He had himself another taste before he turned back to me. "Clumsy," he said, "I'm clumsy as hell. I fell down the stairs, the front stairs, yesterday morning." He tried a laugh that didn't come off. "Fog makes the steps slippery. I just

254

wasn't watching where I was going."

"Looks to me like somebody hit you."

"Hit me? No, I told you . . . I fell down the stairs."

"You're sure about that?"

"Of course I'm sure. Why would I lie about it?"

That was a good question. Why would he lie about that, and about all the rest of it too? There was about as much truth in what he'd told me as there is value in a chunk of fool's gold.

3.

The young woman who opened the door of apartment #4 was not Gianna Fornessi. She was blond, with the kind of fresh- faced Nordic features you see on models for Norwegian ski wear. Tall and slender in a pair of green silk lounging pajamas; arms decorated with hammered gold bracelets, ears with dangly gold triangles. Judging from the expression in her pale eyes, there wasn't much going on behind them. But then, with her physical attributes, not many men would care if her entire brain had been surgically removed.

"Well," she said, "hello."

"Ashley Hansen?"

"That's me. Who're you?"

When I told her my name her smile brightened, as if I'd said something amusing or clever. Or maybe she just liked the sound of it.

"I knew right away you were Italian," she said. "Are you a friend of Jack's?"

"Jack?"

"Jack Bisconte." The smile dulled a little. "You are, aren't you?"

255

"No," I said, "I'm a friend of Pietro Lombardi."

"Who?"

"Your roommate's grandfather. I'd like to talk to Gianna, if she's home."

Ashley Hansen's smile was gone now; her whole demeanor had changed, become less self-assured. She nibbled at a corner of her lower lip, ran a hand through her hair, fiddled with one of her bracelets. Finally she said, "Gianna isn't here."

"When will she be back?"

"She didn't say."

"You know where I can find her?"

"No. What do you want to talk to her about?"

"The complaint George Ferry filed against her."

"Oh, that," she said. "That's all been taken care of."

"I know. I just talked to Ferry."

"He's a creepy little prick, isn't he."

"That's one way of putting it."

"Gianna didn't take his money. He was just trying to hassle her, that's all."

"Why would he do that?"

"Well, why do you think?"

I shrugged. "Suppose you tell me."

"He wanted her to do things."

"You mean go to bed with him?"

"Things," she said. "Kinky crap, *real* kinky."

"And she wouldn't have anything to do with him."

"No way, Jose. What a creep."

"So he made up the story about the stolen money to get back at her, is that it?"

"That's it."

"What made him change his mind, drop the charges?"

"He didn't tell you?"

"No."

"Who knows?" She laughed. "Maybe he got religion."

"Or a couple of smacks in the face."

"Huh?"

"Somebody worked him over yesterday," I said. "Bruised his cheek and cut his mouth. You have any idea who?"

"Not me, mister. How come you're so interested, anyway?"

"I told you, I'm a friend of Gianna's grandfather."

"Yeah, well."

"Gianna have a boyfriend, does she?"

". . . Why do you want to know that?"

"Jack Bisconte, maybe? Or is he yours?"

"He's just somebody I know." She nibbled at her lip again, did some more fiddling with her bracelets. "Look, I've got to go. You want me to tell Gianna you were here?"

"Yes." I handed her one of my business cards. "Give her this and ask her to call me."

She looked at the card; blinked at it and then blinked at me.

"You . . . you're a detective?"

"That's right."

"My God," she said, and backed off, and shut the door in my face.

I stood there for a few seconds, remembering her eyes — the sudden fear in her eyes when she'd realized she had been talking to a detective.

What the hell?

4.

North Beach used to be the place you went when you wanted *pasta fino,* expresso and biscotti, conversation about *la dolce vita* and *il patria d'Italia.* Not anymore. There are still plenty of Italians in North Beach, and you can still get the good food and some of the good conversation; but their turf continues to shrink a little more each year, and despite the best efforts of the entreprenurial new immigrants, the vitality and most of the Old World atmosphere are just memories.

The Chinese are partly responsible, not that you can blame them for buying available North Beach real estate when Chinatown, to the west, began to burst its boundaries. Another culprit is the Bohemian element that took over upper Grant Avenue in the fifties, paving the way for the hippies and the introduction of hard drugs in the sixties, which in turn paved the way for the jolly current mix of motorcyle toughs, aging hippies, coke and crack dealers, and the pimps and small-time crooks who work the flesh palaces along lower Broadway. Those "Silicone Alley" nightclubs, made famous by Carol Doda in the late sixties, also share responsibility: they added a smutty leer to the gaiety of North Beach, turned the heart of it into a ghetto.

Parts of the neighborhood, particularly those up around Coit Tower where Gianna Fornessi lived, are still prime city real estate; and the area around Washington Square Park, *il giardino* to the original immigrants, is where the city's literati now congregates. Here and there, too, you can still get a sense of what it was like in the old days. But most of the landmarks are gone — Enrico's, Vanessi's, The Bocce Ball where you could hear mustachioed waiters in gondolier costumes singing arias from operas by Verdi and Puccini — and so is most of the flavor. North Beach is oddly tasteless now, like a week-old mostaccioli made without good spices or garlic. And that is another thing that is all but gone: twenty-five years ago you could not get within a thousand yards of North Beach without picking up the fine, rich fragrance of garlic. Nowadays you're much more likely to smell fried egg roll and the sour stench of somebody's garbage.

Parking in the Beach is the worst in the city; on weekends you can drive around its hilly streets for hours without finding a legal parking space. So today, in the perverse way of things, I found a spot waiting for me when I came down Stockton.

In a public telephone booth near Washington Square Park I discovered a second minor miracle: a directory that had yet to be either stolen or mutilated. The only Bisconte listed was Bisconte Florist Shop, with an address on upper Grant a few blocks away. I took myself off in that direction, through the usual good-weather Sunday crowds of locals and gawking sightseers and drifting homeless.

Upper Grant, like the rest of the area, has changed drastically over the past few decades. Once a rock-ribbed Little Italy, it has become an ethnic mixed bag: Italian markets, trattorias, pizza parlors, bakeries cheek by jowl with Chinese sewing-machine sweat shops, food and herb vendors, and fortune-cookie companies. But most of the faces on the streets are Asian and most of the apartments in the vicinity are occupied by Chinese.

The Bisconte Florist Shop was a hole-in-the-wall near Filbert, sandwiched between an Italian saloon and the Sip Hing Herb Company. It was open for business, not surprisingly on a Sunday in this neighborhood: tourists buy flowers too, given the opportunity.

The front part of the shop was cramped and jungly with cut flowers, ferns, plants in pots and hanging baskets. A

259

small glass-fronted cooler contained a variety of roses and orchids. There was nobody in sight, but a bell had gone off when I entered and a male voice from beyond a rear doorway called, "Be right with you." I shut the door, went up near the counter. Some people like florist shops; I don't. All of them have the same damp, cloyingly sweet smell that reminds me of funeral parlors; of my mother in her casket at the Figlia Brothers Mortuary in Daly City nearly forty years ago. That day, with all its smells, all its painful images, is as clear to me now as if it were yesterday.

I had been waiting about a minute when the voice's owner came out of the back room. Late thirties, dark, on the beefy side; wearing a professional smile and a floral-patterned apron that should have been ludicrous on a man of his size and coloring but wasn't. We had a good look at each other before he said, "Sorry to keep you waiting — I was putting up an arrangement. What can I do for you?"

"Mr. Bisconte? Jack Bisconte?"

"That's me. Something for the wife maybe?"

"I'm not here for flowers. I'd like to ask you a few questions, if you don't mind."

The smile didn't waver. "Oh? What about?"

"Gianna Fornessi."

"Who?"

"You don't know her?"

"Name's not familiar, no."

"She lives up on Chestnut with Ashley Hansen."

"Ashley Hansen . . . I don't know that name either."

"She knows you. Young, blonde, looks Norwegian."

"Well, I know a lot of young blondes," Bisconte said. He winked at me. "I'm a bachelor and I get around pretty good, you know?"

"Uh-huh."

"Lot of bars and clubs in North Beach, lot of women to pick and choose from." He shrugged. "So how come you're asking about these two?"

"Not both of them. Just Gianna Fornessi."

"That so? You a friend of hers?"

"Of her grandfather's. She's had a little trouble."

"What kind of trouble?"

"Manager of her building accused her of stealing some money. But somebody convinced him to drop the charges."

"That so?" Bisconte said again, but not as if he cared.

"Leaned on him to do it. Scared the hell out of him."

"You don't think it was me, do you? I told you, I don't know anybody named Gianna Fornessi."

"So you did."

"What's the big deal anyway?" he said. "I mean, if the guy dropped the charges, then this Gianna is off the hook, right?"

"Right."

"Then why all the questions?"

"Curiosity," I said. "Mine and her grandfather's."

Another shrug. "I'd like to help you, pal, but like I said, I don't know the lady. Sorry."

"Sure."

"Come back any time you need flowers," Bisconte said. He gave me a little salute, waited for me to turn and then did the same himself. He was hidden away again in the back room when I let myself out.

Today was my day for liars. Liars and puzzles.

He hadn't asked me who I was or what I did for a living; that was because he already knew. And the way he knew, I thought, was that Ashley Hansen had gotten on the horn after I left and told him about me. He knew Gianna Fornessi pretty well too, and exactly where the two women lived.

He was the man in the tan trenchcoat I'd seen earlier, the one who wouldn't hold the door for me at 7250 Chestnut.

5.

I treated myself to a plate of linguine and fresh clams at a ristorante off Washington Square and then drove back over to Aquatic Park. Now, in mid-afternoon, with fog seeping in through the Gate and the temperature dropping sharply, the number of bocce players and kibitzers had thinned by half. Pietro Lombardi was one of those remaining; Dominick Marra was another. Bocce may be dying easy in the city but not in men like them. They cling to it and to the other old ways as tenaciously as they cling to life itself.

I told Pietro — and Dominick, who wasn't about to let us talk in private — what I'd learned so far. He was relieved that Ferry had dropped his complaint, but just as curious as I was about the Jack Bisconte connection.

"Do you know Bisconte?" I asked him.

"No. I see his shop but I never go inside."

"Know anything about him?"

"*Niente.*"

"How about you, Dominick?"

He shook his head. "He's too old for Gianna, hah? Almost forty, you say — that's too old for girl twenty-three."

"If that's their relationship," I said.

"Men almost forty they go after young woman, they only got one reason. *Fatto 'na bella chiavata.* You remember, eh, Pietro?"

"*Pazzo!* You think I forget *'na bella chiavata?*"

I asked Pietro, "You know anything about Gianna's roommate?"

"Only once I meet her," he said. "Pretty, but not so pretty like my Gianna, *la bellezza delle bellezze*. I don't like her too much."

"Why not?"

"She don't have respect like she should."

"What does she do for a living, do you know?"

"No. She don't say and Gianna don't tell me."

"How long have they been sharing the apartment?"

"Eight, nine months."

"Did they know each other long before they moved in together?"

He shrugged. "Gianna and me, we don't talk much like when she's little girl," he said sadly. "Young people now, they got no time for *la familia*." Another shrug, a sigh. "*Ognuno pensa per sè*," he said. Everybody thinks only of himself.

Dominick gripped his shoulder. Then he said to me, "You find out what's happen with Bisconte and Ferry and those girls. Then you see they don't bother them no more. Hah?"

"If I can, Dominick. If I can."

The fog was coming in thickly now and the other players were making noises about ending the day's tournament. Dominick got into an argument with one of them; he wanted to play another game or two. He was outvoted, but he was still pleading his case when I left. Their Sunday was almost over. So was mine.

I went home to my flat in Pacific Heights. And Kerry came over later on and we had dinner and listened to some jazz. I thought maybe Gianna Fornessi might call but she didn't. No one called. Good thing, too. I would not have been pleased to hear the phone ring after eight o'clock; I was busy then.

Men in their late fifties are just as interested in *'na bella chiavata*. Women in their early forties, too.

6.

At the office in the morning I called TRW for credit checks on Jack Bisconte, George Ferry, Gianna Fornessi, and Ashley Hansen. I also asked my partner, Eberhardt, who has been off the cops just a few years and who still has plenty of cronies sprinkled throughout the SFPD, to find out what Inspector Cullen and the Robbery Detail had on Ferry's theft complaint, and to have the four names run through R&I for any local arrest record.

The report out of Robbery told me nothing much. Ferry's complaint had been filed on Friday morning; Cullen had gone to investigate, talked to the two principals, and determined that there wasn't enough evidence to take Gianna Fornessi into custody. Thirty hours later Ferry had called in and withdrawn the complaint, giving the same flimsy reason he'd handed me. As far as Cullen and the department were concerned, it was all very minor and routine.

The TRW and R&I checks took a little longer to come through, but I had the information by noon. It went like this:

Jack Bisconte. Good credit rating. Owner and sole operator, Bisconte Florist Shop, since 1978; lived on upper Greenwich Street, in a rented apartment, same length of time. No listing of previous jobs held or previous local addresses. No felony or misdemeanor arrests.

George Ferry. Excellent credit rating. Owner and principal operator, Ferry Temporary Employment Agency, since 1972. Resident of 7250 Chestnut since 1980. No felony arrests; one DWI arrest and conviction following a minor traffic accident in May of 1981, sentenced to ninety days in jail (suspended), driver's license revoked for six months.

Gianna Fornessi. Fair to good credit rating. Employed by Home Draperies, Showplace Square, as a sales representative since 1988. Resident of 7250 Chestnut for eight months; address prior to that, her parents' home in Daly City. No felony or misdemeanor arrests.

Ashley Hansen. No credit rating. No felony or misdemeanor arrests.

There wasn't much in any of that, either, except for the fact that TRW had no listing on Ashley Hansen. Almost everybody uses credit cards these days, establishes some kind of credit — especially a young woman whose income is substantial enough to afford an apartment in one of the city's best neighborhoods. Why not Ashley Hansen?

She was one person who could tell me; another was Gianna Fornessi. I had yet to talk to Pietro's granddaughter and I thought it was high time. I left the office in Eberhardt's care, picked up my car, and drove south of Market to Showplace Square.

The Square is a newish complex of manufacturer's showrooms for the interior decorating trade — carpets, draperies, lighting fixtures, and other types of home furnishings. It's not open to the public, but I showed the photostat of my license to one of the security men at the door and talked him into calling the Home Draperies showroom and asking them to send Gianna Fornessi out to talk to me.

They sent somebody out but it wasn't Gianna Fornessi. It was a fluffy looking little man in his forties named

Lundquist, who said, "I'm sorry, Ms. Fornessi is no longer employed by us."

"Oh? When did she leave?"

"Eight months ago"

"Eight *months?*"

"At the end of September."

"Quit or terminated?"

"Quit. Rather abruptly, too."

"To take another job?"

"I don't know. She gave no adequate reason."

"No one called afterward for a reference?"

"No one," Lundquist said.

"She worked for you two years, is that right?"

"About two years, yes."

"As a sales representative?"

"That's correct."

"May I ask her salary?"

"I really couldn't tell you that . . ."

"Just this, then: Was hers a high-salaried position? In excess of thirty thousand a year, say?"

Lundquist smiled a faint, fluffy smile. "Hardly," he said.

"Were her skills such that she could have taken another, better paying job in the industry?"

Another fluffy smile. And another "Hardly."

So why had she quit Home Draperies so suddenly eight months ago, at just about the same time she moved into the Chestnut Street apartment with Ashley Hansen? And what was she doing to pay her share of the rent?

7.

There was an appliance store delivery truck double-parked in front of 7250 Chestnut, and when I went up the stairs I found the entrance door wedged wide open. Nobody was in the vestibule or lobby, but the murmur of voices filtered down from the third floor. If I'd been a burglar I would have rubbed my hands together in glee. As it was, I walked in as if I belonged there and climbed the inside staircase to the second floor.

When I swung off the stairs I came face to face with Jack Bisconte.

He was hurrying toward me from the direction of apartment #4, something small and red and rectangular clutched in the fingers of his left hand. He broke stride when he saw me; and then recognition made him do a jerky double-take and he came to a halt. I stopped, too, with maybe fifteen feet separating us. That was close enough, and the hallway was well-lighted enough, for me to get a good look at his face. It was pinched, sweat-slicked, the eyes wide and shiny — the face of a man on the cutting edge of panic.

Frozen time, maybe five seconds of it, while we stood staring at each other. There was nobody else in the hall; no audible sounds on this floor except for the quick rasp of Bisconte's breathing. Then we both moved at the same time — Bisconte in the same jerky fashion of his double-take, shoving the red object into his coat pocket as he came forward. And then, when we had closed the gap between us by half, we both stopped again as if on cue. It might have been a mildly amusing little pantomime if you'd been a disinterested observer. It wasn't amusing to me. Or to Bisconte, from the look of him.

I said, "Fancy meeting you here. I thought you didn't know Gianna Fornessi or Ashley Hansen."

"Get out of my way."

"What's your hurry?"

"Get out of my way. I mean it." The edge of panic had cut into his voice; it was thick, liquidy, as if it were bleeding.

"What did you put in your pocket, the red thing?"

He said, "Christ!" and tried to lunge past me.

I blocked his way, getting my hands up between us to push him back. He made a noise in his throat and swung at me. It was a clumsy shot; I ducked away from it without much effort, so that his knuckles just grazed my neck. But then the son of a bitch kicked me, hard, on the left shinbone. I yelled and went down. He kicked out again, this time at my head; didn't connect because I was already rolling away. I fetched up tight against the wall and by the time I got myself twisted back around he was pelting toward the stairs.

I shoved up the wall to my feet, almost fell again when I put weight on the leg he'd kicked. Hobbling, wiping pain-wet out of my eyes, I went after him. People were piling down from the third floor; the one in the lead was George Ferry. He called something that I didn't listen to as I started to descend. Bisconte, damn him, had already crossed the lobby and was running out through the open front door.

Hop, hop, hop down the stairs like a contestant in a one-legged race, using the railing for support. By the time I reached the lobby, some of the sting had gone out of my shinbone and I could put more weight on the leg. Out into the vestibule, half running and half hobbling now, looking for him. He was across the street and down a ways, fumbling with a set of keys at the driver's door of a new silver Mercedes.

But he didn't stay there long. He was too wrought up to

get the right key into the lock, and when he saw me pounding across the street in his direction, the panic goosed him and he ran again. Around behind the Mercedes, onto the sidewalk, up and over the concrete retaining wall. And gone.

I heard him go sliding or tumbling through the undergrowth below. I staggered up to the wall, leaned over it. The slope down there was steep, covered with trees and brush, strewn with the leavings of semi-humans who had used it for a dumping ground. Bisconte was on his buttocks, digging hands and heels into the ground to slow his momentum. For a few seconds I thought he was going to turn into a one-man avalanche and plummet over the edge where the slope ended in a sheer bluff face. But then he managed to catch hold of one of the tree trunks and swing himself away from the bluff, in among a tangle of bushes where I couldn't see him anymore. I could hear him — and then I couldn't. He'd found purchase, I thought, and was easing himself down to where the backside of another apartment building leaned in against the cliff.

There was no way I was going down there after him. I turned and went to the Mercedes.

It had a vanity plate, the kind that makes you wonder why somebody would pay $25 extra to the DMV to put it on his car: BISFLWR. If the Mercedes had had an external hood release I would have popped it and disabled the engine; but it didn't, and all four doors were locked. All right. Chances were, he wouldn't risk coming back soon — and even if he ran the risk, it would take him a good long while to get here.

I limped back to 7250. Four people were clustered in the vestibule, staring at me — Ferry and a couple of uniformed deliverymen and a fat woman in her forties. Ferry said as I came up the steps, "What happened, what's going on?" I didn't answer him. There was a bad feeling in me now; or maybe it had been there since I'd first seen the look on Bisconte's face. I pushed through the cluster — none of them tried to stop me — and crossed the lobby and went up to the second floor.

Nobody answered the bell at apartment #4. I tried the door, and it was unlocked, and I opened it and walked in and shut it again and locked it behind me.

She was lying on the floor in the living room, sprawled and bent on her back near a heavy teak coffee table, peach-colored dressing gown hiked up over her knees; head twisted at an off-angle, blood and a deep triangular puncture wound on her left temple. The blood was still wet and clotting. She hadn't been dead much more than an hour.

In the sunlight that spilled in through the undraped windows, the blood had a kind of shimmery radiance. So did her hair — her long gold-blond hair.

Goodbye Ashley Hansen.

8.

I called the Hall of Justice and talked to a Homicide inspector I knew slightly named Craddock. I told him what I'd found, and about my little skirmish with Jack Bisconte, and said that yes, I would wait right here and no, I wouldn't touch anything. He didn't tell me not to look around and I didn't say that I wouldn't.

Somebody had started banging on the door. Ferry, probably. I went the other way, into one of the bedrooms. Ashley Hansen's: there was a photograph of her prominently displayed on the dresser, and lots of mirrors to give her a live image of herself. A narcissist, among other things. On one nightstand was a telephone and an answering machine. On the unmade bed, tipped on its side with some of the contents spilled out, was a fancy leather purse. I used the backs of my two index fingers to stir around among the spilled items and the stuff inside. Everything you'd expect to find in a woman's purse — and one thing that should have been there and wasn't.

Gianna Fornessi's bedroom was across the hall. She also had a telephone and an answering machine; the number on the telephone dial was different from her roommate's. I hesitated for maybe five seconds, then I went to the answering machine and pushed the button marked "playback calls" and listened to two old messages before I stopped the tape and rewound it. One message would have been enough.

Back into the living room. The knocking was still going on. I started over there; stopped after a few feet and stood sniffing the air. I thought I smelled something — a faint lingering acrid odor. Or maybe I was just imagining it . . .

Bang, bang, bang. And Ferry's voice: "What's going on in there?"

I moved ahead to the door, threw the bolt lock, yanked the door open. "Quit making so damned much noise."

Ferry blinked and backed off a step; he didn't know whether to be afraid of me or not. Behind and to one side of him, the two deliverymen and the fat woman looked on with hungry eyes. They would have liked seeing what lay inside; blood attracts some people, the gawkers, the insensitive ones, the same way it attracts flies.

"What's happened?" Ferry asked nervously.

"Come in and see for yourself. Just you."

I opened up a little wider and he came in past me, showing reluctance. I shut and locked the door again behind

271

him. And when I turned he said, "Oh my God," in a sickened voice. He was staring at the body on the floor, one hand pressed up under his breastbone. "Is she . . . ?"

"Very."

"Gianna . . . is she here?"

"No."

"Somebody did that to Ashley? It wasn't an accident?"

"What do you think?"

"Who? Who did it?"

"You know who, Ferry. You saw me chase him out of here."

"I . . . don't know who he is. I never saw him before."

"The hell you never saw him. He's the one put those cuts and bruises on your face."

"No," Ferry said, "that's not true." He looked and sounded even sicker now. "I told you how that happened . . ."

"You told me lies. Bisconte roughed you up so you'd drop your complaint against Gianna. He did it because Gianna and Ashley Hansen have been working as call girls and he's their pimp and he didn't want the cops digging into her background and finding out the truth."

Ferry leaned unsteadily against the wall, facing away from what was left of the Hansen woman. He didn't speak.

"Nice quiet little operation they had," I said, "until you got wind of it. That's how it was, wasn't it? You found out and you wanted some of what Gianna's been selling."

Nothing for ten seconds. Then, softly, "It wasn't like that, not at first. I . . . loved her."

"Sure you did."

"I *did*. But she wouldn't have anything to do with me."

"So then you offered to pay her."

". . . Yes. Whatever she charged."

272

"Only you wanted kinky sex and she wouldn't play."

"No! I never asked for anything except a night with her . . . one night. She pretended to be insulted; she denied that she's been selling herself to men. She . . . she said she'd never go to bed with a man as . . . ugly . . ." He moved against the wall — a writhing movement, as if he were in pain.

"That was when you decided to get even with her."

"I wanted to hurt her, the way she'd hurt me. It was stupid, I know that, but I wasn't thinking clearly. I just wanted to hurt her . . ."

"Well, you succeeded," I said. "But the one you really hurt is Ashley Hansen. If it hadn't been for you, she'd still be alive."

He started to say something but the words were lost in the sudden summons of the doorbell.

"That'll be the police," I said.

"The police? But . . . I thought you were . . ."

"I know you did. I never told you I was, did I?"

I left him holding up the wall and went to buzz them in.

9.

I spent more than two hours in the company of the law, alternately answering questions and waiting around. I told Inspector Craddock how I happened to be there. I told him how I'd come to realize that Gianna Fornessi and Ashley Hansen were call girls, and how George Ferry and Jack Bisconte figured into it. I told him about the small red rectangular object I'd seen Bisconte shove into his pocket — an address book, no doubt, with the names of some of Hansen's johns. That was the common item that was missing from her purse.

273

Craddock seemed satisfied. I wished I was.

When he finally let me go I drove back to the office. But I didn't stay long; it was late afternoon, Eberhardt had already gone for the day, and I felt too restless to tackle the stack of routine paperwork on my desk. I went out to Ocean Beach and walked on the sand, as I sometimes do when an edginess is on me. It helped a little — not much.

I ate an early dinner out, and when I got home I put in a call to the Hall of Justice to ask if Jack Bisconte had been picked up yet. But Craddock was off duty and the inspector I spoke to wouldn't tell me anything.

The edginess stayed with me all evening, and kept me awake past midnight. I knew what was causing it, all right; and I knew what to do to get rid of it. Only I wasn't ready to do it yet.

In the morning, after eight, I called the Hall again. Craddock came on duty at eight, I'd been told. He was there and willing to talk, but what he had to tell me was not what I wanted to hear. Bisconte was in custody but not because he'd been apprehended. At eight-thirty Monday night he'd walked into the North Beach precinct station with his lawyer in tow and given himself up. He'd confessed to being a pimp for the two women; he'd confessed to working over George Ferry; he'd confessed to being in the women's apartment just prior to his tussle with me. But he swore up and down that he hadn't killed Ashley Hansen. He'd never had any trouble with her, he said; in fact he'd been half in love with her. The cops had Gianna Fornessi in custody too by this time, and she'd confirmed that there had never been any rough stuff or bad feelings between her roommate and Bisconte.

Hansen had been dead when he got to the apartment, Bisconte said. Fear that he'd be blamed had pushed him into a panic. He'd taken the address book out of her purse — he hadn't thought about the answering machine tapes or he'd have erased the messages left by eager johns — and when he'd encountered me in the hallway he'd lost his head completely. Later, after he'd had time to calm down, he'd gone to the lawyer, who had advised him to turn himself in.

Craddock wasn't so sure Bisconte was telling the truth, but I was. I knew who had been responsible for Ashley Hansen's death; I'd known it a few minutes after I found her body. I just hadn't wanted it to be that way.

I didn't tell Craddock any of this. When he heard the truth it would not be over the phone. And it would not be from me.

10.

It did not take me long to track him down. He wasn't home but a woman in his building said that in nice weather he liked to sit in Washington Square Park with his cronies. That was where I found him, in the park. Not in the company of anyone; just sitting alone on a bench across from the Saints Peter and Paul Catholic church, in the same slump-shouldered, bowed-head posture as when I'd first seen him on Sunday — the posture of *la miseria*.

I sat down beside him. He didn't look at me, not even when I said, "*Buon giorno*, Pietro."

He took out one of his twisted black cigars and lit it carefully with a kitchen match. Its odor was acrid on the warm morning air — the same odor that had been in his granddaughter's apartment, that I'd pretended to myself I was imagining. Nothing smells like a Toscana; nothing. And only old men like Pietro smoke Toscanas these days. They

275

don't even have to smoke one in a closed room for the smell to linger after them; it gets into and comes off the heavy user's clothing.

"It's time for us to talk," I said.

"*Che sopra?*"

"Ashley Hansen. How she died."

A little silence. Then he sighed and said, "You already know, hah, good detective like you? How you find out?"

"Does it matter?"

"It don't matter. You tell police yet?"

"It'll be better if you tell them."

More silence, while he smoked his little cigar.

I said, "But first tell me. Exactly what happened."

He shut his eyes; he didn't want to relive what had happened.

"It was me telling you about Bisconte that started it," I said to prod him. "After you got home Sunday night you called Gianna and asked her about him. Or she called you."

". . . I call her," he said. "She's angry, she tell me mind my own business. Never before she talks to her goombah this way."

"Because of me. Because she was afraid of what I'd find out about her and Ashley Hansen and Bisconte."

"Bisconte." He spat the name, as if ridding his mouth of something foul.

"So this morning you asked around the neighborhood about him. And somebody told you he wasn't just a florist, about his little sideline. Then you got on a bus and went to see your granddaughter."

"I don't believe it, not about Gianna. I want her tell me it's not true. But she's not there. Only the other one, the *bionda*."

"And then?"

276

"She don't want to let me in, that one. I go in anyway. I ask if she and Gianna are . . . if they sell themselves for money. She laugh. In my face she laugh, this girl what have no respect. She says what difference it make? She says I am old man — dinosaur, she says. But she pat my cheek like I am little boy or big joke. Then she . . . ah, *Cristo,* she come up close to me and she say you want some, old man, I give you some. To me she says this. Me." Pietro shook his head; there were tears in his eyes now. "I push her away. I feel . . . *feroce,* like when I am young man and somebody he make trouble with me. I push her too hard and she fall, her head hit the table and I see blood and she don't move . . . ah, *mio Dio!* She was wicked, that one, but I don't mean to hurt her . . ."

"I know you didn't, Pietro."

"I think, call doctor quick. But she is dead. And I hurt here, inside" — he tapped his chest — "and I think, what if Gianna she come home? I don't want to see Gianna. You understand? Never again I want to see her."

"I understand," I said. And I thought: Funny — I've never laid eyes on her, not even a photograph of her. I don't know what she looks like; now I don't want to know. I never want to see her either.

Pietro finished his cigar. Then he straightened on the bench, seemed to compose himself. His eyes had dried; they were clear and sad. He looked past me, across at the looming Romanesque pile of the church. "I make confession to priest," he said, "little while before you come. Now we go to police and I make confession to them."

"Yes."

"You think they put me in gas chamber?"

"I doubt they'll put you in prison at all. It was an accident. Just a bad accident."

Another silence. On Pietro's face was an expression of the deepest pain. "This thing, this accident, she shouldn't have happen. Once . . . ah, once . . ." Pause. *"Morto,"* he said.

He didn't mean the death of Ashley Hansen. He meant the death of the old days, the days when families were tightly knit and there was respect for elders, the days when bocce was king of his world and that world was a far simpler and better place. The bitterest of woes is to remember old happy days . . .

We sat there in the pale sun. And pretty soon he said, in a voice so low I barely heard the words, *"La bellezza delle bellezze."* Twice before he had used that phrase in my presence and both times he had been referring to his granddaughter. This time I knew he was not.

"Si, 'paesano," I said. *"La bellezza delle bellezze."*